Freak 'N' Gorgeous

Sebastian J. Plata

Sky Pony Press
New York

First Edition

This is a work of fiction. Names, characters, places, and incidents are from the author's imagination, and used fictitiously.

Sky Pony Press books may be purchased in bulk at special discounts for sales promotion, corporate gifts, fund-raising, or educational purposes. Special editions can also be created to specifications. For details, contact the Special Sales Department, Sky Pony Press, 307 West 36th Street, 11th Floor, New York, NY 10018 or info@skyhorsepublishing.com.

Sky Pony® is a registered trademark of Skyhorse Publishing, Inc.®, a Delaware corporation.

Visit our website at www.skyponypress.com.
www.sebastianjplata.com

10 9 8 7 6 5 4 3 2 1

Library of Congress Cataloging-in-Publication Data available on file.

Cover illustration by Kirsten Ulve
Cover design by Kate Gartner

Hardcover ISBN: 978-1-5107-3210-0
Ebook ISBN: 978-1-5107-3214-8

Printed in the United States of America

Dla moich ukochanych Rodziców.

CHAPTER 1

KONRAD

I SWEAR, IT'S LIKE EVERYTHING *shrank* overnight.

First my feet dangled off the bed. Then the doorknobs seemed too small for my hands. Now I'm in the bathroom, about to pee, and the toilet's mocking me like a junior version of its former self. What the hell is going—

Hold on. Nope. Not everything.

I blink the rest of the sleep away and bend down for a closer look. Little Konrad not only feels too bulky in my hand, he actually appears bigger than usual, too.

I shut my eyes and suck in a deep breath. Am I still drunk? I don't *feel* hung over, but I must be, right? That's it. Lauren can call me a pussy all she wants. I'm never letting her shitty tequila near my mouth again.

I focus on the bathroom mirror, and my heart rate speeds up another notch. I sidestep to the left so I'm standing directly in front of my reflection.

For a good minute, I just stare at myself. And then I stare some more. Finally, I close my eyes and give each of my cheeks three good smacks.

I open my eyes again. Other than the rapid reddening of my skin, the image staring back at me hasn't changed at all.

All right. There are three possible explanations for what I'm witnessing. Number one, Lauren sprinkled her disgusting tequila with some serious magic mushrooms and didn't tell us. Number two, my dreams have come true. Or, number three, I've gone batshit insane.

Praying it's not the last one, I march to the living room to get a second opinion. Arthur's on the couch, a half-eaten Pop-Tart dangling from his hand, *Dragon Ball Z* blaring from the TV. But he's no longer focused on the screen. My brother's gawking at me.

We hold a silent staring contest. The Pop-Tart slips from his fingers and lands on the carpet. He doesn't even flinch.

"Whoa," he says, chewed-up mush spilling over his tongue. "An Inexplicable Development? For real?"

I race back to the bathroom, heart pounding.

Never have I used the word in reference to a guy before—and not in a million years would I ever have thought to use it in relation to myself—but it's the only way to describe what's reflecting back at me.

I'm gorgeous.

GORGEOUS.

Ripping off my T-shirt and boxers, I climb onto the edge of the bathtub so I can see my whole body in the mirror above the sink. My head bumps the ceiling. It's never reached the ceiling when I did this before.

There's no denying it—I'm gorgeous from the tip of my head down to my toes. I have muscle definition in my arms, my stomach is a brick wall, my thighs look like they belong to a soccer player. Every insecurity I've ever mulled over vanished overnight, replaced by this upgrade. Even my nipples look more appealing. How can nipples look more appealing?

Holy shit. It's true. Inexplicable Developments really can happen to anybody.

Detecting movement on my right, I rip my attention away from the mirror. Mom's standing just outside the threshold, a rag and plate in her hands. But she's not wiping. She's not doing anything. She's too busy trying to keep her eyeballs in their sockets.

I leap down from the tub in my birthday suit and slam the door shut in her face.

"Konrad . . ." she says through the wood, her voice sounding too thin.

Burning with humiliation, I slip back into my boxers and open the door again, coming face-to-face with my mother, who's just seen me checking myself out completely naked. But the embarrassment vanishes as quickly as it came. So what if she saw me naked? If I really look like I think I look now, then *everybody* should see me naked.

She blinks. "Konrad? Is that . . . *you*?"

"Hi, Mom . . ." She's so much shorter than me now.

She shakes her head, trying to form words but failing.

I clench my fists in triumph. "I KNOW, RIGHT?"

I wait for her to speak until I realize my bladder is about to explode. While all of this was happening, I never actually got a chance to pee. "Okay," I say, pushing on the door. "I know this is incredible and all, but I *really* have to use the bathroom now."

From the other side, all I hear is: "I'm calling your father."

My mom, brother, and I sit at the kitchen table waiting for Dad to drive his taxi back from the city to our little suburb. The two of them never stopped staring.

Mom's features scrunch together. She shakes her head. "I don't even know what to say."

"What do you mean?" I ask. "There's nothing to say. Just be happy for me!"

Watching her, I can literally see the buildup. It starts with the heaving of her chest and climbs to the twitch of her lips. A few seconds later, she's bawling. "You didn't like the way you looked?" she asks.

I'm taken aback by the accusation in her question. "No, I did. It's just that . . ."

She takes the towel she was using to wipe the plate—the one she's now holding onto for dear life—and blows her nose. "Just that what?"

"Just . . . I don't know . . . I always wanted to be better looking."

"But you were already good-looking!"

I consider telling her that I wasn't. That I wasn't good-looking enough. But this is probably not the best moment to throw insults at my family's genetic pool. "Mom, I didn't think it would actually happen, okay?"

She's rocking back and forth a little. "An Inexplicable Development," she laments, more to herself than to me. "In our family . . ."

A moment passes in silence. Arthur decides to cut it short. "So . . . are we going to school today or what?"

"No," Mom answers. "You're not."

Arthur's fist pumps through the air. "WOO-HOO!"

I'm both relieved and disappointed. I want to spend the whole day checking myself out in the mirror, but also get to school and show myself off as soon as possible. Although, now that Mom's put a damper on things, I'm not sure either is appropriate.

"Can I text Alan and Lauren?" I ask, already plotting in my head how I'll attach a selfie with the caption I WOKE UP LIKE THIS. They're going to shit themselves.

Before Mom can answer, the back door swings open into the kitchen and Dad walks in. I'm facing away, so at first, he doesn't notice anything different. "What's the emergency?" he asks in his thick accent. "I was already on the highway, Julia. I had to turn around."

I peek over my shoulder. Once his shoes come off, he takes one good look at Mom and his annoyance fizzles. He walks around the table and sits in the last empty chair. When his eyes finally land on me, they turn into two large globes.

"Hi, Dad," I say, my lips pulled back in an awkward smile.

I let him take me in. His mouth opens and closes. I keep looking at his big Polish nose, the one he passed on to me. The one I don't have to deal with anymore.

"How?" is the only thing that comes out of his mouth.

Arthur butts in to explain. "It's an Inexplicable Development, Dad. Konrad thought he was ugly and wished to be better looking and it came true."

Dad's eyes never leave me. "You wished for this?"

"Duh," Arthur goes on. "Of course he did. That's what the main ID theory says. Don't they teach you that stuff back in the motherland?"

Dad doesn't seem to hear him. But he doesn't need to. He knows the theory well enough, just like everybody else. The theory that claims IDs happen because the people they happen to *want* them to happen. What Dad is waiting to hear is for me to confirm it.

"I guess," I answer with a shrug. I don't mention that I've fantasized about this happening pretty much every day since I hit puberty.

"It's so strange," he says, as if I haven't spoken. "It's you, it's definitely you. But it's like you're airbrushed or something."

"Exactly! Isn't it great?" At least his reaction isn't as bad as Mom's. Except, about a second later, his head starts shaking, too. "You *wanted* this?"

Gah! Hell yeah, I wanted this! Who wouldn't? Maybe if I shout it out at the top of my lungs then they'll finally believe me.

"I don't understand," Dad continues. "You've always been such a confident kid. You have friends, and girls like you. There was Sara. And you still have Lauren."

My heart twists at the mention of Sara.

"Lauren's a lesbian," Arthur says flatly.

"I'm still me," I say, because they're kind of making me feel like I'm not.

Dad presses his lips into a line. His eyes twinkle in the morning light coming through the window. And then, like he couldn't be any more melodramatic, like he couldn't just be happy for me, he chokes up this little gem: "But you don't even look like us anymore."

My frustration spills over. "Oh, come on! This is awesome and you know it. It's a dream come true. You're going to tell me you never wished you looked different?"

"I did," Mom admits. "Sure. I'm sure most people your age do. But you must've wanted it a lot more than most people. I never woke up beautiful."

"Julia," Dad scolds, "you *are* beautiful."

Mom's lips turn up at the edges and she starts sobbing again. Arthur and I exchange grimaces. Forehead wrinkled, Dad snaps his gaze back to me and starts shaking his head like I've committed an unforgivable crime.

Seriously, what the hell? IDs have been happening since forever. In Poland, where my parents grew up. In the States. All over the world. Both Mom and Dad know this, so why are they acting this way? And it's not like mine's even that weird. At least I'm not like that Estonian girl who grew wings from her back. Or that Thai dude who developed the ability to turn invisible.

I feel a pinch of dread in my chest. True, the Thai dude turned invisible once and could never turn back again. But maybe that's exactly what he wanted. Inexplicable Developments are inherently good. Isn't that what they say? For Christ's sake, they're supposed to be people's *wishes* coming true. What's more positive than that?

CHAPTER 2

CAMILLA

Numb.

Not hysterical. Not suicidal. Numb.

You want to know the first thing I did when I flung off the covers this morning and saw what I looked like underneath? I laughed. That's right—*laughed*. Like, out loud, no-holds-barred guffawed. I thought: there's no way this is not a joke. The world can't possibly be this cruel. Not even to me. Right?

Well, I'm not laughing anymore. Not that I'm freaking out either. I'm done with that part, too. I guess that "calm after the storm" saying is true. Or is it "calm before the storm"? Maybe the main storm, the bigger one, just hasn't arrived yet.

I could just stay in my room forever. Why not? Get Mom to buy me a little electric stove for cooking. Construct a dumbwaiter at the window so I can pull up groceries after ordering them online. That way, I'll never have to leave. That way, no one will ever have to see me.

I should look again. I don't want to, but I should.

Based on what I know, those *things* don't happen unless you really want them to, so maybe whatever happened to me is something else. Maybe it's only temporary.

I have to check. I need to pee, anyway, and my stomach's been grumbling for a while.

Before I push myself up from the floor where I've spent the past hour hugging my knees, I check my phone to see if Jodie replied yet. She hasn't. But she will. And she'll listen to my endless pleas to come over as soon as school lets out.

I couldn't bear to see Mom this morning. How could I face her reaction when I was still reeling from my own? When she knocked on my door to make sure my alarm went off, I was already up. A shame so potent I thought I'd combust silenced all the evil voices in my head. Before she could come in, I gathered all the energy I had left and yelled, "I'm up, Mom! Love you! Have a great day!" At least one of us still could, right?

Now I'm ready for someone I trust to see me as soon as possible. Jodie's frank. Oftentimes, a little too frank, but if there was ever a time I needed her honesty, it's now.

As I heave myself up, I do my best not to look down. It hurts to even remember the warped impostor that's swapped places with my runner's body.

Shaking, I sneak over to the door. My plan is to go to the downstairs bathroom, use the mirror there, and then steal something from the fridge. The house is quiet. Mom won't be home from the hospital until eight and, obviously, Dad is never coming back.

On the first floor, I flip on the bathroom light and creep inside. Resting my hands on the sink, I take a deep breath, and look up.

My stomach drops. Nothing's changed. Everything's still wrong. Not just wrong—*obscene.* It's as if some sadistic deity rearranged the layout of my entire face while I slept, smashed some features down, exaggerated and distorted others, all with the ultimate goal of making me look as disgusting as humanly possible.

Lips quivering, I reach up to run my fingers over the bulbous, asymmetrical nose. Around the beadier eyes, farther apart than they used to be. Then the new bumps surrounding them on my olive complexion—the formerly spotless complexion I inherited from my Turkish dad and one of the few things I had actually liked about my appearance.

Not a single redeemable trait remains. None. But what hurts even more, what I can't stomach, is that, even among all these hideous new features, I still recognize myself.

With shaking hands, I yank open the mirror and snag a razor off a shelf. I smear shaving cream above my nose and start slashing at the patch of hair connecting my eyebrows. I don't worry about cutting myself. In fact, I secretly hope I do.

I splash some water on my face, but there's no relief. If anything, I feel even worse. There's nothing else I can try. No other improvements to be made. And even if there were, they would be meaningless in the grand scheme of things.

I refuse to cry. I didn't cry when I broke my arm in sixth grade. I didn't cry when one of my best friends made out with the guy I'd been secretly in love with for years. And I didn't cry after Dad's accident. I'm not going to start now. In the end, I don't stop at the fridge. I go back up to my room, close the door behind me, and lie down.

Maybe, if I go back to sleep, this will all just end up being a nightmare.

The incessant chime of the doorbell rips me awake. I grab for my phone. 3:40 P.M. Six missed calls from Jodie. Eleven unread messages.

I race downstairs, refusing to so much as glance at any reflective surface, forcing myself not to think about how it takes my muscles so much more effort to cover the same distance. Peering through the peephole, I unlock the door, but instead of opening it, I back into the living room, gripped by the same shame I'd been experiencing since I first woke up this morning.

After a moment, there's a tug on the knob and the door flies open. "Camilla?" Jodie yells. "Are you okay? What hap—"

The moment she lays eyes on me, she freezes. Both of her perfectly manicured hands fly up to her face. That's how I know the nightmare is real. Nothing ever shocks Jodie.

Tears climb my throat, but I hold them back. My knees buckle. Jodie lowers her hands, her forehead in a knot, her naturally large eyes even wider. Still, she doesn't say a thing. For the first time in seven years of friendship, Jodie is speechless.

My lower lip trembling, I wring my hands and wait. Jodie takes a wary step toward me, as if she's trying to corner a frightened but potentially dangerous animal.

"My life is over," I say, because I can't stand her silence.

I see her searching for words, turning them over in her head. For a second, I think she might even agree with me. *Yup, it is, Camilla. Your life is completely over. See you around? Or probably not.* But then she wouldn't be Jodie.

In one burst, she closes the distance between us. As she swoops me into a hug, all I can think is how she's slightly taller than me now. She cradles me in her arms, but I just hang there in her grasp like a limp rag doll, my cheek against the strap of her backpack. I like the smell of her perfume. It's familiar. Comforting. It helps.

Eventually, she pries me away.

I look up at her face, at the bold mascara smudged on her brown cheeks. She's crying. An urge to do the same stings my eyes, but I blink it away.

Jodie's lips twist to one side. She scans me from head to toe and back up again. "It's not *that* bad," she says.

The manic laughter from earlier this morning returns. Now I've seen it all. Jodie is actually *lying* to try to make me feel better. My giggles, however, are only temporary. I drop to the couch and put my disgusting new face in my disgusting new hands. Jodie joins me, her long fingers landing on my shoulder, giving it a gentle rub.

"So I'm guessing you didn't wish for this, huh?" she asks.

My head snaps up. I'm too weak to get defensive. "Jodie, please."

"Isn't that how these things usually happen, though?"

"I don't know."

She thinks for a moment. "Maybe someone else wished it?"

A cold shiver ripples down my spine. Could it be? Is this some kind of punishment for what I did? But I apologized. I was a bitch, I reflected on it, and everybody moved on. Ashley even told me so herself. She wouldn't do this to me.

"What did your mom say?" Jodie asks quietly when I don't reply.

"She doesn't know yet," I whimper. "Nobody knows."

Jodie's face lights up. "You have to go to the hospital and tell her. If you didn't wish for this, then it might be something else. Someone there will be able to figure this out for sure."

A spark of hope flickers in my chest. No sane human being would ever wish for this. Maybe this is some kind of disease after all? Oh God, I hope it's some kind of disease. Then maybe it can be cured. The other explanation is forever.

With one of her fingers pointed at my chest, Jodie shoots up. "Wait right there." A couple of minutes later, she's back with my jeans and gray hoodie. I don't point out that it's almost eighty degrees out as I slip into both, then drop my butt back onto the couch.

Jodie peels off her backpack and settles beside me, then puts her bag on her lap and starts digging through it.

Facial wipes come out first. Her fingers grab my chin to steady it and she goes to town cleaning my face. She's a little rough, but I kind of like the feeling. I want her to rub the ugly off my face.

She spends a long time applying makeup. I've never been a big fan of the stuff; it gets messy when I run. But Jodie always carries an extra bottle of foundation for my skin tone. "Just in case," she'd always say. I'd laugh it off, but I guess "just in case" is finally here. Jodie'd probably deny it, but I bet Ashley's shade is still in there, too.

My heart bursts with gratitude.

When she's done, she takes a moment to examine her work. She reaches for a mirror, but I shake my head. I don't want to see.

"Well, anyway," she says, flashing her perfect set of white teeth. "I think you look great." The smile, even if it's forced, warms my chest. At this point, I'll take anything that sounds even remotely positive. "Okay," she says. "Let's go."

Maybe she's right. Maybe things aren't as bad as they seem. Maybe I'll just wear more makeup from now on and everything will be fine.

I get up.

"Oh," Jodie says, reaching into her bag one last time. Her hand returns with a pair of sunglasses. Not just any sunglasses. Oversized, round, seventies-style shades with lenses so big I bet if you put one on a record player it would play disco. "These will look so cute on you." Her teeth are on display again and her eyes are trying to convey enthusiasm.

Emphasis on *trying*.

Forget what I said. Things are definitely as bad as I think.

I do my best to pretend I'm an A-list celebrity. Between the hood over my hair, my oversized sunglasses, and Jodie rushing me from my house to her car and her car to the hospital lobby like a bodyguard, I might as well be hiding from the flashing cameras of the paparazzi.

But who am I kidding? I feel like the freak show that I have become. Like I'm so unbelievably ugly now, people would pay to see me. Showing myself to the public for free would just be bad business.

Arm hooked in mine, Jodie leads the way as we pass through the automatic doors of the hospital waiting room. "Hi, Darnell!" she calls to the security guard.

"Hello, sweetheart." His eyes land on me. "Who's your friend?"

Jodie hesitates, so I answer for her. "It's me, Darnell," I whisper. "Camilla."

Darnell's face tightens into an awkward smile, his confusion crossed with concern. "Oh. Hi, honey. Sorry, I didn't recognize you."

Before I can melt into a puddle of shame, Jodie jerks me away, flagging down Mariah, the head nurse. Mariah took my mom under her wing almost twenty years ago and they've been friends ever since. I've known her my whole life.

"Mariah!" Jodie says. "Where's Mrs. Hadi?"

Mariah stops fiddling with her clipboard and lowers her chin. She observes us over her thick-framed glasses. Her gaze lingers on me, but she doesn't ask questions. I love her for that.

"She's assisting with surgery right now. Should be out in a couple of minutes. Can you wait?"

Jodie nods and scans the room for empty seats, but the waiting room's full. She drags me to a nearby corner where we stand next to a young mother and her son. A big bandage covers the kid's left hand. He holds it with his right one like it'll fall off if he lets go. I wish I were here with a cut-up hand. Hell, I'd cut off my hand if it meant getting my old self back.

We don't have to wait long. Not even ten minutes. Mom rounds the corner, and as soon as she spots us in the crowd, she runs over.

"What is it?" Her voice is so full of concern. My face burns and the urge to cry lurks just below the surface. I can't bear to look at her, so I keep my eyes on the hospital floor. What do you say to your mom when her heart is guaranteed to break anyway?

It turns out I don't have to say anything. All it takes is one look and her arms fling around me. She presses me to her bosom, her hand sliding up and down along my back. I breathe her in. If I could, I'd stay like this forever.

Eventually, in one gentle motion, she pries us apart. A cold draft of air sneaks between us. With one hand on my arm, she reaches over to pull down Jodie's sunglasses with the other. I force myself to look my mom in the eye.

Shock flashes across her face, but it's immediately replaced by pain. So much pain. She stifles a sob. "Oh, Camilla." Again, she pulls me into a mighty hug, rocking me back and forth. "My baby, my baby." She holds onto me so tight, I have trouble breathing.

Everything that happens next is a blur. I hear the woman who came in with her son complain that she got to the emergency room first. Mom shushes her and leads me to an isolated bed. Dr. Jackson arrives, takes my temperature, then listens to my heartbeat. I answer his questions. But I'm running on autopilot. I just want him to say it already. Make it official.

Just as he's about to, the world around me comes back into focus. I'm still sitting on the bed, my now-shorter legs dangling above the floor. Jodie stands next to Mom. Mariah lingers behind them. They all look like they're at a funeral. I guess, in a way, they are.

Dr. Jackson clears his throat, pulls up a chair, and settles into it. I get the feeling he doesn't do this for all of his patients. Mom shuffles over, takes my fingers from my lap, and wraps them in hers.

"Camilla, sweetheart," he says with a sigh, "you're perfectly healthy." I nod, urging him to just spit it out. "I know how you must feel—"

Um, no, I think to myself. *No, you don't.*

"—but there's nothing medically wrong with you."

Mom's eyes are brimming. I think, at this point, she's even more distraught about this whole thing than I am. And I get it. I do. The child she gave birth to, watched grow over a span of sixteen years, looks nothing like she did up until last night. God already took the love of her life. Now he replaced her daughter with a monster.

"It's very strange," Dr. Jackson continues. "I've never personally seen a case like this before. It's so far outside the usual paradigm. But it just goes to show that there are so many things we don't understand about this particular phenomenon yet." He pauses and tries to soften the blow. "Sometimes, unlucky things happen to the best of people."

"It's okay, Dr. Jackson," I blurt. "Just say it."

Mom's fingers squeeze harder around my hand. Mariah's gaze drops. Jodie gives me a small smile, but a tear skids down her cheek. Everyone braces for it. Everyone except me.

"Unfortunately, there's no doubt in my mind that . . . that this is an Inexplicable Development."

Even though I knew the words were coming, they echo inside my head. They feel so formal. So burdensome. So exhausting.

Inexplicable Development.

The name says it all.

Something that just happens. Has been happening for centuries. Inexplicably. Irreversibly. Once or twice in a blue moon. In this little town or that faraway country.

Something you read about in biology, occasionally hear about on the news. Something people commonly chalk up to wishing, but clearly even doctors don't fully understand.

Something that's supposed to be *positive.*

Something I *definitely* did not wish for.

And yet, something that still weaseled itself into my life and destroyed it.

CHAPTER 3

KONRAD

TODAY IS AN IMPORTANT DAY. Not only is it the one-day anniversary of my Inexplicable Development (yay!), it also marks my grand return to school. I kind of wish my transformation happened before the first day of the year, and not a random two weeks into September, but hey, not *everything's* going to be perfect, right? *Wink-wink.*

Mom's at the stove, flipping eggs. I wait, my mouth formed into a giant grin, my leg pumping under the kitchen table. Arthur and Dad are both still asleep. I've been up for an hour. If they looked like me, I'm sure they wouldn't waste their time sleeping either.

Call it cocky, call it douchey, whatever. I don't care. I'm calling it "embracing my fate." Because, yeah, there's no way

I'm feeling guilty about something this awesome. I hit the ID jackpot and I'm going to let myself enjoy it.

Yesterday, I took a shitload of selfies. Yes, *selfies*, and no, I'm not ashamed. I need some kind of outlet for my new hotness. Of course, I didn't just do it because I'm in love with myself. There's a method behind my narcissistic madness. As soon as I make my appearance at school, I'm going to update all of my social media. Delete everything that came before and start all over with my new mug. It's time for a new beginning and I'm going to start with a bang.

In between all the selfies, I went to the mall. Most of my old clothes don't fit me anymore, so I got new jeans, three T-shirts, and a new pair of Vans. By the way, my shoe size went from a ten to a twelve. Yes, this is important.

I drove a little farther out than necessary, all the way to the mall downtown in the city. I didn't want anybody from school seeing me before I was ready. I want the big reveal to be nothing short of perfection.

Also important, strangers notice me now. Like, *actually* notice me. My final tally for two hours of wandering from store to store was five glances, two smiles, and a 'sup from some random dude. A dude. Even floor staff treats you differently when you're good-looking. Before the ID, the only attention I got from strangers was an occasional *move it, kid*.

Today is going to be epic. I'll be the man of the hour. Man of the year, even. People might be a little weirded out by the circumstances, sure, but that'll pass.

A squeal of joy escapes my lips. Thankfully, the hiss of frying bacon drowns it out and Mom doesn't hear a thing.

"I'm going to call the school and let them know," she says through a yawn. "Just to be on the safe side."

"I know," I mumble. "You said that forty thousand times already." What does she think the school's going to do about it, anyway? Assign me a pair of burly bodyguards because I'm so beautiful people won't be able to restrain themselves?

"I'm glad you met up with Alan yesterday," she adds.

"Yeah," I lie. "Me, too."

Mom thinks Alan came with me to the mall. Technically, he was supposed to, so I'm not a total fraud. But he canceled on me last minute—his cousins invaded his house. Of course, I could've told Mom that, but considering she thinks this is more of a curse than a blessing, I thought it would ease her mind to know that I already had Alan's support. Truth is, he knows nothing about it. *Yet.* He'll be finding out soon enough.

"You're going to need your friends," she says, standing over me and scraping the eggs onto my plate. "Now more than ever. You might think this is the best thing that's ever happened to you, but not everyone will agree."

"Mom," I say with a sigh, "how can anything but the positive come out of this?"

Suddenly enveloped in a dramatic silence, she returns the pan to the stove and makes her way back to sit across from me at the table. Great. The lectures continue. As if I didn't get enough of them last night.

"Honey, everything's going to change."

I unleash a *tsk*. "I *know*, Mom."

"People will treat you differently. You had time to grow into yourself. Now you almost have to start from scratch. It's like getting a new car. It takes time to learn how to navigate it."

"You don't navigate cars, Mom. You drive them."

"Well, you better drive carefully."

I roll my eyes.

"Konrad, I just want you to remember who you are. You can't let this go to your head. Looks are not everything."

"I won't."

"You promise?"

"I promise," I say, just so I can get back to my food.

Looks are not everything. Yeah, right. What world is she living in?

After breakfast, I drive over to Alan's. He has no idea I'm coming. I never pick him up like this. It would be super eco-friendly and all, but he lives on the other side of town, has his own car, and, most importantly, hates the way I drive.

I park in front of his house. The sun feels so good on my face I decide to snap another selfie. I swear, it's like an addiction. Before, on the rare occasion I'd snap one, I needed at least five takes before I settled on something acceptable. Now I can have my eyes closed, my tongue out, and my mouth gaping mid-sentence, and still rock the photo.

Checking out my latest self-portrait, I ring the doorbell. After a couple of seconds, Mrs. Nguyen opens the door. She's squinting, scrubbing her glasses on her robe.

"Is that you, Konrad?"

"Morning, Mrs. Nguyen!"

"It's 7 A.M. What in the world got into you?"

"Can I go up?"

Shaking her head, she steps aside and tilts it toward the staircase. I paste on a smile and wait, hoping she'll put her glasses back on and say something about my transformation. She doesn't. She just shuts the door and walks off. I can't say I'm not disappointed.

I run upstairs.

There's a slight chance that, at this very moment, Alan is playing with himself. He has a policy and it goes something like this: polishing your knob in the morning polishes your mind for the day. If I do catch him in the act, it'll only make this day better.

I barge into his perpetually clean-freak room without knocking.

Alan's not playing with himself. He's not even moving. He's sprawled out on his bed in his boxers and a Hanes T-shirt, a limb at each corner of his bed, his snores the only indication he's alive. An Xbox controller sits at his feet and his TV screen displays a frozen enemy soldier.

I launch myself onto his mattress and scream into his ear, "GOOD MORNING!"

He totally freaks out, shrinking away and covering his head with both hands. "WHAT THE FUCK?" he yells in a creaky voice. "Get off me!" Unfortunately for him, telling me to get off only encourages me. I drop my arm around him and spoon him from behind, my face zoning in on his giant crop of pitch-black hair. This works like a charm. He rockets off the bed.

As soon as he does, I prop my head up with one hand, strike a sexy pose, and bat my eyelashes. "Are you sure you want to reject *this*?"

"Huh?" Alan growls, turning his back to me and plucking his basketball shorts from his desk chair in an obvious attempt to hide his morning wood. Once they're on him, he gropes for his glasses. Like mother, like son, I guess.

Patiently, I wait, my teeth on full display. When he can finally see the world around him, he looks at me. He takes me in. He sees the new me.

I don't move, enjoying the delight bubbling up inside.

His annoyed snarl vanishes. Within seconds, his face becomes a slideshow of different emotions, changing like a kaleidoscope. First his eyes go big, then his brow wrinkles, his lip twitches. He opens his mouth, closes it again.

I can't contain myself any longer. I jump from the bed and immediately remove my T-shirt. "Check this out." I flex and spin around. "Dude, look at my stomach!" I babble about what happened, about what's different, not missing a single detail. I make him squeeze my biceps, get up in his face and point out the inch I gained on his height. Alan has gotten plenty of ignorant *you're really tall for an Asian* comments in his life, including some tongue-in-cheek but secretly envious ones from me. He'd always just shrug in response, but I know he liked hearing them. Well, he's not the tall one anymore and I'm making sure he knows it.

Alan doesn't speak, but I can tell he's following every word. "Dude," I finish, spreading my arms out in a *ta-da*. "Isn't this *insane*?"

Something like a groan escapes his lips. He opens his mouth again, but the words take a while to come out. "Yeah," he finally says. "It is."

"Well? What do you think?"

He shakes his head, taking a while to answer. "Dude, this is so . . . random." His eyes jump all over my body. "You look so weird."

"Not weird," I correct him. "Gorgeous."

"You look like a Disney prince version of yourself."

"Good," I say. "That means I can get all the Jasmines!"

He forces out an awkward chuckle.

"What?" I ask.

"You wished for this?"

I shrug. "Yeah."

"Why?"

"Um . . . because I'm a human being with a pulse?" My ass plops down to his bed. Doubt and disappointment creep up on me. First my family and now my best friend, too? Why is everyone trying to guilt me into regretting this?

"Dude," he says, coming over to sit beside me. "Sorry, I'm just not sure what to say. Congratulations?"

"Forget it."

"Oh, come on. If this is what you wanted, I'm happy for you."

"Doesn't seem like it."

He snorts. This time it's more genuine. I think. "I'm just confused," he says. "My best friend looks like a totally different person."

I sigh. He's right. And I think I get it. I just need to give those closest to me some time. How would I react if I were in Alan's shoes? Besides, there's a big difference between *it happened to me* and *it happened to my friend or son or brother*. Eventually, though, he's going to have to accept and support me. Because there's no going back.

"Well, this is me now," I say.

Alan nods. "This is you now."

"Yup."

"Does Lauren know?"

"Not yet."

"I'm the first friend you told? I'm flattered."

"You should be."

For a moment, we sit in silence. Alan clears his throat. "So," he says, "do you have a giant schlong now, too?"

My lips tug upward.

"You do! Let me see!"

I snort. "No!"

We both laugh, and I let the relief wash over me. After a moment, when I glance at him, I see he's still smiling, but his hands are clenching and unclenching in his lap. He looks like he wants to say something and he's trying to find the right words. The silence stretches on, and I dread finding out what it is. When he finally speaks, his voice is softer. "Does Sara have anything to do with this?"

My head snaps in Alan's direction. "What? Why would she?"

He's shaking his head a little too fast. "Just wondering."

Frowning, I study the floor. "Dude, she has nothing to do with this. Trust me."

"Okay."

I clench my jaw. I'm not lying. I didn't want to be better looking because of Sara. That girl doesn't even deserve space in my thoughts anymore. Sara? *Pff*, please . . .

Now that he mentions it, though, if she happens to regret crushing my heart, then, well, *good*. That will only add icing to my already sexy cake.

CHAPTER 4

CAMILLA

"You ready?" Jodie asks from behind the wheel of her Nissan. Her sleek hair is gathered into an elegant bun at the back of her head. From her clothes to her makeup to her mannerisms, everything about Jodie is perpetually meticulous.

I'm in the passenger seat, wearing my paparazzi getup. I have to say, I kind of appreciate the mysterious vibe her giant sunglasses create. I might have to get special permission to wear them in school when I go back.

If I go back.

"Give me a couple of seconds to think," I say.

There's only one other car in the diner's parking lot. It's four o'clock, so that makes sense—too late for lunch, too early for dinner. Ashley should have some time to talk. If she even talks to me in the first place.

"She probably just started her shift," Jodie says.

I nod. Not probably. Ashley always works at four on Wednesdays. I know because I know her schedule by heart. We used to make plans around it all the time.

"What are you going to say?" Jodie asks, giving her Diet Coke a slurp. On numerous occasions, I've tried to tell her that Diet's not as healthy as she thinks, but she doesn't listen. She listens when it really matters, though. She even skipped school today to spend the day with me.

"I'm just going to ask her straight up," I say with a sigh.

"What if she lies?"

"I'll be able to tell."

Jodie snorts. "Yeah, right." After a moment, she adds, "To be honest, I doubt she had anything to do with this. You more than made things up to her. And she's not *that* evil."

My throat tightens. I know Jodie doesn't mean to be hurtful, but her words are a blaring reminder of what I have to live with now.

She catches herself almost immediately. "I'm sorry. I didn't mean it like that."

I turn to face her and force a small smile. "I know." Jodie smiles back, but I can tell she's beating herself up. "I just need to make sure." I can't spend the rest of my life wallowing in my room. If there are no confirmed rules about how or why

IDs happen, then who's to say someone other than yourself can't play a part in bringing one about? I need to know if Ashley had anything to do with mine. I need answers. I need there to be a reason this happened to me.

"Maybe there *is* no explanation," Jodie says, as if reading my thoughts.

"There has to be."

"What are you going to do if she says she did it?"

"I don't know."

"Are you going to beat her ass?" The edges of Jodie's lips lift, and then she slurps up the rest of her Coke. "You should."

Obviously, I'm not going to beat Ashley's ass. If she does admit to playing a part in my ID, I'm going fall to my knees and beg her to take her wish back. I don't care if all documented IDs in the past have been permanent.

The slurping stops. "You sure you don't want me to come with you?"

"No. It's better if I do this alone. I don't want Ashley thinking we're ganging up on her again."

"Oh, come on. We didn't gang up on her."

I stare at the decrepit building in front of me. People call the restaurant—officially named Dory's—the Shack for a reason. It's really close to our school, though, and the food is cheap. It's the best option for when you're broke and don't feel like crossing the border into the city. I don't think there's a kid in town who hasn't been here at least fifty times. For me and Jodie, it's closer to five hundred. "Yeah, Jodie," I say. "Yeah, we did."

She shrugs and shifts her attention to her phone. "Whatever. I'll be here if you need me."

Up until three months ago, Jodie was as close to Ashley as I was. To everyone who knew us, we were the JAC team— Jodie, Ashley, and Camilla. Jodie played a part in the breakup of our little group, too. The difference is, Jodie wasn't in love with Lance Dietrick. I was. And she didn't hit the SHARE button on that video. I did.

I take a deep breath and pop open the car door. Trudging toward the building, I spot Ashley and her breathtaking Afro almost immediately. She's behind the register in her white waitress skirt—a perfect contrast to her dark skin. As always, she looks stunning. Jodie is beautiful, too, but not in that effortless way Ashley has been for as long as I remember.

A pang of the same type of jealousy that led to the end of our friendship pinches my insides. I quickly squash it down. Why do people feel things they don't want to feel? I want nothing but the best for Ashley and I'd do anything to undo what I did, yet, no matter how hard I try, I still can't kill the envy. Maybe this, right here, is the reason I'm a freak of nature now.

Even before I push open the glass door, Ashley's flashing me her polite smile. "Welcome to Dory's," she says. It feels like it's been so long since I heard her voice. "Just one?"

She has no idea who I am.

I stare at her from behind my shades. "Hi, Ashley."

Her smile dips. "Hello?" It sounds more like a question than a greeting. Slowly, I remove my sunglasses. Her smile vanishes completely.

"Can you talk?" I manage to squeeze out.

Her eyes are glued to my face. Feeling exposed, I slip my sunglasses back on.

Ashley doesn't answer. Her forehead wrinkles and she dashes around the counter. Instead of running away after seeing me for the monstrosity I've become, she closes the distance between us, scooping me into a big hug.

This feels weird. Weird, but wonderful. Ashley hasn't touched me, hasn't given me the time of day, since the beginning of summer, at Gina's end-of-school party.

Where it all went down.

It was so wrong of me to call her a slut when she made out with Lance. To film it. To share the video. Even if it wasn't fair to me. Why should Ashley get two guys at once—a devoted (albeit a little douchey) boyfriend in Mike Rogers, and Lance, *my* Lance—when I can't even find one? To be honest, I still don't think it was fair.

But Ashley didn't deserve what I did to her.

My body responds on its own. I lean in, my hands wrapping around her, my cheek brushing against her hair. I came here to get an answer. I've already gotten it before even asking the question.

Ashley's head snaps toward the floor of the restaurant. "Christine!" she yells to the skinny girl wiping down an empty table in the back. "I'm just going out for a smoke, okay?"

Christine nods a few times. She's as much taken aback by Ashley's open admission that she smokes as I am. Ashley's smoking had always been a secret we shared. One of many.

She grabs my hand and drags me out the door, toward the big dumpsters behind the diner. I barely even register the smell. Her hand still clenching mine, she whirls around to face me. "What happened?"

My lips go on auto-quiver again. I'm sobbing, but without the tears. "I don't know."

She runs her gaze all over my new features, her eyes getting more and more blurry with every passing second. "Is it an ID?"

"I missed you so much," I tell her. And I mean it.

Ashley pulls me into another embrace. "I missed you, too."

"You're not mad anymore?" I whisper into her shoulder.

I feel her body tense. She pulls away, as if she's just remembered what I'd done. Her hand reaches into the pocket of her skirt and she yanks out a pack of Parliaments. Through one of them on her lips she says, "No."

"But everyone thinks you're a slut," I say. "All because of me."

Ashley shrugs. The cigarette lights up orange at the tip as she inhales. "It doesn't matter," she says, blowing out a cloud of smoke. "The past is in the past. When did this happen?"

"Yesterday."

Her frown tightens. "Do you know why?"

"No. I thought you cursed me or something."

Ashley's expression softens, then tightens right back up. "You think I'd do that?"

"No."

"Then why are you here?"

"I don't know." I look her in the eyes, pleading as if she has all the answers. "Why did this happen, Ashley? I didn't want this. So *why*?"

"I don't know. But I would never do that to you, Camilla. *Never.*"

Her words give me some relief. But they also flood me with another powerful emotion. A much less desirable one.

It's not disappointment. It's not despair or sadness.

It's anger.

Because if Ashley isn't responsible for my change, then who is?

CHAPTER 5

KONRAD

"HI, KONRAD," BECCA LIPOWSKA SAYS to me out of freaking nowhere. "I never noticed how hot you were before."

She's obviously being sarcastic, but that doesn't stop me from exchanging looks of disbelief with Alan and Lauren anyway. I scramble to reply with something intelligible. "Uh, you never noticed me, period." (Gah. I'm such a dork.)

Becca's laugh is accompanied by a wink. Flanked by her cheerleader posse, she struts off down the hallway. Alan's and Lauren's eyes latch on to her butt as it wiggles away. "Damn," Alan says. "She actually said *words* to you."

It's my second day back and the stares, compliments, adds, and follows haven't stopped. If anything, they're multiplying.

Ours is a pretty small school—900-something students—but with all this new attention, it feels so much bigger.

I guess I shouldn't be that surprised, though. After all, I'm the local miracle. Jackie Baker even asked me to do an interview for the school blog. The only person who isn't really celebrating, besides Alan—who says he's happy for me but is clearly not—is Lauren. That makes two friends who are not happy for me. (I only have two friends.) I'm giving Alan some time to come around, but with Lauren, I'm not even sure there's hope.

"You could've wished for anything in the entire universe and you wished for this?" she asks, eyebrow raised. Lauren missed my big debut yesterday because she was ditching the entire day. She does that a lot.

"I wish for things all the time," I reply. "How was I supposed to know that out of all of them, this would be the one that would come true?"

"Hm. I had no idea you were so incredibly shallow."

I feel my face burning up, even though I'm not surprised. That's Lauren for you. No filter. Probably no soul either.

When I don't say anything, she adds, "I liked your big nose. I thought it gave you character and made you look very handsome."

"Yeah," I mumble. "Too bad no straight girl has ever said that about me . . ."

Lauren gives me a cutting look. "Did you want to make Sara jealous or something?"

I slam my locker shut. "No! Can you two stop mentioning her? She has nothing to do with this."

"Jeez," Lauren says. "Don't get your nut sack in a twist, Pretty Boy."

"Don't call me Pretty Boy."

"But that's what you are now." She tilts her head. "I mean, come on, that was a pretty narcissistic wish." I glare at her, and she flashes her teeth in a cheeky smile. "So what are you going to do next? Quit school and model underwear for a living?"

I'm overwhelmed with a huge desire to accuse her of jealousy. Except that wouldn't be much of an argument. Lauren's super comfortable in her own skin, which is probably the reason she has more than a few admirers. And she's the only true redhead in school, so she gets points for that, too. I bite my tongue and look at Alan, hoping he backs me up and tells her I'm not a self-obsessed douchebag. That *everyone* wishes to be better looking.

But he doesn't.

"I'm going to class," I say, turning my back on them. Neither joins me or mentions anything about lunch.

Whatever.

As I make my way to the second floor, I let the stares and *hi*'s sink in. Now we're talking. And why shouldn't I enjoy the attention? Why is everyone I know trying to make me feel bad? My ID happened, and there's nothing I can do about it.

In history, Mr. Connick pushes shut his desk drawer and looks me up and down. "The man of the hour," he says, giving me a smile.

"Hi, Mr. Connick," I reply, smiling back. *See? Even the teachers are more supportive than my own friends.*

I make my way to a desk in the middle of the room. For as long as I can remember, I've always sat in the middle. It's a neutral approach, I know, but then I've always occupied a neutral space in school. I wasn't cool, and I wasn't a pariah, so the middle worked.

I'm not so sure it still will now that the whole school—including, ahem, Becca Lipowska—knows my name.

Once my butt's in my chair, Mr. Connick averts his eyes, but everyone else is less polite. Or maybe, by staring, they're being polite? I'm not sure what the etiquette should be under these circumstances. You'd think the novelty of my ID would've faded a bit after a day, but that doesn't seem to be the case at all. I smile at as many people as I can without seeming like a creep and focus on pulling my books out of my backpack.

"Konrad?"

I turn toward the voice. "Hey, Eric, what's up?"

Now Eric Stewart's social status has always tended toward the bottom rung. I like him, though, and have partnered up with him by default a bunch of times in the past.

"Can I ask you something?"

The bell rings, and I hesitate. But Mr. Connick is busy writing something on the board. "Uh, sure."

"How did it happen?"

"No idea," I say. "It's an ID."

"I mean, was there anything specific you did? Beforehand?"

I try to remember if I did anything out of the ordinary the night before my transformation. All I can come up with is downing Lauren's nasty tequila, but neither Alan's nor Lauren's wishes came true, so I'm pretty sure that had nothing to do with it. "Not that I can recall. Why?"

Eric's face flushes red. "I wish something like that would happen to me."

I take in his big glasses and the pimpled landscape of his bony face. Mother Nature has been even less kind to him than she's ever been to me. Poor guy. If I could help him, I would. Unfortunately, there's nothing I can do. I flash him an apologetic smile and face the front.

Five minutes into Mr. Connick's lecture on the demise of the Mayan empire, a folded-up piece of paper lands on my desk. I turn just in time to see Eric slip back into his seat. A sense of dread prickles my chest, but I hunch my shoulders and discreetly unfold the note.

Scribbled in blue pen are the words: *Can you please write down everything you did the day before it happened? Please? I'll pay you for your time.*

Okay, now he's just being annoying. I don't want to be an example or an advocate or some kind of symbol of hope for the less fortunate. I just want to live my life. I crush the paper in my fist and stare straight ahead for the rest of the class.

As soon as the bell rings, I jump from my desk. Just when I think I can make it out of the room without interruption, Mike Rogers's fist hovers between me and the door.

Ugh. Mike Rogers is one of the few people at school I genuinely despise. Like, *despise* despise. And not just because he gets to snuggle up against my ex-girlfriend's breasts whenever he wants to. Rogers has always been the definition of *douchebag.*

"Welcome to the good-looking club, K," he says.

I wince, but fist-bump him out of politeness anyway. *K?* No one's ever called me that. Ever. And *good-looking club*? I'm sorry, but Mike's not even that attractive. All he has going for him is his bulgy muscles and unwarranted popularity. Okay, and his parade of hot girlfriends like Ashley Solomon, and now Sara. Whatever. His buzzed head still reminds me of a potato.

I force a smile and leave.

In the hall, I'm greeted by the now-usual shy smiles, *heys*, and *Hi, Konrads*. Since it's lunchtime, I get a group text from Alan asking Lauren and me if we're going to the Shack like we did last Thursday. I'm about to reply with a yes when the sound of a familiar voice stops me.

"Hi, Konrad."

My skin goes taut and a sense of déjà vu ripples through my body.

After a long breath, I look up. "Hi, Sara."

Here she is. My ex-girlfriend of seven months and four days. The girl who apparently only went out with me out of boredom, just until someone more worthy of her time came along.

The girl who destroyed my heart.

"You're so tall now," she says, her eyes sparkling.

I'm tense all over. I can't help it. I never thought I'd see her from this up close again, much less speak to her. "Yeah," I say, injecting as much frost into my tone as I can. How can she even do this? How can she act like nothing happened?

"Look, I'm sorry things ended the way they did between us. I was kind of a bitch ignoring you like that."

"Kind of?"

She laughs, as if I made a great joke. My stomach churns with disgust. I don't even bother hiding it.

"Anyway," she says, "congratulations. You're really, really good-looking now."

I just want her to go away. "Thanks."

"Maybe we can talk soon?"

"What about Mike?"

She shrugs. "What about him?"

"Okay."

"See you in gym class?"

"Bye."

She walks away, and I'm left standing before my locker feeling angry at myself. Why did I even give her the time of day? I should've just brushed her off without a word. She deserves to feel at least a fraction of the crushing rejection I did.

Shaking my head, I pull out my phone. There's a message from Lauren: **Let's meet in the parking lot.**

Still dazed from Sara stooping to such a low level, I'm walking toward the exit so I can meet up with my friends when a smooth hand lands on my arm.

"Come have lunch with us," Becca Lipowska says, twirling her long, straight hair around the fingers of her other smooth hand.

Whoa. First Sara gives me an apology—a half-assed apology, but still—and now Becca is not only making physical contact, she's inviting me to lunch. Seriously, everybody is totally into my transformation except my own friends.

I remember I'm supposed to be on my way to see them and that I still haven't replied to our group text. "I'm sorry," I say to Becca, regretfully sneaking a peek at my phone.

There's a new message from Lauren on my screen.

Guess you're too busy, PRETTY BOY. We're off!

I grit my teeth. Lauren didn't even wait five-freaking-minutes for my reply. I could probably catch them if I hurry, but I'm pissed that she called me Pretty Boy again, and Becca's still lingering in front of me, as if sure I'll change my mind.

"Actually," I say, slipping my phone in my pocket, "never mind. Let's go."

"Great," she says, a smug grin etched on her face. "Come on."

She waits for me to fall into step with her and we start strutting down the hallway, Becca on my right and her hot friend Carrie on my left. The crowd in the hall starts parting like I'm a pop star with two sexy dancers at my side. I'm riding the wave, relishing our three-person parade of cool, when I see something that sticks out like a brown leaf on a healthy houseplant.

A cold chill scuttles up my spine.

Among the looks of envy from the guys and adoration from the girls, I catch one face that draws me in like a black hole. That face belongs to Jodie Mathews, and I don't think she likes what she's seeing. In fact, between the rage in her eyes, the twisted disgust on her lips, and the stiffness of her posture, I'd bet she thinks I'm Satan himself.

CHAPTER 6

CAMILLA

"Konrad?" I squeak. "Konrad Wolnik? Sara Hernandez's ex?"

"Yeah," Jodie says, focused on typing his name into the search bar. We're at my desk, in the Lair of the Forsaken— also known as my room. After visiting Ashley at the diner, I've been hiding out here until I decide my next move. I only leave the house at dawn to run, and I'm back before the world is awake to see me.

Yesterday, Mom delivered a note—a very lengthy one—to Principal Marks from Dr. Jackson. I'm temporarily excused from school because of "emotional distress due to an Inexplicable Development."

Jodie angles the laptop my way. When I see what's on screen, I suck in a breath and hold it. The guy in the profile picture *is* Konrad Wolnik, but it's also not. It's the boy I've seen around the hallways at school, the one I had physics with last year, but the Konrad grinning back at me doesn't have a big nose, a round face, and wiry hair. This Konrad has high cheekbones and eyes that could slay any functioning person attracted to men.

"He's taller and his body is, like, perfect, too," Jodie explains frantically. *"And,"* she adds with emphasis, like she's about to say the most important thing of all, "he's hanging out with Becca Lipowska now."

At first, I'm in awe; an average guy has transformed into one of the best-looking people I've ever laid eyes on. It's incredible. But then I'm hit with an onslaught of jealousy, quickly followed by misery and, finally, an explosion of anger.

"You all right?" Jodie asks.

If wanting to see Konrad's breathtaking eyes bulge and his movie star lips struggle for air as I strangle him to death counts as all right, then yes, Jodie, I'm very all right.

"He did this to me," I say. "He's the reason."

Before Jodie can reply, the door opens and Mom strides in. She's been cutting her shifts short so she can be around more. Over and over, I assure her I'd never do anything dangerous to myself, but she's a single mother, not to mention a nurse. Her care-meter is more alert than most.

Mom sees me practically growling. "What is it, honey?"

Jodie decides to answer for me. "This kid we know—"

"It's nothing," I interrupt. I don't want Mom to find out about Konrad. Not yet.

"What kid?" she asks.

"This kid in our class," I say before Jodie can speak, trying to come up with a convincing lie. Mom's bullshit detector is pretty well honed, so I tread carefully. "Someone pushed him down the stairs at school. He's fine, though. He just broke his arm."

"Oh my God," Mom says. "That's terrible."

Jodie's gives me a sideways glance. "Yeah," she says. "So terrible."

"Oh!" Mom blurts. Smiling, she peeks back into the hallway. "Come on in, Ashley."

Ashley pushes her glowing face around the doorframe. At first, I'm happy to see her, but that changes pretty quickly. As far as I know, unlike Jodie and me, it's been school as usual for her. As far as I know, she already knew about Konrad Wolnik when I saw her at the diner yesterday.

Mom asks the standard *do you girls need anything?* questions, then finally finds the door. Halfway out, she turns and says, "This is so great. I'm so happy seeing the three of you spending time together again."

With Mom gone, Ashley crosses to the computer screen to see what Jodie and I are looking at. And her smile falls. I give it a moment for her guilt to sink in as deep as possible before starting my interrogation. "Why didn't you tell me yesterday?"

Ashley silently backs up, then sets her butt on my bed. "I thought you knew," she replies. There's a creak to her voice. "Everybody's been posting about it since, like, Tuesday."

I aim my narrowed eyes at Jodie next.

She looks offended. "What? I barely look at stuff online at all. You know that. Plus, I was with you almost the whole time!"

Jodie might be our very own fashion icon, but she's a surprisingly light social media user. I believe her. As for me, it's painful enough to have to see the few photos of Old Me scattered throughout my room. I haven't exactly been itching to revisit my old life online.

I inhale deeply, but my breath turns into a half sob. Angry and frustrated, I jump from the chair and start pacing around my room. I'm so mad I don't even care that I'm parading my shapeless, unattractive body in front of my friends.

The girls let me quietly fume. After a while, Jodie says, "It's so weird, though. Why him? It's not like he was ugly. He was just . . . average. Nothing wrong with that. He seemed pretty chill, too, and it didn't seem like he wanted to be more popular. Sara dated him. Sara's cute."

"Yeah, but Sara dumped him for Mike," Ashley reminds us.

I stop pacing and plop back into my chair. The memory of Gina's party hangs in the air, thick and unpleasant. Sara left Konrad for Mike, sure, but Mike left Ashley for Sara.

Because of me.

Jodie breaks the silence. "He's *definitely* the reason."

"We don't know that," Ashley says.

Both Jodie and I turn to stare at her.

Jodie's face scrunches up. "Are you defending him, Ashley?"

"No," Ashley quickly replies. "It's just that . . . nobody knows for sure how IDs happen. And they happen so rarely and so randomly. No one has ever found a pattern to them. I looked it up last night." She pauses. "I'm just saying, maybe this is just one big, twisted coincidence."

Jodie shakes her head with certainty. "He obviously wished for this."

"That's really unlikely," Ashley goes on. "There is a ton of research out there, old and new. The theory that someone can wish something upon someone else has been basically debunked." She pauses, then continues a little more gently. "Besides, I don't think Konrad specifically thought, 'I wish I was insanely attractive and I wish the complete opposite for Camilla Hadi.' He's never been a mean person."

"We don't know what he's really like!" Jodie says. "Or what he thought. At the very least, whatever happened to Camilla is collateral damage. However you look at it, *he's* the reason. I've never heard of two IDs happening at the same time. There is *obviously* a correlation." She turns to me, eyes full-on puppy dog. "He stole your beauty, Camilla."

I look away. "What beauty?"

I was never beautiful. It's a fact; I'm not going to pretend otherwise. I've never even had a boyfriend. I was just as average as Konrad, if not more so.

"Don't be like that," Jodie says.

My eyes fall to the now-stubby fingers in my lap. I make my hands into fists so I don't have to look at them anymore. I never did anything to Konrad Wolnik, and certainly never gave him a reason to do something like this to me. And yet, he did. Whether intentionally or not, he made me this way.

"Let me talk to him," Ashley says.

I tense up. "What would you say?" I'm not ready for news of my ID to spread beyond those few who already know about it. At this point, I'm not sure I ever will be.

"I'll try to find out as much as I can."

"*I* should talk to him," Jodie interjects. "Konrad's not going to trust you since you're kind of the reason Sara broke up with him. If you hadn't given Lance a hand job at Gina's party, Mike wouldn't have broken up with you, and Sara would still be with Konrad."

"I *didn't* give him a hand job," Ashley says through her teeth. "We made out. Kissed. That's it."

Jodie huffs. "That was one hell of a kiss then. Since when does kissing involve slipping your hand down a guy's jeans?"

Ashley flinches, and then her expression goes hard. "Maybe if you hadn't stabbed me in the back and posted that video, Konrad and Sara would still be together."

"That was my idea," I say, my eyes downcast. "I shared the video."

"Yeah, but Jodie's the one who made sure everyone knew about it. Plus, you're actually sorry, Camilla. Jodie's obviously not."

Jodie's eyes fall to her nails. "Whatever. I apologized already. Plus, you knew Camilla had a thing for Lance."

Ashley slaps both of her hands on my bed. "NO, I DIDN'T!"

"She didn't, Jodie," I say for the millionth time. "I never told her."

"Whatever," Jodie mumbles. "If Ashley didn't know, then she was one clueless friend."

"*Ugh!*" Ashley says. "I didn't know!"

I give her a weak smile. None of it matters anyway. Lance was never interested in me before, and he sure as hell won't be interested now.

"Okay," I say.

Both girls turn my way. "Okay, what?" Jodie asks.

"You can talk to Konrad, Ashley."

I might not have been beautiful, but what I was—what I had—was mine and mine alone. No one had a right to mess with that but me. Especially not a human being who is so vain, and so self-centered, that his greatest wish in the whole world was to be *better looking*. Whether he meant to or not, Konrad Wolnik ruined my life for his own selfish gain.

And there's no way I'm going to let him get away with that.

CHAPTER 7

KONRAD

It's lunchtime. Every time I touch the bleachers the metal scalds my palms. I try to keep my hands in my lap, but I can't stop fidgeting. Also, I'm sweating like a construction worker. The sun burning through my jeans is playing a part, yeah, but it's got nothing on Becca Lipowska.

"So how many girls have you been with?" she asks.

We've been out here for ten minutes. Out on the field some of Mike Rogers's douchebag friends are throwing a ball around. They're all pretending not to, but I can tell they're totally watching us.

"Oh, I only dated Sara."

Becca slaps my arm playfully. This is the fourth time she's done that since we sat down. "No, stupid," she says. "I mean, like, *been* with."

Truthfully, it's only been Sara and my hand, but Becca doesn't need to know that. "Hmm, like maybe five or so," I lie. "You?"

She giggles. "Girls?"

My cheeks burn, and I chuckle like a goat.

"Well," she says, leaning in even closer. I feel the hair on my neck spring to life in sync with something else in my jeans. "This is a secret, but I did sort of hook up with Carrie once. But there was this college boy with us, so it wasn't a full-on lesbian thing, or anything."

I whip my bulging eyes her way, but then jerk back because her barely visible freckles are, like, an inch away from my face. "You had a threesome?"

She shrugs, clearly enjoying my bewilderment. "Yeah, I guess."

"Nice." I swallow hard.

"It wasn't my thing, though."

"I see," I say, thinking of a good topic to follow that up with. Nothing good comes to mind, so I just go with: "So tell me something about yourself."

"What do you want to know?"

"Hmm. Like . . . do you know what you're going to study in college?"

Becca's face goes deadly serious. "Yes."

"What?"

"Premed. I'm going to be a neurosurgeon."

My mouth pops open. I didn't think anything could top her threesome story, but here we are. I was expecting her to say something like, "I want to try modeling." But no, Becca Lipowska wants to be a freaking brain surgeon.

"That's intense."

"Yeah. I've always had a thing for brains. Like, I used to buy rats at pet shops, or mice—you know, like the ones they sell for snake feed?—and then kill them and cut open their skulls. These days, I'm mostly interested in the human brain. The whole human nervous system."

"Oh, wow," I say, slightly disturbed. "That's . . . pretty sick. I mean, like, in a good way."

She slaps my arm again. "I got it." Her tongue brushes over her shiny lips and her gaze drops to my lower half. "Come over to my place tomorrow night," she says. "My parents are going to see some play at seven. We'll have a couple of hours."

On behalf of the soldier in my pants, I immediately agree.

"Great," she says, getting up with a satisfied grin on her face. "We should probably get something to eat now. Lunch is almost over."

I don't move. Partly because I'm sure even the guys on the field will be able to see my boner, and partly because there's something I want to ask her, even if it will probably make me sound like a loser. "You'd never talk to me if my ID hadn't happened, right?"

Becca's smile dims but doesn't disappear completely. "Look, I'll be real with you," she says. "You weren't my type before. Now you are. Plus, you seem like a really cool guy. I'd like to get to know you better."

"But you wouldn't have before?"

She shrugs. "No, probably not."

My lips pinch, but I nod. I appreciate her honesty. It's so much better than Sara's fake "I'm just trying to reconnect with you" bullshit.

Smiling up at her, I say, "Tomorrow."

Becca and I hug (she insists) and we part ways. I buy a hamburger at the cafeteria and look for Alan outside the gym.

The gym building has these creepy-looking protruding eaves. The place looks like a spaceship from a Soviet-era science fiction novel. The overhang does provide a lot of shade, though, and it attracts kids from all walks of life. Most of them stare at me as I approach.

Alan's squatting with his back against the wall, one hand wrapped around a sandwich and the other attacking his phone. Mouth bobbing up and down, he glances up from the screen. His eyes narrow. "What took you so long?"

I throw my thumb over my shoulder and shake my head. "Becca..."

His eyes drop back to his phone. Unwrapping my burger, I rest my back against the wall and slide down next to him. "Sorry."

"We really did wait for you in the parking lot yesterday."

"Yeah," I mumble through a bite. "For, like, a minute."

"Dude," he says in a tone I'd only heard from him once before, when he snapped at Mark Andrews for asking if his sister was already bald. This was before she even started chemotherapy. Snapping at people is not something Alan usually does. "Lauren and I haven't changed," he goes on. "You have."

I stop chewing and turn to him. It's so obvious he's been waiting to say these words to me for a while. I'm guessing he's speaking for Lauren, too.

"No," I say, trying to stay calm, "I didn't. I'm the same exact person."

"Uh, no, you're not. You're talking to people you used to make fun of. Everybody's freaking staring at you all the time." He glares at two passing freshmen who are, indeed, staring—but what am I supposed to do about that? "You're the one who was unhappy with your life, with how things were, and you wished them to be different. Well, now they are."

I'm stunned. Four days into my transformation and I'm fighting with my best friend. Okay, not fighting with him yet, but I will be in about two seconds. "Did you ever stop to think about what I'm going through?" I ask. "I have zero control over any of this."

"Oh yeah, like it's so tough becoming the most attractive dude at school. Plus, you *wished* for it."

"It's a big change. It's not all peaches and cream."

"You wished to be hot, Konrad. I mean, how messed up is that?"

I try to keep my breathing under control. Alan rips a bite out of his sandwich and chews hard. He's only pretending to be busy tapping his phone screen, because he says, "You were our best friend. This is a big change for us, too, you know.

Even though Alan's not looking, my hand flies into the air, traffic cop style. I get to my feet. "Excuse me? I *was* your best friend? Past-fucking-tense?"

Alan's face twists in annoyance. "You know that was just a slip of the tongue."

"I don't think it was." I don't want to listen to any more of this bullshit. "You know what, Alan? Fuck you," I say. "And tell Lauren that Pretty Boy is sending her the same message."

Stomping away with my half-eaten hamburger in hand, I ignore a *hi* from Ashley Solomon and head around the gym to the sidewalk out front. I need to get off school grounds and I need to do it now.

Five minutes later, I'm sitting on the curb on one of the quiet residential streets nearby. My burger's cold, but I shove the whole thing in my mouth anyway.

What's Alan's problem? He and Lauren are the victims here? Please! They're supposed to be happy for me. They're supposed to be supportive. What the fuck was that "this is a big change for us, too" bullshit? Not only do I have to deal with my own parents glancing at me through a film of suspicion like they never really knew me during dinner at home, I need to keep defending myself to my so-called friends when I'm at school, too.

Since when is being insecure in your appearance and wishing to be good-looking such an evil thing? Everybody's guilty of that. Everybody.

Fuck Alan. And fuck Lauren. If they don't want to be friends with me anymore, I'm fine with that. I'm the king now, and the student body is my dinner table. I mean, Becca Lipowska wants to get into my pants tomorrow night. Enough said.

I'm so angry, I don't notice Ashley Solomon approaching until she's almost in front of me. My head snaps her way.

Disclaimer: Ashley's really cute. I had a mini-crush on her back in seventh grade. I still think she's great, but I'm not feeling very friendly right now.

"Did you follow me?"

Ashley's long brown legs take a couple of reluctant steps forward. "Yeah." She looks very serious, which is odd. I can't remember the last time I didn't see Ashley Solomon smiling. She even managed to remain positive after that party video everyone at school saw of her making out with Lance Dietrick while she was dating Mike Rogers the Douchebag.

"What do you want?" I ask.

"Can you talk for a second?"

"About what?"

"About something huge. So huge I need you to promise not to tell anyone else."

"Fine," I mumble. The sooner I let her spill, the sooner she'll leave me alone.

"Do you promise?"

"I promise."

She sits on the curb a couple of feet away. "Do you mind if I smoke?"

Huh. Interesting. I never considered her the type. "Go for it."

Ashley offers me a cigarette. After I decline, she lights one up, both hands shaking. I watch her take a long drag. "You know Camilla Hadi, right?" she asks.

"Not really. Why?"

"Have you noticed that she hasn't been coming to school?"

"Um. No. Have you noticed that I have a lot going on lately?"

Ashley nods to herself. She aims her gaze at a yellow-brick bungalow across the street and puffs out another cloud of smoke. "Camilla had an Inexplicable Development happen to her, too."

For a second, my heart seems to stop. Then it picks up again, beating faster. "Huh?"

"You're not the only one. She went through an ID, too."

I let Ashley's words sink in. "Really?"

"Really."

Swallowing, I look down at the ground. "What was it?"

"The opposite of you."

I turn to her, my brain stuck in a fuzzy limbo. "What do you mean?"

Ashley sighs. "She woke up less attractive."

"What?"

She closes her eyes. "She woke up ugly."

"When?"

"Same day as you."

I examine her expression, searching for a hint, anything to say Ashley's fucking with me. I don't find it. "Are you serious?"

"Yeah."

Ripping a few blades from someone's perfectly cut lawn, I throw them into the nonexistent wind. "That's messed up."

We sit in silence for a while. Finally, Ashley says, "So, did you have anything to do with it?"

My shoulders lock. "With what?"

"With what happened to Camilla."

"Of course not!"

"What did you wish for exactly?"

I puff out my cheeks. This question. Again. "Lots of things," I say, annoyed. "I wished I could self-heal like Wolverine. I wished I could swim better. I wished I could read people's minds. And yeah, I wished I was better looking." I pause. "Honestly, I don't even think wishing has anything to do with it. I just got really lucky."

"And what? Camilla was really unlucky?"

I take a moment to answer. "I guess."

"You don't think it's strange that Camilla's ID happened on the same day as yours?"

"I do, but what do you want me to say? I don't know how to fix her, if that's what you're after."

"*Would* you fix her?"

"If I could, sure."

I can feel Ashley willing me to look her way, so I do. As soon as our eyes meet, she asks, "Really? You'd undo what happened to you to help her?"

Alan and Lauren's faces flash into my mind. I hear Alan's words: *Lauren and I haven't changed. You have.*

But then I think about all the attention I've been getting. And Becca's breasts, which I'll get to see bouncing around *au naturale* tomorrow night.

I stand up, brushing the stray hamburger crumbs from my pants. "I didn't say that." Without another word, I start back to school.

CHAPTER 8

CAMILLA

EVERY MORNING, BEFORE THE SUN is even up, I run. And every time afterward, I aim the hot stream of the showerhead at my face. I imagine it cleansing me of my new flaws. Washing them away to reveal the old me underneath.

It never helps, no matter how hot the water gets.

Every morning, I stand in front of the mirror and try to push my features back into place. Mold them into something less grotesque.

So far, that hasn't worked either.

I keep telling myself if I run enough, I'll be able to get my body back in shape. Just because I'm ugly doesn't mean I have to be unhealthy, too. I can still finish this race, even if I know there's no gold medal waiting for me at the end.

Down in the kitchen, I make an egg-and-avocado salad, eat my share, and wrap the rest up for Mom. It's one of her rare Saturdays off, but I'm letting her sleep in. There's only so much of a mother's worry a person can take.

Last night, I ordered Jodie and Ashley to take the day off. My life might be over, but they still have theirs. It's time I face this thing head-on. On my own.

First thing I do when I return to the Lair of the Forsaken is collect all my photos. I stare at the one framed on my desk: Jodie, Ashley, and me at Six Flags, three years ago, all gums and teeth. My skin is glowing. Every feature so right, so *me*. Of course, at the time, I wouldn't have agreed. How petty and ungrateful of me to have had insecurities back then. I wish I loved myself more when I still had the chance.

My eyes fill with tears. Dropping the photo in an old shoebox, I reach for another picture—the one from my fourteenth birthday where my arms are tight around my dad's neck, a time when I was naive enough to believe he'd never be dumb enough to drink and drive.

I throw the photo on top of the pile in the box, put the lid on, and stow it deep in the back of my closet. It isn't easy. This is me in these pictures. This is my story. But how can I move on if my old self keeps staring back at me everywhere I look?

My online presence is next. I glue myself to my laptop and delete every single photo I'd ever uploaded with me in it and I untag myself from all others where possible. Once that's done, I click on the most liked photo in my feed—Becca

Lipowska and Konrad Wolnik sitting together at lunch. I swear, if she could scoot any closer, she'd be inside him.

Anger rises within me. It's not fair.

The clank of dishes in the kitchen snaps me back to reality. Since this means Mom is up, I blast "We're Never Gonna Disappear" by the Leaky Lizards and continue my crazed clicking from one post to the next. The selfish, shallow life-ruiner is everywhere I look. He's like a spreading virus. Minutes pass. When a hand touches my shoulder, I startle.

"GOD! You scared me," I gasp, slamming my laptop shut.

"Sorry," Mom says, standing over me. "Morning."

I heave a breath of relief. "Morning."

Mom's lips twist to one side and I tense right back up. She's about to say something I'm not going to like. "What?" I ask.

"You have a visitor."

I throw my head back and sigh at the ceiling. My guess is it's Jodie. She's more the type to ignore everything I say. "Why didn't you let her up?"

A small grin forms on Mom's face. "It's not a *her*."

I blink. "Huh?"

"It's a boy."

My heart jumps, nudging my throat. "You're kidding, right?"

She shakes her head.

"What boy?"

She lowers her chin. "He's really handsome, by the way."

I jerk my shoulder from under her hand. "What *boy*, Mom!"

"His name is Konrad. He says he needs to talk to you. Did I mention he's really handsome?"

Suddenly, I'm having trouble breathing.

"I think you should talk to him," Mom goes on. "It'll do you good."

At first, I can't even bring myself to speak. My mind is blowing up with questions. Ashley must've talked to him. And she must've said too much.

"Jesus, Mom. You let him into OUR HOUSE?"

"Yes. Why wouldn't I?"

"What's WRONG with you?" I'm screaming. "Do you seriously want me to end up in a MENTAL INSTITUTION?"

Her eyes fill up with confusion and pain and I immediately regret my outburst. She has no idea who Konrad Wolnik is or why he's here. But does she actually believe that a boy would just swing by to say hi, especially in my current state?

"Sorry," I mumble. "It's just . . ."

"Camilla," Mom interrupts before I can make something up. "Sooner or later, you're going to have to deal with people. Just talk to him. Please." She flashes me a hopeful smile. "Can I let him up?"

My jaw drops. She wants him up here? Unless you count my cousins and playdates from kindergarten, no boy's ever been over to my house. Let alone been in my *room*. No way is Konrad Wolnik, the vile human responsible for my ID, going to be the first.

And yet, I don't say no. I'm too curious to see what he wants.

"Okay, fine. You can let him up."

Mom's beaming, but I push her into the hall before she can say anything else. What she doesn't know is that just because I agreed to let him *up*, doesn't mean I have to let him *in*.

Once she's gone, I shut the door, flip the lock, and dart toward my desk where Jodie's sunglasses are sitting. I have no intention of showing myself, but I slip them on anyway. Pressing my back to the door, I wait. My heart's pounding a million times a minute.

When I hear the creak of the stairs, I hold my breath.

The creaking stops.

"Camilla?"

The only words Konrad Wolnik has ever said to me were, "Can I borrow your pencil?" in physics last year. Maybe there had been a *thanks* after that, but that's it. I know of him, and he knows of me, but we're practically strangers.

My voice comes out a lot weaker than I want it to. "Yeah?"

"It's Konrad. Konrad Wolnik."

I clear my throat. "How do you know where I live?"

"I got your address from Ashley Solomon."

Oh, Ashley. You're so dead to me.

"What do you want?"

He doesn't reply right away. I press myself harder against the door in case he tries to open it or something. Eventually, he says, "Were you just listening to the Leaky Lizards? They're pretty badass, aren't they?"

It's as if the words turn off a boiling kettle in my stomach. *Random*, I think. But also unfortunate. Because if he heard that, he definitely heard me screaming about mental institutions.

Heat spreads through my cheeks. I don't want him to think I'm on the verge of insanity. Worse, I don't want him to think I'm weak.

"What do you want, Konrad?"

"Can I come in?"

"No."

"Look," he says, hesitating, "I heard about what happened."

I swallow, imagining his face, the one I've been staring at on my computer screen for the past hour. That flawless, beguiling face.

"I was thinking about it all day yesterday," he continues, "and I just wanted to come and let you know I had nothing to do with what happened to you."

I remain quiet, unsure how to respond, even though that's pretty much exactly what I expected him to say.

"It sucks, I know. I mean, I know it's not the same thing or anything, but I understand."

Rage floods my body. He's got to be kidding me. This kid is even more self-centered than I ever imagined. "Oh, do you now?" I snarl.

I hear him sigh on the other side of the door. "What happened to me might sound glamorous or whatever, but it's not as great as you'd think. People look at me differently.

My family's acting like I'm an impostor in my own home. My friends are being assholes about it. Like I'm a complete stranger, you know? All of it, it's just . . . this whole thing is just so weird."

That's the last straw. *Your life is weird? You're the victim? You? With your perfect new appearance and newfound popularity?* How dare he come into my house and tell me his life is tough? After what his selfish act did to mine?

"Anyway," he says when I don't reply. "I'm here if you want to talk."

My whole head is throbbing with angry heat. "LEAVE!"

"Do you want my number?"

"GET OUT OF MY HOUSE!"

For a couple of beats, he's completely silent. I brace myself, expecting him to say more, but then I hear the creak of the stairs. Relieved, I wait at the door, my ears pricked, until Mom's muffled voice travels up to me and the front door closes with a thud.

Konrad's gone.

Next thing I know, I'm at my window, peeking from behind the curtain at the street below. Konrad marches to his car like he's in a hurry. He looks even better in person than he does in pictures. Before he dips behind the wheel, he glances up.

I let the curtain go, my heart rate spiraling out of control. I stand there, my teeth shredding my nails, unsure whether he saw me or not. But then, I realize, I don't really care. In fact,

I'm kind of hoping he did. He *should* see me. Hell, everyone should see me. Everyone should know what Konrad's perfect new life has done to mine. Everyone should know what an awful human being he is.

I make up my mind. Monday, I'm going back to school.

CHAPTER 9

KONRAD

Saturday afternoon, my follower count hits 1,200. Prior to my ID, it was 418, which means it's almost tripled. I don't know half of these new people.

Twelve new notifications call my name, but before I check what they're all about, I type the name *Camilla Hadi* into as many search bars as I can.

Her social media accounts are all there, but all her photos and videos are gone. When I try googling, a couple of local articles pop up about track meets and high school athletics.

I don't want to think about her, but I can't stop myself. It's like I have this new, amazing skin, right? But ever since I learned about Camilla's ID from Ashley, it kind of feels like I discovered a tumor on it.

Yes, it's odd that whatever happened to Camilla Hadi happened on the same day as whatever happened to me. And yes, it's odd that her ID, like mine, was related to her appearance. I know how it looks from the outside. I'm not an idiot. That's why I went over to her house. I wanted her to know I had nothing to do with it.

Because I *didn't*.

I can understand why she kicked me out. Why she's angry with me. Why she and Jodie Mathews, and who knows who else, might even blame me. And it's only going to get worse. If people didn't think I was selfish for wishing to be hot before, they definitely will after word spreads about Camilla. Next to her, I'm going to look like an asshole.

But why do I feel like *I'm* blaming me, too? I did nothing wrong.

Inexplicable Developments are a mystery. Mine happened because, I guess, I wanted it to. But there's no proof that that's the case *every* time. That whole wishing thing is just a theory. It's not a fact. And Camilla Hadi's case basically proves it wrong, anyway. No one would ever wish for themself to become less physically attractive.

Is it possible that someone else wished that upon her? But IDs made on other people's behalf have never been documented before. And even if someone did wish that awful transformation upon her, it sure as hell couldn't have been me, because there's *definitely* no record of one person who had *two* wishes come true at once. I checked.

Camilla's ID could very well be a biological mistake. A glitch. An anomaly in the process. Like a third nipple or premature balding or something. But even if it is somehow collateral for my own transformation, that's not my fault either. I'm not responsible for the actions of the damn *cosmos*. There's no reason for me to feel guilty about any of this.

I find a picture in one of the articles and zoom in, my heart picking up speed. Camilla is—was, I guess—pleasant-looking. Not beautiful, but not unattractive either. Dad would probably call her a "plain Jane."

The two main things I know about Camilla are that she's a track star and that she hangs out with Ashley Solomon and Jodie Mathews. Or she used to, anyway, before the whole "Ashley gave Lance Dietrick a handy j" video scandal thing.

I wish I'd known Camilla liked the Leaky Lizards before. I would've totally talked to her about them. When it comes to music, Lauren, Alan, and I could never really find common ground. Alan listens to pop, Lauren likes obscure early nineties hip-hop, and I listen to the Leaky Lizards. Maybe Camilla and I might've even become friends.

I close the article and try to shake Camilla from my mind. Glitch, coincidence, whatever it was that caused her ID, it wasn't something I had anything to do with. I know this better than anyone, and there's no reason to dwell on it. Or on her.

I turn my attention to the notifications on my phone. Many of them are direct messages. There are some hellos and some invitations to hang out—mostly from girls who don't have the courage to ask for my phone number in person. But one name stands out.

Eric Stewart.

A cold chill runs up my spine. Yesterday, he tried talking to me again about the same thing. I got kind of short with him. I was worried that otherwise, he'd never leave me alone.

I take a deep breath and click the message open:

You don't have to be such an asshole.

The door flings open and Arthur barges in. "Quit jerking it," he says. "There's no need for you to do that anymore. Not with all that hot ass lining up for you!"

Eric vanishes from my mind and Becca takes over. More specifically, Becca and what'll probably happen when I see her tonight.

Heat explodes in my cheeks. "Shut up! How do you know about that, anyway?"

"Everyone's talking about you at my school, too, bro. Your fame's rubbing off on me. Even *I'm* getting more action."

I wipe my palm down my face. "You're thirteen. You're not getting any action for at least three more years."

"Just 'cause you were a late bloomer doesn't mean I have to be."

That makes me laugh. And then I realize how much I needed to laugh. "What do you want?"

"Lunch is ready."

As if on cue, my stomach growls.

"Why isn't Alan here today?" Arthur asks as I follow him through the kitchen and out to the backyard.

"He's not around this weekend."

Outside, smoke from the grill tickles my nostrils. Mom's leaning against the fence, talking to our thousand-year-old neighbor, Bonnie. Bonnie's husband passed away when I was a kid. These days, she only leaves the house to go to church. She hasn't seen the new me yet.

"My, my," she says as I jump down the porch steps. Her thick glasses magnify her surprise. She steadies herself on her cane.

"Hi, Bonnie," I say.

"The Lord has truly blessed you." She makes the sign of the cross. "This is miracle, if I've ever seen one."

"I guess," I say, getting a whiff of dog shit from her yard. Not even the smoke can mask it. Bonnie's dog is an ancient rottweiler named Delilah. This cute college girl comes over to clean her place once a week and picks up the turds outside while she's at it. Unfortunately, dogs shit more often than once a week.

"I just read an article about how taller, good-looking people get better jobs," she continues. "Your life will be so fruitful."

I fake a smile. Bonnie's an old lady. I'm sure she doesn't mean to suggest my life would've been unfruitful otherwise.

Mom looks uncomfortable. "Oh," she says, "Bonnie, would you mind taking our photo? It's been a while since we took one as a family."

"Of course not!"

"No . . ." Arthur growls, pretend-banging his head on the picnic table. Dad doesn't seem too thrilled with the idea either, but he puts down his barbecue tongs and shuffles over. They all gather around me, forcing me into the center.

Lately, I've been feeling like an out-of-town relative they haven't seen in years. Or, worse, like I just got adopted. Like I'm a new addition to the family. I'm sure Mom and Dad don't act like I'm a stranger intentionally, but why can't things be exactly like they were before? Why do they both have to keep reminding me that I look different now?

Well, guess what. I'm *not* a new addition to the family. I'm me. Nothing that should matter, to them at least, has changed. At school, I'm all for reinvention. But I never asked for a fresh start at home. I just want one constant in my life. Is that too much to ask for?

"What do I press?" Bonnie asks, examining Mom's phone like it's some kind of James Bond gadget. Mom shows her what to do. Tilting her head back, Bonnie points the camera. "Okay, smile!"

I don't.

Mom retrieves her phone and checks the photo. I catch a small scowl on her lips. When she sees me looking, she blushes and asks, "Why the serious face?"

"Yeah," Arthur says. "Why are you hiding those million-dollar molars?"

"Should I take another one?" Bonnie asks.

"No, it's okay," I say, turning toward the table.

"Hey, Mom," Arthur says, making sure I hear him. "Think of all the money we could've saved on Konrad's braces."

Bonnie calls Delilah and they both go back inside to hibernate. Mom brings over the sausages on a big flowery plate and Dad prepares the utensils.

"What's wrong?" he asks me.

"Nothing."

Mom sits down, her ears perking up. Dad goes on, "*Coś się stało?*"

"Yeah, bro," Arthur says. "Why the frown? Something happen?"

For a second, I consider telling them about Camilla. Ashley swore me to secrecy, but I assume it only applies to people at school. How would my parents take the news? Would they blame me, too? At the last minute, though, I change my mind. "Nope. Everything's fine."

"Well," Mom says, "we're here if you want to talk."

"Thanks," I say, but think: *Like you'd get it. . . .*

I stop chewing and stare at my plate. *We're here if you want to talk.* That's pretty much the same exact thing I said to Camilla this morning.

God, I feel so stupid. As if I actually understand what she's going through. My life's going to be fruitful—at least according to Bonnie. Camilla? Camilla's been handed a tragedy. I must've come off as such a condescending prick.

After I gobble up the rest of my grilled sausages, I sit on my bed eating Oreos and binging on *Game of Thrones*. A favorite scene comes on and I almost shoot Alan a text out of habit. It's almost unnatural, watching the show alone, without his hilarious commentary.

We've fought and gone days without talking before, so it's not like this is a first. There was that time I ditched him to hang out with Sara. Total "bros before hoes" fail. Eventually, I apologized and we made up. But this time, it feels different. This time, I doubt sorry will cut it. No matter which one of us is the one saying it.

Before I know it, it's seven o'clock. Mom makes me eat some of her lasagna ("I don't cook for myself!") and I drive over to Becca's. I make a pit stop at Walgreens to pick up a box of condoms. You know. Just in case. I'm pretty sure I have an idea what Becca invited me over for, but you can never be one hundred percent sure.

Side note: condoms are freaking expensive. Everyone tells you to use protection and practice safe sex, but what if you're trying to do that on a measly twenty bucks per week allowance and your parents won't let you get a job before you turn seventeen?

Becca lives in a large two-story house with cream-colored siding. When I pull up to her driveway, she comes out to meet me wearing a big blue T-shirt. Her shorts are so short, it looks like she's not wearing anything below the waist.

I slam the car door. "Hey."

She catches me staring at her long, exposed legs and grins. "Hey."

Blushing, I clear my throat. She gestures for me to follow.

This is so obviously a booty call it's not even funny. She knows it and I know it. That should make things easier, but I've never been in a position like this before. Guys like me—or guys like the former me—are never guaranteed sex. Now, though, it's as good as done.

As she climbs the stairs, she blesses me with a fantastic view of her ass. Bonnie was right. My life is definitely going to be more fruitful.

"Want something to drink?" Becca asks, swerving into the spacious open kitchen. I don't know what her parents do, but judging from all the fancy-looking furniture and the gigantic fridge, they're obviously well-off. I make a mental note to ask her later. It'll give us something to talk about. God knows I don't have any other topics lined up.

"Uh, yeah, sure," I say.

"Coke, juice, 7UP, water. Or beer. I'm having a beer."

"Your parents won't mind?"

"No, they know I drink." Her mouth forms into a smirk. "Just like they know I'm sexually active. They'll probably be happy I'm doing it at home."

I swallow, wondering which part she's referring to. "Ha, yeah."

Becca hands me a beer. After the slightly unpleasant incident with Lauren's cheap tequila the night before my ID, I think I might've developed a slight aversion to alcohol. But I don't want to seem like a buzzkill, so I take it. She twists the cap off of hers and raises the bottle, brushing it against her lips before taking a sip. I don't think I need to explain what this does to my imagination. "So what do you want to do?" she asks.

I look at the shiny tiles. "Whatever you want."

"Do you want to see my room?"

I look up, willing the redness I'm pretty sure takes over my entire face to disappear. "Sure."

The pursuit of Becca's beautiful cheeks up more steps continues. Framed photos hang on the wall along the staircase, most of them of her in her cheerleading uniform. She must be an only child. Jeez, I know practically nothing about this girl.

Becca's room is surprisingly tame for a girl with such high social status and so much personality. I don't find a single shade of pink. But there are a lot of books. Not just books—tomes—most with the word *neuro* written somewhere on the cover. The only predictable thing about the space is her fluffy maroon carpet. I wonder if she ever dissected a hamster brain on it.

Becca grabs her laptop and plops onto her bed. "Sit down."

My eyes search for any surface to sit on that isn't her bed. It'd be weird if I sat on her bed, right?

"Come here!" she orders, patting the duvet beside her. "What do you want to listen to?"

"Um." I lower myself beside her. "The Leaky Lizards?"

"The what?" She starts typing. "The Leaky Lizards? I don't think I know them."

"You can put on whatever you want."

But Becca's apparently more considerate than I thought, because the opening strings of "We're Never Gonna Disappear" start blasting from her speakers. When I glance over to gauge her reaction, though, she looks like she swallowed a large insect. "Let's just listen to Rihanna," she says. The song stops and a new one comes on.

"Okay."

Becca chuckles. "God, you're so shy. I like that."

"Thanks," I say, because I don't know how else to respond. There's an awkward silence that keeps stretching on and on. Becca makes it even worse by staring at me in what I can only describe as a porn-star-in-action kind of way.

"So . . . what do your parents do?" I ask.

"Take off your shirt."

My eyes crash into hers. "What?"

"Your shirt."

"Are you serious?"

Without a word, Becca pulls her own shirt up over her head and reveals a lacy black bra. Her breasts are at least twice as big as Sara's. At least.

My brain shuts off. My beer's on the floor. My shirt is off. Throwing her laptop aside, Becca slides down to the carpet and gets on her knees. She shimmies over, closing the short distance between us, her elbows squeezing her breasts together like two wrestling peaches.

Before I know it, my back's parallel to her bed and my shorts are around my ankles. Becca's still on the floor, only now she's creating magic. With her mouth.

This is too much.

Just when I try to warn her, Becca jerks away.

"Sorry!" I say, my voice squeaky, my entire body in shudders. "God!—I'm so sorry!" The whole thing, from start to finish, couldn't have lasted more than three minutes. Turns out I didn't need the condoms after all.

I am the most pathetic dude in the whole world.

"It's fine," Becca says, shooting up. She skips over to her desk, reaches for the tissue box, and tosses it at my exposed belly. While I clean up, Becca chatters about something, but I'm just nodding along, only pretending to listen because this is the most embarrassing moment of my life.

Becca stops talking and sits down on the bed.

"Sorry," I say again. "That doesn't usually happen." I *have* gotten a blow job before, I swear. It's just that Sara must have twice as many teeth as Becca does.

I can feel her stare on me so I lift my eyes to meet hers.

"Do you want to be my boyfriend?" she asks.

"What?" I blurt with an awkward chuckle. I look to check if she's joking, but it doesn't appear she is. "Shouldn't we get to know each other a little first?"

"Why? We look perfect together."

"But—"

"Do you want me to do what I just did again?"

I think about it for about a second. "Yes."

"Good. Then you're my boyfriend."

CHAPTER 10

CAMILLA

My feet are stuck to the parking lot pavement. I can feel my sweat glands working overtime. I don't think my original plan of making an entrance by strutting down the school hallway with Jodie and Ashley flanking my sides like Queen Bees in a high school movie is going to work.

Jodie's arm is hooked into mine. She'd stopped to study me with her smoky eyes, her features suddenly tight with suspicion. Ashley locks her car and comes to stand on my other side. "Everything all right?" she asks.

My breaths are wobbly. "Um, yeah. Totally all right. I became too-ugly-to-look-at-straight-on, nobody except for my teachers knows, and what the hell am I doing, again?"

"Camilla," Jodie says. "It's going to be okay."

"I don't think I can do this."

Ashley reaches up to massage my shoulder. "You can."

I didn't expect this. The girls didn't either. Coming to school today had been my idea. One I thought I could pull off, but I'm not so sure I can anymore.

I look around. Through my sunglasses, I can see a couple of heads already turned my way. Observing me from the stairs, one girl leans her mouth toward her friend's ear. Her lips start moving and the friend smiles. Swallowing, I scan the grounds for Lance. Even though I'm (mostly) over him, he's the person I dread seeing the most. Thankfully, he's nowhere in sight.

"I'm not ready," I say. And then more to myself, "What am I trying to achieve?"

Ashley twists my body to face hers and looks me right in the eyes. "Camilla, listen to me. You're not trying to achieve anything. You're just being you."

But I am, I think. I am trying to achieve something. I want to prove I'm not going to disappear into oblivion while Konrad Wolnik has the time of his life. I want everyone to know the true scope of his selfishness.

"Everyone's going to talk about me."

"Good," Jodie says. "You're going to be more popular, then."

"Negative attention is worse than no attention," I mumble.

"No," Jodie says dismissively. "That's not how the saying goes. 'Bad press is better than no press at all.'" She tugs at my arm. "Who cares, anyway?"

Ashley gives Jodie the eye. Her expression softens when she looks back at me. "You're not going to get any bad attention. I promise. If I hear anything negative, I'm going to do some serious ass whooping."

I can't help but chuckle. I've got two amazing friends who have my back. They're also the reason Mom isn't with us right now. When she found out I wanted to come back to school, she insisted on coming along, but after a lengthy three-way call with Ashley and Jodie, she gave in. And thank God for that. If Mom came, I'd feel like even more of a disaster.

Jodie pulls at my arm again. "Come on, hon. Let's do this."

I give in. My feet propel me forward. Two reluctant steps later, I'm marching toward the entrance, my chin held high, my two best friends at my sides. Adrenaline pumps through my veins. The starting shot has been fired. Nothing to do now but run.

Right before we get to the door, I remove my sunglasses and slip them into the pocket of my flannel. Go big or go home, right?

As we make our way through the hallway toward my locker, I'm convinced people are staring for two reasons: one, I'm ugly now, and I didn't used to be—at least not this ugly; and two, they're surprised to see me, Jodie, and Ashley together again after what happened with Ashley and Lance and the video.

Or maybe I'm wrong and people just think Jodie and Ashley have found a new, unattractive wing-woman to replace me.

A part of me wishes that last thought were actually true. That people didn't recognize me. That I could have a fresh start. Unfortunately, that's the least likely explanation. I know this because a minute after I get to my locker, I'm cornered by half of the track team.

"Camilla?"

The voice belongs to Anna. For a moment, I just keep my nose buried in my locker.

It's weird, but I never got close to the other girls on the team. We're on friendly terms, and we do have fun when we're together, but I've never considered any of them my true friends. Jodie and Ashley have been a part of my life way longer than track has. I guess I've always seen it as a work-life balance thing. Track's work and Jodie and Ashley are my life.

Still, these girls have been nothing but nice to me, even if it is only because I'm the fastest runner on the team. Shutting my eyes for brief moment, I suck in a deep breath and turn around. "Hi, Anna."

Behind her are three other girls from the team: Jen, Amanda, and Eve. They're all huddled together, like they knew they were about to come face-to-face with a monster.

They look so ridiculously on edge, I almost want to shout, *Boo!*

As soon as they process what they're seeing, they gasp in unison and their faces twist in shock. Eve's hand flies up to her mouth, but she catches herself and forces it back down into a fist at her side. She's trying to be polite, but that doesn't make her gaze any less scrutinizing. I feel like I'm naked on a hospital bed and her eyes are doing the operating.

Meanwhile, Ashley and Jodie have tensed up. They're like two soldiers willing to jump in front of a moving bullet for me. All the kids passing us slow their pace, the phones in their hands temporarily forgotten, their mouths gaping open, eyes locked on me. I do my best to pretend they don't exist.

"Camilla . . ." Anna says. She looks like she really needs to go to the bathroom and take care of a very persistent number two. She doesn't even get this red-faced after we run five miles.

Eager to get this over with, I try to smile.

Anna trades a few nervous looks with Eve and Amanda and Jen. She has no idea what to say. None of them do. They just stand there, little baby lambs from a petting zoo thrown into the wild. Not that I blame them.

Eventually, Anna opens her mouth again. "Are you okay?"

I wish she'd just say it. Stop running circles around the elephant—or should I say, ogre—in front of her.

"I've had better days," I joke. Jodie giggles beside me.

Now Anna looks like she might cry. It's so obvious she's itching with questions. She wants to know how it happened. When and why. But she doesn't ask.

"Sorry I didn't reply to any of your texts," I say in another attempt to make a crack in the Great Wall of Awkwardness.

Anna's quick to reply. "It's fine! Don't worry about it!"

"We missed you at practice," Amanda says, taking over since Anna seems to have reached her limit. "No one would tell us what was going on." She gives Jodie some side-eye.

I respond quickly before Jodie can rip her to pieces. "I was laying low for a while. Trying to get used to the new me. But I'm back now."

"Can you still run?" Eve blurts. If there's an airhead on the team, it's always been Eve. Anna's elbow jabs her in the side.

"She *has* legs," Jodie says through her teeth.

I flash Jodie an "I got it" smile. "Yeah," I say. "I've been running a lot. I'm not quitting the team or anything. Not sure I'll make it today, though."

"Take all the time you need," Anna says, unleashing a series of rapid, red-faced nods.

"Thanks."

There's more awkward silence. Everybody's fidgeting. We all want to be done with this conversation, including the for-ever-clueless Eve and all the kids quietly observing from the sidelines. Thankfully, the chime of the first bell saves us all.

"Great," Ashley says. "Time for class!"

I give my teammates a small wave-and-smile combo. "Let us know if there's anything we can do," Amanda says as I walk off into the pool of surrounding pity.

Even though the bell rang, nobody's rushing to class. Apparently, it's okay to be late on Let's Look Sad for Camilla Day. My stomach clenches. Someone should have the balls to say something about my transformation already. But all they do is stare, putting on the best funeral expressions they can muster.

Well, everybody, I'm not fucking dead.

Jodie and Ashley walk me to first period. I wish at least one of them was in class with me, but I'll have to wait until third period for biology with Jodie.

Ashley gives me a hug. "Like water off a duck's back," she says into my ear. When we pull apart, I smile at her, assuring her I'll be fine, then squeeze Jodie's hand, and walk into the classroom.

"Good morning, Camilla," Ms. Walker says. She's facing the door, hands folded in front of her like I'm the guest of honor she's been anticipating all week. "Good to have you back." Her stiff posture betrays her discomfort, but I detect some relief there, too.

"Good morning," I say, beelining over to my seat. The teachers are probably glad the cat's out of the bag. Now they can officially pity me in public.

As people settle into their seats, I'm assaulted by more sad smiles, more reluctant waves. I adopt a neutral smile, but underneath it I'm screaming. I'd rather have people laugh at me or be disgusted by me. Anything would be better than this godawful pity party.

Ms. Walker gets class started, but her voice does little to kill the tension in the room. Most of the kids are facing forward, but Melissa Rojas is still staring at me over her shoulder like I'm a homeless orphan on the street in winter.

I reach my limit and lift my middle finger.

Melissa's face flushes with color and she whirls back to face the board. I'm pretty sure Ms. Walker saw, but if she did, she doesn't say anything. Great. Even the teachers think I need special treatment.

The classroom door opens, and in walks Lauren Batko in her tight jeans and even tighter black leather jacket, her face framed by her red curls.

Konrad Wolnik's good friend, Lauren Batko.

Ms. Walker's expression clouds over. "You're late, Ms. Batko."

Even though I know it's only temporary, I'm grateful for the distraction.

Lauren shrugs. "Sorry. Just got my period."

The class erupts in giggles and a couple of ewws from the guys. Lauren being late to class isn't exactly unusual. She's late more often than she's not—if she decides to grace us with her presence at all. What is unusual is that on the way to her seat in the back of the room, she stops in front of my desk and stands there.

I look up and our eyes meet.

"Holy shit," she says, grinning. "What the hell happened to you?"

The words crash into me, leaving me blindsided. I don't know whether I should feel relieved or insulted.

Ms. Walker's voice thunders over the room, ordering Lauren to her seat. But Lauren doesn't oblige. Not right away. Not before she shakes her head and says, "Damn, girl. You sure got the short end of the stick."

CHAPTER 11

KONRAD

AFTER FIRST PERIOD, BECCA swoops down on me in the hallway and snags my hand like she owns it. She does this in the most conspicuous manner possible.

We walk together, entwined like the happiest couple ever. Mike Rogers waves us down and Becca drags me over to where he stands by his locker with his equally annoying buddy, Tom Dempsey. Considering Becca shares the same popularity rung with these douchebags, I'm not surprised she wants to talk to them. I don't like it, but interacting with Becca means I have to interact with the jocks, too.

"Wowza," Mike says. "Congrats, kids." Tom follows this up with an annoying whistle, which is kind of fitting, I guess, since he has a very unfortunate-looking gap between his front teeth. "When did this happen?"

Becca makes a show of swinging our entwined hands. "Saturday."

"Nice," Mike says. He turns his buzzed head to me, suddenly serious. "Dude, I hope there's no hard feelings between us. About Sara. I had no idea you guys used to date. She just told me about it last night."

Heat surges to my cheeks. "Really?" I ask. "You never noticed us together?" Even if Mike never paid me any attention before, I'm sure he noticed Sara. All the guys did. And I was with Sara for a long time. We weren't exactly puritans when we were at school together either.

"Nah, man," he says. "I didn't know."

I call bullshit, but before I can interrogate him further, Becca interrupts. "Who cares? The past is in the past."

Tom is looking past my shoulder. "Speaking of Sara . . ."

I turn and follow his line of sight to find her approaching our group. Something's off in her walk, though—I notice that immediately. I know her body language better than anyone. She's already crying, "OH MY GOD," from a few feet away.

"What happened, babe?" Mike asks.

Sara's eyes are already huge, but when they land on Becca's hand in mine, they get even bigger. She looks at me like I ran her over with my car. My chest sticks out and I beam with pride. Becoming good-looking was worth it for moments like this alone.

Sara flashes Becca a sheepish smile. Becca wears the crown at our school and Sara's still a little reluctant around her. Mike might be Sara's link to the popular crew, but it looks like she still hasn't gotten her permanent membership card. I, on the other hand, seem to have been granted mine the moment Becca started talking to me.

Once my new relationship with Becca seems to sink in, Sara straightens her back and sucks in a deep breath. "Did you guys hear about Camilla Hadi?"

My stomach goes into free fall.

"What about her?" Becca asks.

"She's . . ." Sara hesitates. "She's really unattractive now."

"What do you mean?" Mike asks.

"Yeah." Tom snorts. "She was always unattractive."

I narrow my eyes at him. "No, she wasn't."

Tom's annoying grin drops.

"Yeah," Mike says, backing me up, which takes me by surprise. "She's not exactly a catch, but she's always had a pretty tight body because of track."

"Well," Sara continues. "Not anymore. She had an ID, too. She, like, turned *awful-looking*. Her face is all distorted and stuff. It's really disturbing."

"How do you know?" I ask, my heart thumping.

"She's here. I saw her this morning. The poor girl."

My feet are moving before I know it. Camilla's here. She came to school.

"Konrad?" Becca says to my back after I've freed myself from her grip. I ignore her. I have to find Camilla. I have no idea what I'm going to say to her, or if I'm going to say anything at all, but I have to at least see her.

I quicken my step, tuning my ears for whispers and gossip, searching for a hint as to where she might be. If she really did come to school, then people must be talking about her.

Everyone I pass notices me, even more than usual. I still see the awe and adoration I've come to expect, but today some of their looks are sprinkled with something else. Something like uncertainty and maybe even suspicion. Are people starting to blame me for Camilla already?

I turn a corner and spot Jackie Baker. If anyone knows where Camilla might be, it's our local journalist. I get up in her face. "Have you seen Camilla Hadi?"

Jackie takes a step back. The something I've been noticing couldn't be more clear on her face. "She was at her locker. Why?"

"Where's her locker?"

Just as Jackie throws a thumb over her shoulder, a hand sneaks into mine and I startle. "Did you find her?" Becca asks. Mike and Tom are right behind her. I'd been so absorbed in my search for Camilla, I didn't even notice them following me.

I'm about to tell them no when Mike's hand flies up. "Whoa!" he says as he points.

Dread swallows me whole.

I turn.

And I see Camilla Hadi.

And then she sees me.

She's standing in front of room 114, backpack hanging from her shoulder, like she was just about to go in but something stopped her. I notice that even though she no longer looks like an athlete, she still carries herself like one. Her chin is held high, her chest puffed out, pushing back all the gawking around her.

Her features are different and, yes, less traditionally appealing. But it's not at all what I'd been imagining. In my head, I'd envisioned a female Frankenstein's creation, but Camilla's not a freak. She might not be pretty, but she's no monster either.

I get a good look at her, and she eyeballs me. Me, with the most popular kids at my side—Becca's hand again connected to mine. Me, next to Mike, who's still pointing.

It's only when I see the shift in Camilla's expression—like an airplane shadow catching on her face—that I realize what I must look like. Not only to her, but to the entire school. Here I am, the luckiest guy around, hanging out with my hot new girlfriend and popular new friends, pointing and gaping at the unluckiest girl like she's some kind of rare animal in a cage.

Camilla breaks our eye contact first. She slips into the classroom, leaving Ashley and Jodie standing outside. I hadn't noticed they were there until now. I shiver. Their combined glares could turn a large mammal to stone. Jodie gives me the finger and turns away. Ashley, on the other hand, starts stomping in my direction. I'm frozen before she even arrives.

"You just had to rub it in, didn't you?" she says.

"He's not rubbing anything in," Becca replies icily. "What's your problem?"

"Speaking of rubbing," Tom chimes in, "when's it my turn, Ashley? And can we make a video like you did with Lance?"

"Fuck you, Tom," she spits. Then she turns back to me. "Just stay away from her."

"It's not like that," I say, but my voice is too small, and Ashley's already turned away.

"Don't listen to her," Becca says, dismissing Ashley with a wave of her hand. "It's not like you wished for Camilla's ID or anything." I stiffen up even more. A sudden fear grips my insides and I look Becca right in the eyes. Her smile wavers. "Did you?"

"No!" I almost yell. "Of course not!"

Her face lights up. "Good." Leaning in, she gives me a peck on the cheek. "Then it's not your fault. It's just an unfortunate coincidence. See you at lunch?"

I mumble a goodbye. The warning bell echoes through the hallway. Everyone disperses.

Me, I stay where I am, until I'm the only person left.

Becca's right. It's just a messed-up coincidence. It's not my fault.

So why do I feel like it is, now more than ever?

This is just great, isn't it? Camilla hates me. Her friends hate me. *My* ex-friends hate me. And now, with the way people glance at me, half the school seems to hate me, too. And what did I do to deserve any of this? I was a sixteen-year-old teenager insecure about the way he looked.

What. A. Crime.

In geography, Mr. Miller's voice is a monotonous drone. I keep sneaking glances at my phone—for which Mr. Miller actually scolds me twice. Clearly, I'm not the only one using my phone in class, though, because the hashtag #IStandWithCamilla is exploding everywhere I look.

My leg keeps bobbing up and down under my desk. What am I going to do? My ID was supposed to make more people *like* me. But line me up next to Camilla and I'm a selfish douche who, very likely, may have played a part in another person's misfortune. If I were an outsider looking in, I'd think so, too.

A notification pops up on my screen and I tap it without even catching who it's from.

Did you have anything to do with Camilla Hadi's ID?

It's from Eric Stewart. Instinctually, I turn around, but then remember that the kid isn't in this class with me. I return my attention to my phone and block him.

So even Eric thinks I'm to blame. That's just fantastic. I'm pretty screwed, aren't I?

But then it comes to me.

I look up from my screen and carefully glance around to see if anybody else has been struck by the same spark of enlightenment. All I get is Mr. Miller's scowl.

I obediently drop my gaze to appear low-key, but what's happening within me is anything but. Because I think I just came up with a solution.

It's so simple. I just have to become Camilla's friend. Get close to her, be nice to her and the people she hangs out with, show her that I'm not a narcissistic bastard. If she likes me, if she approves of me, then everyone else will have no choice but to like me, too.

As soon as the lunch bell rings, I spring from my seat and head for Camilla's locker. The first step in getting on Camilla's good side should be an apology for sounding like an ass when I visited her house. Hopefully, I'll be able to catch her alone. Going through Jodie Mathews and Ashley Solomon seems like a lot of work.

Hands in my pockets, I keep my eyes on the floor, trying to be as inconspicuous in the hallways as possible. My phone buzzes against my hand. I pluck it out to find a text from Becca, but my mind's pretty preoccupied at the moment, so I ignore it.

As I round a corner, I hear a whistle—not unlike a catcall a woman walking down the street might hear from a creepy dude. Curiosity wins, and I look up.

Lauren's fingers fall away from her face, revealing a smirk. She's looking right at me. Alan is beside her. His head turns just in time to avoid catching my eye.

I realize I've slowed my pace, nearly stopping, so I hurry on with every intention of walking past them without a word.

"Hey," Lauren calls out. "Pretty Boy. Wait up."

Clenching my teeth, I whirl around. "I told you to stop calling me that."

"Sorry," she says, her hands up in the air in apology. There's a hint of mischief in her expression and I already regret acknowledging her. Alan's still busy examining the lockers next to him. Lauren's arms cross at her chest. "Did you hear about Camilla Hadi?"

"Hasn't everyone?"

She nods. "It's pretty messed up."

"Yeah," I say, "it is."

"What do you think?"

I feel my face warm up. "What do you mean, what do I think?"

"Well," Lauren says, shrugging. She's always been a pro at shrugging. "Rumor has it her ID happened on the same day as yours."

I swallow. "So?"

"So, you don't think that's weird?"

"No."

"Do you want to talk about it?" she asks. Alan's gaze jumps my way, but as soon as his eyes meet mine, he drops them to the floor again, his cheeks red as a beet.

I shake my head.

"Come on. It's all over your beautiful face," Lauren says. "It's obviously bothering you."

"No," I say. "*You're* bothering me."

I turn my back to them and shuffle away so fast I'm practically speed walking. See? I knew those two would blame me for what happened to Camilla. That's obviously what Lauren was implying. She's suddenly worried about my feelings? My ass.

A large form advances in my direction. I stop and look up. Mike Rogers—or his huge chest, rather—is coming right at me like a cannonball. Before I can step aside, he bumps into me and I stumble back. If I were still my old, scrawny self, I bet I would've flown across the hallway and smacked into a locker.

"What the hell, Mike?"

He doesn't seem to think he's done anything wrong. Tom takes a spot behind him. "Becca's looking all over for you. She's in the cafeteria."

I straighten to my full height to remind him I'm taller. "Thanks, I'm heading over there now. Did you happen to see Camilla Hadi anywhere?"

"Camilla the Gorilla?" Mike asks, inspiring a guffaw from Tom. The two bump fists.

"What did you call her?"

Mike turns back to me. "It's just a joke, man. What happened to her totally sucks."

"Not a very good one," I mumble.

Tom rips off a piece of beef jerky with his teeth, talking through a full mouth. "She left for lunch with Handy Ashley and that other black chick, the stuck-up lipstick one."

More uncreative nicknames? But what else would you expect from boneheads like these two? I wonder what they call *me* behind my back. "Okay," I say. "Thanks."

"Why do you care so much about that girl, anyway?" Mike asks.

"I don't. I mean, we both had IDs, so I guess it's a camaraderie thing."

Tom stops chewing. They're both staring at me. "It's a what thing?"

"Never mind."

"Like I said," Mike goes on, "it sucks what happened to her. I feel for her, for sure. But I mean, what are you going to do? She'll be fine. Life's a bitch."

"Yeah," I say. "Thanks for those wise words, Mike."

He nods, clueless to my sarcasm, and pats me on the back. "No problem. Now go find your fine piece of ass, you lucky dog."

I nod and watch them walk off. My new—quote, unquote—friends.

Yup. I'm a lucky dog indeed.

CHAPTER 12

CAMILLA

"I STAND WITH CAMILLA?" I spit.

Jodie has just handed me her phone. I scroll from post to post, each one a selfie of one of my classmates, each with a hand covering most of his or her face, their eyes peeking out from between their fingers.

My heart is pounding. My whole body shakes. I drop my chicken sandwich back into the fast-food bag. I've completely lost my appetite. "Who started this shit?"

Ashley's on her own phone in the backseat. "Looks like Jackie Baker was one of the first," she says. "There're over fifty of these posts now."

"Of course," I say flatly. Jackie Baker is famous for sticking her nose where it doesn't belong. I hate to admit it, but she's going to make a great journalist one day. "What is this supposed to even be?"

"Well," Ashley explains, taking a bite out of her burger, "some of the pics are accompanied by another hashtag, **#looksmeannothing.**"

A huff escapes my lips. "'Looks mean nothing,'" I repeat. "What am I? A freaking natural disaster? A charity case? What's wrong with people?"

"No," Jodie says. She takes a sip of her Diet Coke. Her voice is composed, but her eyes are big with excitement. "This is good."

"Huh?" I practically throw the phone back at her. "How is any of this good?"

Ashley leans forward, reaching between the front seats to squeeze my hand. I focus on my breathing to calm myself down.

"Look at it this way," Jodie says. "You have everyone on your side. Sympathy can be a powerful tool. At this pace, you might become a national sensation. Global, even. You can probably make money off of this."

"I don't want to be a sensation!" Worldwide pity is the last thing I want. I got more than a lifetime's worth already. I came to school to show that I'm strong and to make Konrad Wolnik look like the selfish asshole he is while I'm at it. Not for this. And aren't high school kids supposed to be cruel? Why are they acting like goddamn activists all of a sudden?

"Trust me," Jodie continues. "We should act fast."

"Jodie," Ashley says, "just be quiet."

"This is all *his* fault," I mumble, remembering Konrad and his perfect face, his perfect girlfriend, and his perfect group of friends, pointing at me in the hallway like I'm some sort of mutant sideshow. Why are people doing this crap instead of blaming him like they're supposed to? Why can't they see this is not a coincidence? *He* did this to me.

"Konrad's?" Jodie asks.

"Yes Konrad's!" I bark. She's basically proving my point. "Who else's? I bet if everyone didn't glorify his ID as some sort of miracle when they first found out, they wouldn't be acting like this now. These people just want to make *themselves* feel better. Nobody cares how *I* feel or what *I* think." I huff. "And did you see that interview he did with Jackie?"

"Ugh," Jodie says. She clearly has, because she starts quoting it in a mocking voice: *"I know that I'm lucky, and I'll never take that for granted."*

I add a quote of my own, the one that bothered me the most: *"I want to believe these things happen for a reason."*

Jodie snorts, but Ashley's not paying attention. She exhales at her phone, her lips veering to one side. "What?" I ask. This can't possibly get any worse.

Hesitating for a second, Ashley twists the device so I can see the screen. It's another pic of a guy covering his face. It appears he's in class; you can see the desk and the white ceiling tiles as his phone camera is angled upward. Although only the eyes are visible, I recognize them immediately. I don't even have to look at the screen name.

Konrad Wolnik.

Tears of frustration sting my eyes. "You've got to be kidding me." My hatred for him multiplies like cells splitting in a time-lapse video.

Jodie scoffs. "What a high-and-mighty asshole."

"Camilla," Ashley says, "just ignore it."

"No!" I snap. "I'm going to start my own campaign."

"Ooo!" Jodie says. "What kind?"

"The I'm-going-to-ruin-him kind. I just need to think of a good hashtag."

"YASS, GURL!" Jodie yells, raising her palm. I smack it with mine.

I turn to look at Ashley, expecting to see her hand in the air, as well, but she's leaning back against her seat. "What?" I ask.

Ashley slowly shakes her Afro from side to side. Her big brown eyes meet mine—they're the opposite of supportive. "I hope you're kidding," she finally says.

My ears start burning in shame. I look out the window at the long lunchtime line at the Shack. "Of course I am." Talking about ruining people using hashtags is probably not the best idea around Ashley. No matter how much they deserve it.

"You need to ignore him, Camilla," Ashley insists. "Get past this. It'll all die down with time. Trust me."

But I can't. I can't get past this. Konrad's faux-solidarity snap stays on my mind the whole ride back to school and it follows me to class. Konrad gets to live his precious, good-looking life while I'm immortalized as the face of some bullshit "looks don't matter" campaign? Without my permission? No one's even consulted me about how *I* feel. Everyone is just assuming I'm some kind of victim. How can people think that's okay?

And now Konrad Wolnik's contributing from up on his high horse? I get that Inexplicable Developments are a mystery, but mine's pretty damn explicable to me.

He's responsible.

I'm scarring my notebook with an angry doodle, thinking about going home early, when the school aide walks through the door and whispers in the teacher's ear.

Ms. Reilly's eyes lock on me immediately. She clears her throat. "Camilla? Sweetheart? The counselor would like to see you."

I stare at her with my mouth open. This is probably the last thing I expected to hear today. I slide my chair back and stomp out of the classroom.

Our school has two full-time counselors. The last time I saw one—the forever-rambling Mr. Sanders—was when I got a C on my algebra test. Everybody freaked out because they thought track was interfering with my schoolwork. It totally wasn't. I just didn't feel like studying for the stupid test.

When I barge into the counselor's office I'm expecting to see Mr. Sanders again, but find Ms. Hughes waiting for me instead.

Ms. Hughes is this tiny woman, barely older than me. Her mouth and nose assemble at the bottom of her face, almost to a point. She reminds me of a rabbit. I've never spoken to her, but I don't even bother with introductions. "My mom specifically said I didn't need a counselor."

"Hello, Camilla," she says, barely opening her tiny, lettuce-munching mouth. "Please come in, sweetheart."

Ugh. Can people stop calling me that? I'm about to explain to her that I'm not her goddamn sweetheart, but she's already holding the door open. Sucking down my frustration, I march through it and plop down into a chair. Even before Ms. Hughes can sit on the other side of her desk, I'm repeating myself. "I don't need a counselor. Did you not get the note? I'm pretty sure my mom can sue you for this."

Ms. Hughes gives me that pitiful look I don't think I'm ever going to get used to. I think I hate it even more coming from an adult. "I got the note," she says, "but the situation has changed dramatically. I thought it might be good for us to talk."

"How did it change dramatically?"

She lowers her chin at me. Not in a threatening way. In that, condescending "I'm here for you" manner counselors think is encouraging, but totally isn't. She doesn't wear glasses, but she's one of those people who look like her face is missing something without them.

"Hashtag #IStandWithCamilla?" she says.

My eyes widen. "How do you know about that already?"

"I'm on social media, too. It's a gateway into understanding students."

I cross my arms and sink back into the chair. "Whatever. I don't even care about that."

"I think you do."

"No, I don't."

"Your Inexplicable Development caused quite a stir within the school, Camilla. That's a lot of attention for one person. Direct contact is one thing, but social media attention—and on this scale—is another. I just want to make sure you're handling it okay."

I grind my teeth. "I'm handling it just fine. Can I go now?"

She's studying me. I fidget under her gaze. "Yes," she says. "But before you do, I want you to promise me to think of this as a positive thing. Remember, it's not personal. Your peers don't know how to handle things they're unfamiliar with. This is them reacting in the best way they know how." She smiles. "You're having a wonderful influence on them."

I want her to stop talking so I stand. "Bye, Ms. Hughes." I'm already walking away when she says, "I'm here if you need me!"

I don't return to class. Instead, I sprint toward the closest bathroom and lock myself in a stall. Dropping down onto the seat, I shut my eyes.

Everyone's got opinions about what's best for me. My life is ruined and I'm supposed to think positive thoughts because I'm having a wonderful influence on people?

Balling my trembling hands into fists, I take a long, deep breath. *Stop*, I tell myself. *Calm down. You will not cry. You are not a quitter. You are not that girl.*

I need to run. Not as in escape. I actually need to run. I need to get this frustration out of my system, and running my ass off until I can't feel my legs anymore is the only way I know how to do that. Then I'll be able to figure out what to do.

With the promise of track to look forward to, I make my way back to class. I'm two doors away from Ms. Reilly's classroom when the door to my left opens and spews out my former crush, Lance Dietrick.

I screech to a halt. He's wearing a white Sonny & Cher T-shirt I've never seen before. Must be a new addition to his wardrobe. He looks amazing.

In the past, Lance has never looked at me for longer than four seconds at a time. Well, today, it's already been five. "Hi, Lance," I blurt.

His lips pinch together like he swallowed a bitter grape. The hall pass in his left hand travels to his right. I had apologized about the video I took of him and Ashley at Gina's party, and he'd said it was cool, so, technically, we are supposed to be on speaking terms.

But he doesn't speak. What he does do is this:

His face rearranges into that funeral home expression I've seen countless times today, and just when it seems like he's about to say something, his palm travels up to mask most of his face, his fingers parting to reveal his eyes. As he starts walking past me, he raises his other hand and gives me a thumbs-up.

A thumbs-up.

I want to die.

The last bell ricochets through the school. Somehow, I made it through the day. Fingers trembling, I text Jodie and Ashley to let them know I'm going to practice, then make my way to the locker rooms.

None of the other girls from the team have arrived yet. I change into my running clothes and go out to the field to stretch.

It feels so good to be out here. Normal, almost. Like I traveled back in time and I'm my old self again, the sun a familiar presence on my face, the smell of grass and rubber all around me. But the illusion only lasts a few seconds. All I have to do is glance down at my distorted body to remember my reality.

I finish stretching with my eyes closed.

An unusually large crowd of spectators has gathered around the field. I tune them out. As soon as I start running, I hear someone shout, "GO, CAMILLA!" but I focus only on my breathing and the swooshing sound my shoes make every time they hit the track.

This is my element. This is where I'll always belong.

I run three laps without stopping. When I reach the finish line on the final one, I'm covered in sweat. Bent over, hands on my knees, I get lost in the sound of my own panting.

When I hear my name again, it sounds different from the cheers that reached my ears earlier. It's both more urgent and more tentative at the same time. I look up.

Not twenty feet away from where I stand, Konrad Wolnik is gripping the chain-link fence with both hands. He's alone. And he looks desperate.

"Camilla," he calls. "Please. Just one minute."

CHAPTER 13

KONRAD

HOLY SHIT. SHE'S COMING MY way.

What the heck do I do? I thought I'd have to work harder to get her to talk to me. I didn't expect her to start charging at me like an angry bull as soon as I opened my mouth.

Camilla stops a couple of feet away from the fence. Her hands are balled into fists at her sides, her chest is heaving, and her expression is tight with fury.

"That was pretty intense," I say, hoping to break the ice—there seems to be a lot of ice between us. It's more than just small talk, though. Earlier, every time she sped past me as I watched, I was genuinely impressed by the concentration on her face, the complete devotion.

Camilla's gaze lurches away for a second. Her right hand travels to push back a strand of hair behind her ear. Her post-run blush seems to intensify. Did I embarrass her or is she getting even more pissed off? She hasn't told me to fuck off yet, so that's good, right? Plus, the last time I talked to her, there was a door between us. Now it's just a fence. Progress.

"I wish I was as passionate about something as you are about running," I continue, but I want to slap my own face as soon as the words leave my mouth. Can I sound any cheesier?

She looks me straight in the eye. "Your one minute's up."

"Wait! Okay! Look, I'm sorry about what I said at your house. I *don't know* what this is like for you. I have no idea what you're going through."

"No," she says, matter-of-factly. "You don't."

"I just want you to know that I really don't know why this happened to us. I swear. I'm as surprised at how things turned out as you are."

Camilla's face twitches. "Why do you even care? You got what you wanted. Why don't you just leave me alone? And posting about me online? Do you even have a fucking heart?"

I stare at her through the chain-link. I swallow and start to speak, but my voice comes out small and shaky. "I don't want you to hate me."

Camilla feigns surprise. "Oh," she says, "I see. So you're after forgiveness?"

"It's not like that . . ." I try, even though I'm pretty sure the conversation just swerved into unsalvageable territory.

"No," she says, "you want me to give you a pass or whatever, so you can have your happily-ever-after with Becca without what you did to me on your conscience." Something stings inside my chest, but before I can defend myself, she hisses, "Well, you're not going to get it. No matter what people say, no matter how 'inexplicable' IDs may be, this wouldn't have happened to me if it weren't for you. *You* did this to me and I'm never going to forgive you for it. *Never!*"

I blink. "Can't we be friends?" I whimper.

Camilla laughs like a maniac, then turns away. But before leaving, she shakes her head as if she could never believe I'd say something so ridiculous.

I stay there, fingers hooked in the fence, watching her trot over to her teammates. I realize they've all been observing our conversation—if you can even call it that—for a while now. Others, too. I catch two freshmen girls in the bleachers, staring, and shove my hands into my pockets before walking away from their scrutiny.

So. My plan to befriend Camilla Hadi did not go well. I figured it wouldn't be smooth sailing, but I didn't expect a shit storm of this size. Instead of getting her to like me, I probably got her to hate me even more. And so many people saw that. Can we say epic fail?

Shuffling back to my car, I try to process what happened.

Camilla's upset. Like, *seriously* upset. She blames me. She blames me for everything. Her words settle in my stomach, heavy, toxic, stirring together into a brew of guilt—even though I know I had nothing to do with her ID.

What the hell am I supposed to do now?

I turn to my phone, craving a distraction. There's a text from Becca: **My parents are out again**, followed by two winking emojis. I might as well take her up on her offer.

"That was really sweet of you," a voice I recognize says.

I stop walking and check over my shoulder to confirm that it, in fact, belongs to Sara.

"What was?" I ask, looking around for Mike, for anybody. Most people have gone home by now. There are just four cars and a news van still in the parking lot.

Wait. What's a news van doing at our school?

"Talking to Camilla," Sara says.

I shrug and keep walking. I'm not going to comment, and I'm not going to explain myself. Especially not to Sara.

"You were always such a great guy," she continues, following me.

I stop and turn. "What do you want, Sara?"

Her gaze falls to the ground, and she pushes her hair behind her ear. When Camilla did the same thing, it was real, natural. When Sara does it, it screams *fake-fake-fake.* "Do you want to get tacos?" she asks. "It's so nice outside."

I raise my eyebrows. There's a taco truck downtown, smack in the middle of a huge backyard with white miniature bulbs strung around its edges. It's a fun, romantic spot, especially on summer nights. After I took Sara there the first time, she loved it so much it became our go-to date destination. We'd sit there for hours, talking, sharing one pair of headphones, grossing other customers out with our lovey-dovey cuddles. Now I know it only meant something to one of us.

"You're out of your mind," I say.

"Why are you being so mean to me?"

A huff pops out of my mouth. "You broke my fucking heart, Sara. I was in *love* with you, and you erased me from your life like I was nothing. Now that I'm attractive, you're suddenly talking to me like the whole thing never happened?"

"I'm sorry."

"I don't care."

She drops the act. Real emotions seem to be pushing up to the surface. "I made a mistake, okay? What if I told you I'd like to give it another chance?"

"Then I'd tell you to fuck off."

Sara's eyes fill with tears. Her jaw trembles. I know her too well, though. These are tears of frustration. She's not getting what she wants and she hates it.

I like seeing her hate it.

"Bye, Sara." I say, facing my car.

"Becca only likes you for your looks!" she spits at my back.

I don't even bother to turn around. "I know."

As I drive home, I have a smile plastered on my face. You know that "I'll show them one day" feeling? When you promise yourself you'll prove someone wrong, and even though you're not sure when, you're determined to make it happen? I just had that one day with Sara.

But it's not all relief and satisfaction. I can't seem to get Camilla off my mind. It's not just how she made me feel either. How she shot me down. It's Camilla herself.

If you think about it, she's pretty amazing. It takes humongous balls (ovaries?) to come to school after an awful ID like hers, act like it didn't break you, and tell the guy you think caused it exactly how you feel. After today, I have a whole new level of respect for her.

When I get home to grab something to eat before I see Becca, Mom's outside in the backyard, sitting in a chair on the deck holding a beer. Arthur's butt is on the railing, his feet dangling over the side. I already know something's up. Mom doesn't usually drink, and Arthur only talks to her one-on-one when they're fighting or something unusual has happened.

It doesn't look like they're fighting.

"Your school was on the local news," Arthur says before I can even close the gate. I go around the deck to the steps, recalling the news van in the school parking. "What?"

"They were talking about that girl," Mom says.

I stop on the third step from the top. I don't even have to ask. "Oh."

"Do you know her?"

"Not really."

"Can you believe how brave she is?" Mom asks, shaking her head. "If I had an Inexplicable Development like that happen to me ... And she went back to school? Unbelievable."

"Yeah," I say. "She's pretty brave."

"Did you see her?" Arthur asks. "Does she look like a burnt nuclear bomb victim?"

"Shut up," I snap.

"They mentioned you, too," Arthur says.

My eyes widen. "On the news?"

"They didn't mention *you*," Mom says. "They can't do that, legally. They just brought up the nature of your Inexplicable Development. Mostly for contrast. They're more interested in your classmate's incident because it's so rare, even among IDs. Most of the ones that happened in the past have been, you know, *positive*. Like yours." She's quiet for a moment, her eyes trying to read me. "What's wrong, honey? You're not blaming yourself, are you?"

I shrug. "Camilla's ID happened on the same day as mine."

"Come here," Mom says. Sighing, I shuffle over to her chair and she reaches out to squeeze my hand. I realize that she hasn't really touched me like this since my transformation. "You had nothing to do with it," Mom tells me.

"Unless you wished for that girl's ID, too, of course," Arthur says.

"Arthur," Mom barks, "go inside."

Smirking, he jumps off the rail and walks into the kitchen, closing the door behind him.

Mom focuses her attention back on me. "There's no point in thinking about these things, trying to explain them. They're inexplicable for a reason. Your father and I had a hard time at first. We didn't handle your ID very well, and I want to apologize to you for that. We should've been happy for you, no questions asked."

One of my eyebrows hikes up in suspicion. "So you only realized this after you heard about what happened to Camilla Hadi?"

Mom's face flushes with color. She looks down at the bottle in her hand. "Her situation helped me see things more clearly, yes."

I sigh. At least Mom's being honest.

She gives my hand another squeeze. Neither of us says anything for a moment. I move to the chair across from her and fall into it. Since Mom's opening up, I might as well give a confession of my own. "You were right," I say.

"About what?"

"Things aren't as great as I thought they would be."

She gives a tiny nod but doesn't say anything.

"The popular kids want to hang with me, but I don't really like them much. Alan and Lauren hate me—they think I wanted to be better looking so I'd become popular and ditch them. And I didn't even do anything. I'm just trying to deal with this sudden change, you know?"

"Why can't you just tell Alan and Lauren that, then?"

"Why can't they just see it? They're supposed to be my friends."

Mom sighs. "Honey, miscommunication is a waste of time that will only end in regret. You can't expect people to interpret events and actions the same way you do. Everyone is different. Everyone has different experiences and expectations."

I think for a minute. "I guess."

A small smile creeps onto her face. "Soon after I first started dating your father—this was when I was still in college—I saw him giving this beautiful girl a hug. I got so jealous, it nearly broke me. It turned out it was just his cousin. You know, Aunt Elizabeth—she was even more beautiful back then. She was visiting him from Poland. But I didn't talk to him for a month because of it. A whole month of our lives, wasted."

I watch her remembering, rubbing the neck of her beer bottle with her thumb.

"So what are you saying?"

She looks up. "So I'm saying talk to them. Be clear. If you want your friends back, if you want things to return to the way they used to be, tell them how you feel. Make sure they understand your true intentions. It will help you understand theirs, too."

I nod, remembering what I said to Sara earlier. Telling her everything I felt gave me closure. I'm not so sure I'm ready to get my old friends back just yet, but Mom's story does make me want to make a new one. And for real this time. Not because I think it might help my reputation. Because I want to.

I've said it before and I'll say it again: Camilla is pretty damn amazing. She's strong and confident and devoted. There's a fire within her I admire. A fire, which I wouldn't mind borrowing a few flames from for myself. And, plus, she likes the Leaky Lizards.

I want to get to know her. I want to be her friend. And, this time, I want to make sure she knows my true intentions.

I just have to figure out how to do that.

CHAPTER 14

CAMILLA

ANOTHER ONE OF MY NIGHTMARES is coming true. Wonderful.

In Jodie's words, I'm becoming a "sensation."

Apparently, my story has made national news.

The media can't release my name without permission because I'm a minor, but all you have to do is google our school and my name is all over the comments on all the websites. And don't even get me started on the **#IStandWithCamilla** hashtag. Not only is half my name already in it, the stir around the movement is the worst part. Apparently, it's uniting the student population and beyond. I'm a hero and the inspiration to so many young girls.

What a load of crap.

Twice today, I was accosted by reporters. Not once, *twice*. First, in the morning when Jodie was driving us to school—a news van pulled parallel with us and a reporter leaned halfway out the window, begging us to pull over, screaming at the top of her lungs that she promised they'd blur out my face. Then, at lunch, another reporter, a man this time, pleaded for me to give him two minutes from the other side of the fence.

Like I'd actually do an interview. And even if I did, the reporters would only hate it, because I wouldn't be like *I'm so happy something positive could come out of this bluh, blah, doo-dly-do*. No. Fuck that. I'd tell the truth. I'd tell them how my life sucks now and how the media's making it even worse.

My only hope is to ignore this mess until it dies down. And if it doesn't? Well, then some pretty correspondent will have to put on a somber expression during a special report and explain to the world how the whole thing drove me over the edge.

Or, more likely, drove me to murder Konrad Wolnik. Because after I get three more palms on the face from random kids at school and lock myself in the girls' bathroom to get away from it all, this is what I overhear:

"Cindy said she saw Konrad talking to Camilla Hadi yesterday."

"Aww! For real? How adorable!"

"I know! Seriously, can he be any more perfect? He's, like, actually worried about her. And he doesn't have to be. You know what I mean?"

"Becca Lipowska is so freaking lucky."

"Right? I would seriously, like, pay to be his girlfriend."

"He's not a gigolo, Michelle."

"Did you just say 'gigolo'?"

Giggles.

One of the voices loses steam. "He still hasn't followed me back."

"Maybe he's just not into freshmen?"

I slap my hand down on the flush handle. I can't listen to this. The perfect guy? Are you fucking kidding me? My appearance at school was supposed to make Konrad's life less glamorous, not more so. It was supposed to make everyone see how selfish he really is. Now he's got freshmen fangirling over him even more?

It's official: I'm the only person who can see through Konrad Wolnik's act. Everybody else is blinded by his looks, by his performance. They don't know everything he does is for show, that he doesn't give a crap about anyone else.

But, you know what? That's okay. If me coming to school isn't going to make that clear, I'm going to have to break the spell he's cast on everybody another way. One that's guaranteed to work. How do I know it will? Because it's worked for me in the past.

Since there's no practice today, Jodie gives me a ride home. When we get to my house she turns off the engine and invites herself in.

"I don't know," I tell her, faking a yawn. "I'm kind of tired."

Jodie's hand pets her perfect bun a little more aggressively than usual. "I have to tell you something," she says, "and I can't do that here in the car where you can strangle me."

I stare at her, my heart rate rising. "Oh God. What now?"

"Come on." She prods my side.

Heavy with dread, I open the car door. All the way into the house, I beg her to tell me her grave secret, but she refuses until she has a Diet Coke in her hand. Now I'm sitting on the couch and she's leaning against the wall as far away from me as possible. She's not kidding. This is going to be bad.

"Jesus," I say, bracing myself for the worst. "Just spit it out."

"So, I might've done something without your permission."

"You might've?"

"Okay, I did. Last night."

"Jodie, *what*?"

"You know how I said we could make money off of this #IStandWithCamilla thing?"

I nod. "Uh-huh."

"Well, it turns out we can. I mean, *you* can." She pauses. "Actually, you already did."

My mouth goes dry. "What did you do?"

"I set up a crowdfunding account on your behalf."

A quiet whimper sneaks past my lips. "You did not."

"Camilla, look at this." Jodie already has the page open on her phone. "You made six thousand dollars. *In one night.*"

I spring from the couch and yank the phone out of her hand. The first thing I take in is the number: $6,045.

"You're getting money from people in New York, Camilla. New York!"

Jodie had used a picture of us for the post, but relief washes over me when I see that it was taken from behind. I remember the shot. Ashley snapped it when we went camping last summer. Jodie and I are sitting at the edge of a cliff, our arms wrapped around each other's shoulders, a valley sprawling out below us.

Panic slams into me when I read the message below the photo.

"Hey, guys," I read aloud. "Jodie here. As you may have heard, my best friend recently underwent an unfortunate Inexplicable Development related to her appearance." I pause, trying to control my shaking voice. "My friend is the most wonderful human being in the world. She's kind and determined and she fights hard, no matter what. She deserves to lead a happy life. If you could find it in your heart to help her fight the biggest battle she's ever faced, I know she'll be able to put her life back on the wonderful track it was on. XOXO, Jodie."

I look up from the screen. Jodie's back is pressed against the wall, her eyes wide.

Part of me is moved by the kind words she wrote. And I'm grateful the description is kind of vague—why would people give away their hard-earned dollars based on this message alone? But the biggest part of me really does want to strangle her.

And that part wins.

"How could you?"

"Camilla—"

"You knew I'd hate this!"

"I'm just trying to help."

"You're making my life even worse!"

"If you'd just listen to me—"

"Can you leave now? Please?"

"GIRLS!"

Startled, both Jodie and I whirl toward the kitchen. Mom's standing in the doorway, still in her scrubs, her tote bag hanging from her shoulder. Her head is shaking. "What's going on?"

I clench my jaw. "Nothing. Jodie was just leaving."

"Mrs. Hadil!" Jodie dashes up to her side like my mom will protect her from Hurricane Camilla. "I'm just trying to help."

"Sit down," Mom orders, pointing at the couch. "Both of you."

There's so much authority in her voice, Jodie and I have little choice but to oblige. We sit as far away from each other as the couch allows. Mom drops her bag on the dining table and pulls out a chair. "What is this about?"

"Jodie decided to ruin my life," I say.

Jodie's voice is stronger than mine. "I set up a crowdfunding page. She's already getting all of this attention. We might as well use it. We made six thousand already!"

Mom's lip twitches. "Six thousand? Dollars?"

"Yes! And the number keeps growing!"

"Mom!" I say, raising my voice to drown out Jodie's. "She's even worse than the media!"

Mom shakes her head. "What do these people think they're paying for?"

"That's the thing," Jodie says. "I didn't give any details. Camilla can use the money for whatever she wants." She pauses. "I mean, yeah, there are a couple of weird comments from conspiracy theorists—you know, the ones who think aliens have to rearrange DNA for IDs to happen or whatever. And a few from super religious people who believe IDs are gifts from God. But most people are just kind and want to support her!"

Mom's quiet, looking back and forth between Jodie and me. Instead of getting upset, dipping into her motherly wrath to make her devastated child feel loved and protected, her face flushes with color like she's embarrassed.

"Mom?"

"That's a lot of money."

"So what?" I squeak. "We're doing just fine. I'll get a scholarship for track. I don't want people's charity!"

"You don't know that for sure," Mom says.

"Don't know what for sure?"

"That you'll get a scholarship."

"I'm the best runner on the team!"

Mom takes a long look at me, her eyes softening. "This could be a good thing."

My jaw drops. "OH MY GOD! Are you seriously considering this?"

"Camilla, honey, we're getting by, yes, but we could be doing better. I wish I had money like that for you. But I don't."

"I'll get a job, then!"

Her head shakes a resounding no. "Out of the question. You need to focus on school and track." She pauses. "This could be a wonderful safety net for us. For you."

"Do you not see how humiliating this is for me?"

Mom tries to put on a reassuring smile. "Jodie was just trying to help. Sure, she should have consulted you beforehand." She shoots Jodie the side-eye, but it's obviously more for my benefit than anything else. "But it's a done deal," she continues. "You're not making these people spend money on you. It's their choice."

"But that's a lot of money! What would we even use it for?"

"A lot of things, Camilla," Jodie pipes up. "Maybe for books in college or a prom dress?" She shrugs, but it looks fake. "Plastic surgery? I'm not saying you need it, of course, but maybe you'll want it in the future."

My brain slows down. Once her words seep through me—once I understand the meaning behind them—I glare at her, willing her to spontaneously combust. "What did you just say?"

Jodie's gaze drops to her lap. Her slender shoulders slump, making her look smaller. "Books for college?"

An involuntary growl escapes my mouth. "You said I look fine. You said I don't look that bad. Now you're telling me I need plastic surgery?"

Jodie dares to look me in the eye. A challenge. But it's undermined by her tiny voice. "I'm just being real, Camilla."

I spring to my feet and I'm upstairs in my room in a heartbeat. I know Mom's going to follow me up here, so I lock my door and start pacing to the window and back again, restlessness coursing through every part of my being, until, just as I predicted, I hear my name on the other side of the door: "Camilla?"

"I don't want to talk, Mom. I want to be alone."

A pause. "Open the door."

"NO!"

Mom's quiet for a minute. "I'll come back in a bit," she says. When I don't answer, she adds, "Just tell me you're okay."

My best friend not only betrayed me, she thinks I need plastic surgery. Instead of defending me, my mom took her side. Yeah, I've never been better.

"I'M OKAY!" I yell.

As soon as I hear the creak of the stairs, I bolt to my shelf and snatch last year's yearbook. I need to do something to snuff out this blazing rage. This whole fucked-up day— Konrad, Jodie, this godforsaken world. All of it.

Flicking though the pages, I find what I'm looking for and lay the book down on my bed. I steady my shaking hands, and then aim my phone's camera at the page until Konrad's face fills the entire screen. Once it comes into focus, I snap the photo.

It's not a terrible picture of him. He's grinning, and the angle disguises the real size of his nose. Still, the mug looking back at me is a far cry from the handsome face I saw today on the other side of the fence. It'll do.

It takes a while to set up a fake account. I have to create a new email address and make up a profile. But I'm on fire. And the satisfaction of what I'm about to do fuels me to see my plan through.

When I'm done, I find as many people from school as I can.

I upload Konrad's picture from my camera.

I add the hashtag #uglyforever.

I stare at the screen.

And then I hit POST.

CHAPTER 15

KONRAD

I'VE NEVER BEEN CALLED TO the principal's office before, so when I get to Mr. Connick's class on Thursday and he tells me to go, I'm surprised.

Mr. Connick's expression gives nothing away.

"Do you know why?" I try anyway.

He shakes his head. "Sorry, buddy."

I leave class just as the last of the stragglers enters, and by the time the bell rings the hallways are empty.

Before my ID, I spent most of my time under the radar. Now I'm all over it. Could this have something to do with the interview I gave on my front lawn this morning? But that wasn't a big deal. As soon as I told the reporter I had nothing to do with Camilla's ID, the news crew just left, unimpressed. Turning all the possible reasons for why I've been summoned over in my head, I make my way toward the office near the main entrance.

An elegant woman I've never seen before hovers by the door. As soon as she spots me, she plasters on a gentle smile. "Konrad Wolnik?" she asks.

I'm suddenly a little nervous. "Yes."

"Thank you for coming. This shouldn't take long."

I consider asking what she means by "this," but she has that hard-to-resist air of authority. Plus, she seems nice. I walk through the doorway, and as soon as I step into the tiny waiting area, my eyes lock on a girl sitting in a chair.

Camilla Hadi.

Heat hits my face and spreads down to my toes. Every waking moment, for the past two days, I've spent trying to figure out how to get close to her. Never in a million years did I expect outside forces to bring us together like this.

Camilla shoots up to her feet, her smooth mask of surprise morphing into a grimace. I catch a glimmer of unease there, too, almost like she knows something I don't.

"What's *he* doing here?" she demands.

The lady's smile doesn't waver. "We'll explain everything in just a second. Please." She gestures to the next door. Camilla hesitates, but stomps into the principal's office. I glance at the elegant woman. She urges me inside with another smile.

Framed certificates are hung on the wall and Principal Marks sits in her boss chair, both elbows on her desk. She looks a little unsure, but shifts her smile from Camilla to me.

In addition to the two chairs in front of her desk, there are two extra ones by the wall. They look like the chair in the waiting room, so I'm guessing they've been brought in here just for this occasion, whatever that may be.

Leaning back with his legs crossed is a middle-aged man who instantly gives off a Bill Nye the Science Guy kind of vibe. Introducing himself as Dr. Lin—"But you can call me Steve" —he stands up, shakes Camilla's hand, then mine, and then he gestures for us to take seats in front of Principal Marks. Once both of our butts are in place, the elegant woman closes the door.

"I'm Dr. Hanks," she says, settling herself in the chair beside Steve. They're both smiling now. I'm not sure what to make of this whole nonthreatening atmosphere these people are trying to project, but it does put me a little at ease. I don't think the same can be said for Camilla.

"What is this?" she barks at them.

Principal Marks scratches her temple. "Ms. Hadi, Mr. Wolnik, these nice people have come to pay you a visit, all the way from Washington, DC."

"We specialize in Inexplicable Developments," Steve eagerly explains. "We would've gotten here sooner, but we were in Botswana, interviewing a woman who could suddenly speak one thousand different languages."

Camilla crosses her arms. "We're minors," she says. "I'm pretty sure you're not allowed to talk to us without a parent or guardian present. Is this even legal?"

Principal Marks's face turns red. "Well . . ."

"You're free to leave anytime you like," Dr. Hanks says. "Your participation in this discussion is completely voluntary."

Camilla gets up. "Great."

"*But*," Dr. Hanks continues, her hand flying up in desperation, as if to grab on to Camilla and hold her in place, "we'd really, really appreciate a few minutes of your time. Please, Camilla, we're just trying to understand."

"Understand what?" Camilla lingers on her feet, debating what to do. But the plea on Dr. Hanks's face is so sincere, she grudgingly sinks back down.

Dr. Hanks gives her a tight smile of thanks, while Steve leans forward.

"As you may know," he begins, "it's believed Inexplicable Developments have been happening sporadically for as long as people have been people. Written records of them date back all the way to ancient Sumer. Throughout time, we've seen all sorts of variations, including ones related to physical appearance, of course."

"Can you please get to the point?" Camilla says. I'm watching her from the corner of my eye. I'm not the only one. All eyes are on her. It's like she commands attention, carrying herself like she has nothing to lose. My heart beats a little faster.

Steve and Dr. Hanks exchange a glance. Principal Marks is biting her nails. I don't think she's even aware she's doing it. Dr. Hanks pulls out a notepad and rests it on her knee. "We have no record of two IDs so clearly related to each other happening at the same exact time. Not to mention happening this close in proximity."

Steve jumps in, a spark firing up in his eyes. "The closest recorded—geographically speaking—is one hundred forty-seven miles." He pauses for dramatic effect. "The closest—time-wise—is two months and seven days."

"This is a first," Dr. Hanks says. "Maybe it's a coincidence, maybe it's not. Getting insight from you two as to why this occurred may give us a hint as to why Inexplicable Developments occur in the first place."

I open my mouth for the first time since we entered the room. "I thought they happened because of wishing?"

Dr. Hanks nods. "That's the widely accepted theory, yes."

"So you did wish for this change, Konrad?" Steve asks. He's trying hard to appear patient, but I can tell he can't wait to hear what I have to say.

I shrug. "I guess."

His gaze moves to take in Camilla. "And you, Camilla?"

She sighs and sets her eyes on her lap. She makes us wait like she's about to reveal something huge. "Yes," she says.

Everyone in the room tenses up.

Principal Marks shifts in her chair and pretends to cough. "Really?" she asks.

"Really," Camilla says, nodding meekly. "I can't believe you're even asking me this. Isn't it obvious? I just didn't want to be objectified anymore. By boys, you know? Like every teenage girl, I just wanted to be uglier."

I snort a little too loudly. Everyone snaps out of the spell Camilla's cast, their bullshit detectors back on high. Camilla glares at me for cutting her moment short.

Dr. Hanks looks uncomfortable. "We're not trying to upset you. We just want the facts. For science."

"Here's a fact," Camilla says. *"No one would wish for this."*

"Did you wish for anything else? Anything that might explain—"

"No."

"What do you remember wishing for? Before the Development."

"Let's see." Camilla looks up at the ceiling and starts counting things off on her fingers. "Winning the lottery. Hairlessness, so I could stop shaving my legs. A chocolate fountain. My dad not dying. Should I go on?"

Camilla doesn't even flinch when she says the last thing on her list. I feel a warm pang in my chest. I had no idea Camilla had lost her dad.

Dr. Hanks's gaze falls to her notepad. "I'm sorry," she says.

Everyone in the room shifts uncomfortably. To our relief, Steve decides to change the subject. "Are you two close?" he asks, leaning back again.

It's Camilla's turn to snort a little too loudly. "Nope."

"Were you? Before?"

"Nope," she repeats.

"How would you describe your relationship prior to the Developments?"

I answer this one before she can. "We had a class together last year. We saw each other in the halls. Know some of the same people."

"Did you communicate much?"

I glance at Camilla, then look down. "Not much."

"He asked to borrow my pencil once," Camilla says, a little too cheerfully. "You should all write that down. I have some pencils I can lend you right now, actually. Maybe you'll wake up looking like supermodels, too."

"Camilla," I say to her, scolding. These people are only trying to do their jobs and, honestly, I'm starting to feel bad for them. "Let's just hear them out. Maybe they can help."

Her glare settles on me again, twice as intense as before. I sink deeper into my seat. "Help with what?" she says. "There is no helping! These things, they're irreversible. Permanent! Unlike you, I don't get a happy ending. No matter what."

"Camilla," Dr. Hanks says. "You're angry, we understand, but—"

"I had nothing to do with this!" Her voice cracks. "You're beating a dead horse. Also, it sounds like you know as much about IDs as I do." She rises to her feet. "If Konrad shares something useful, please let me know. I'm done volunteering for the day." And just like that, she storms out of the room without even bothering to close the door behind her.

I have an urge to follow her, calm her down, convince her that people do care. I want to tell her that she doesn't have to go through this alone. But it's not my place. I'm not her friend yet. And at this pace, I never will be. Why couldn't I just keep my damn mouth shut?

The room is quiet. I realize that everyone is staring at me, waiting. Principal Marks looks about a decade older than she did three minutes ago.

"We're just average sixteen-year-olds," I say.

"We know," Dr. Hanks replies. "But what we also know, Konrad, what every single ID has proved in the past, is that there's always a trigger. It's the only common thread among all incidents. And the trigger always comes from the person the ID happens to."

"A trigger?"

"Yes. Usually it's in the form of a powerful desire. More powerful than any other—a powerful *wish*, if you will. In your case, your insecurity led to a vigorous belief that you'd achieve happiness through physical attractiveness. We don't know what it was for Camilla yet, but we know that the trigger had to be there."

I let the words sink in. "It wasn't that powerful," I mumble.

"What's that?"

"My desire to be good-looking," I say. "It wasn't *that* powerful."

"It had to be."

"There's no way it could've been something else?"

Dr. Hanks shakes her head. "Unless there was another powerful desire we haven't yet discovered that might somehow explain your ID, then no."

"I'm just a normal dude. I want the same things everyone else does."

She gives me a sad smile. "There's always a reason, Konrad."

"Well," I say, "what could it have been for Camilla, then?"

Dr. Hanks shrugs. "Honestly, we have no idea. And she might not know what it was at this point either. But, my guess is, eventually, she will."

The conversation leaves me irritated long after Principal Marks wraps things up and sends me back to class. Irritated at pushing Camilla even further away when I had a chance to do the opposite. Irritated at how unfair her life is. Irritated at the so-called experts having absolutely nothing valuable to share. The meeting even makes me irritated at Becca when she finds me at lunchtime.

"Hey," she says.

"Hey."

"Want to go to the Shack?"

"Um." I look around, like I'll find the perfect excuse taped to a wall somewhere. "I have homework to finish. I'm just going to have lunch in my car."

"What's wrong?"

"Nothing."

Her lips twist to one side. "You're still coming to Carrie's party, right?"

"Yeah," I say, even though Carrie's party is the last thing on my mind. I not only forgot about it, I don't even know if I want to go anymore.

"Is it the picture?"

The way she says this makes me tense up. "What picture?"

Becca pulls out her phone. Her nails swipe and tap at the screen while I wait. When she angles the screen my way, my stomach goes into free fall. Staring back at me is my yearbook photo. My gigantic nose. My skinny neck. A reminder of a past I don't know how to feel about anymore. A reminder of a present I know is a lie.

"Who posted this?" I ask, noticing the **#uglyforever** hashtag.

"It's from a fake account. Some guy named Josh Steinberg." She hides the phone back in her pocket. "Someone's just jealous. Don't worry. I'll make sure it doesn't spread."

My irritation morphs into full-out fury. I don't even bother asking how she plans on doing that because I know exactly who this jealous someone is.

"I'll be right back," I say. And then I'm marching though the hallways, each step pounding more anger into my system.

It's not the picture itself that bothers me. It's the loser who thinks he has the right to rile me up, mess with my life because he doesn't have one of his own.

I recognize Eric Stewart's skinny frame almost immediately. His back is to me at first, but my approach draws the attention of everyone around, so he stops and turns to see what everyone's looking at. That's when he finds my face hovering two inches from his. Surprised, he stumbles backward, grappling with a paper lunch bag in his hands.

"What's your problem?" I ask.

He pretends to adjust his glasses. "What do you mean?"

"What exactly did I do to you?"

I see him acting, pretending he doesn't know what I'm talking about. "I don't know what you're talking about," he says. And then he tries to leave.

But I don't let him.

I grab him by the arm to twist him back around. Except my new muscles are more than just decoration. They actually have strength in them that I don't quite have a grip on yet. And Eric's as skinny as they come. I push him off-balance and he stumbles back, falling on his ass.

My mouth opens in surprise as I stare at him splayed on the floor in front of me, an apple rolling out of his lunch bag.

Five seconds later, Ashley Solomon is crouching beside him. The shock in her eyes when she looks at me is a physical force, blasting me in the stomach. She springs to her feet and gets up in my face. "You're a bully now, too?"

I scan the sea of faces, watching me like a herd of frightened sheep. And it dawns on me. These people don't know what Eric did. They only know what they see. To them, I'm the lucky guy whose dreams came true, who got to become super good-looking. The guy who then started dating the most popular cheerleader, hanging out with the jocks. And now, the guy who picks on the weakest kids in school. To them, I'm a cliché.

My focus returns to Ashley, hands on her hips. The rage in her brown eyes is urging me to leave, but I don't want to be a cliché. "I didn't mean to do that," I say. "But he asked for it. He's posting old pictures of me and talking shit. I never did anything to him."

Ashley's face softens. "What pictures?" she asks, glancing over her shoulder at Eric.

"I didn't post any pictures," he says, getting to his feet and wiping his apple on the hem of his shirt.

Ashley turns back to me. "He didn't post any pictures."

"He did. I'm sure."

"I didn't post any pictures!" Eric repeats. Then he sneaks off. I have an urge to go after him, but Ashley's in my way.

"Why do you think it was him?" she asks.

"He's had a problem with me since my ID."

"Come on," she says, crossing her arms. "Eric's not like that."

"You're wrong. He's the only one who could've done it."

A faraway look overtakes Ashley's face. When she comes back down to planet Earth, she still looks angry, but I get a strange feeling that it's not with me anymore.

"No," she says. "He's not."

She leaves without another word.

CHAPTER 16

CAMILLA

No one at school is talking about Konrad's yearbook picture and the **#uglyforever** hashtag yet. I guess I have to give it more time to take off. Patience, Camilla. Patience.

On top of that, my phone's been eerily quiet all day.

Jodie hasn't texted yet to apologize. How am I supposed to torment her for what she's done when she's not even giving me a chance to ignore her? I bet she's counting on the cooldown period. We don't fight often, but when we do, time always brings us back together. She'll probably text me out of the blue soon acting like nothing ever happened.

Well, she can try. But this time, I won't be letting her slide that easily—even if she freezes that awful crowdfunding campaign. This time, she went too far.

Jodie's a straightforward person. I get that and I respect her for it. But criticizing my shoes or the shirt I'm wearing is one thing. Dismissing my physical appearance—something I have zero control over and something forced on me on top of that—is another. Even if it's true. Even if she knows it and I do, too. You don't imply that your friend might want to go under the knife to look better. You don't make your friend feel this insufficient. And the worst part? Plastic surgery is constantly in the back of my mind now, and it didn't used to be. My life was so much easier when I didn't need to think about my appearance every second.

Now Jodie may expect a cooldown period, but Ashley hasn't talked to me since last night when I spent an hour complaining to her about Jodie's little stunt either. So when I spot her by her locker, I practically scuttle up to her like a lost fawn that's finally found its mother.

"Yo," I say. "Where've you been?"

Ashley doesn't even blink. She keeps piling books inside her locker like I'm a fruit fly, not even making a sound.

"Ashley?"

Slamming her locker door, she swings her backpack onto her shoulder and whirls to face me. Her clenched jaw and the look in her eyes makes me want to crumple up into a tiny ball and disappear. "What?" I ask, quietly.

"How could you do that?" she demands. I realize that the tone in her voice is more heartbreak than fury. I already know I would've preferred fury.

My mouth goes dry. "Do what?"

"Hashtag #uglyforever?"

I wince, but try to act cool, even though inside I'm panicking. My first instinct is to lie. "What's that?"

Ashley huffs in disbelief. "And you're going to *deny* it, too? I thought you'd at least have the guts to own up to your actions."

My eyelids feel as heavy as marble. "It's just a reminder."

"Oh yeah? Is that all it is? You're not trying to hurt Konrad? Make him squirm?"

When I posted that pic, I never thought anyone would trace it back to me. I never expected Ashley to read me like a book. I can't lie to her.

Ashley shakes her head. She looks disgusted by me, like she might spit right into my face. I wouldn't blame her if she did. "After what you did to me, Camilla? How could you?"

My throat is tight. "He deserves it, Ashley. You didn't."

"Oh yeah? Why does he deserve it?"

How dare she not know the answer? But she doesn't balk. I raise both of my hands and frame my face with them. *"This!"* I say. "He did *this* to me!"

"You don't even know the guy."

"I don't have to know him."

"You know what he did today?" she says. "Because of *you*? He almost beat up Eric Stewart. He thought Eric was the one who posted that yearbook picture. Konrad's not that guy, Camilla. Do you understand? You're messing up his life."

"Pff—oh, because he didn't mess up mine?"

"We don't know that he's responsible for your ID."

"You're taking his side?"

Ashley sucks in a deep breath. "Maybe you should get to know the guy first, huh? Before you decide that he 'deserves' it."

I glare at her. She better be kidding.

"You know what, Camilla?" she continues, her eyes drilling into mine. "You're getting uglier and uglier every day. And your ID has nothing to do with it."

Frozen, I watch Ashley's back as she walks down the hall, and the whole time, I keep thinking: This is *his* fault, too. Now he's trying to turn Ashley against me.

I'll admit it, Ashley has every right to be angry. Posts can hurt people, and after what I did to her, I should know better than anyone. And I do. She's right about that, too.

But that's exactly *why* I did it.

Because Ashley's wrong about Konrad.

Was there another way to put a dent in his undeserved golden reputation? Maybe. Do I regret doing what I did? No. Ashley didn't deserve it when I posted about her. Konrad does.

But fine. Whatever. I *will* get to know Konrad Wolnik better, just like Ashley said I should. Then, once and for all, I'll *prove* to her and to Jodie and to the rest of the school just how shallow and selfish he really is.

I pull out my phone and pull up Konrad's profile. I open up the direct message screen, type the words "**Free tomorrow?**" and hit SEND before I can change my mind.

For a couple seconds, I hold my breath. Heat blasts through my body.

Did I just invite Konrad Wolnik to hang out?

"CAMILLA!"

Startled, I look up. Tom Dempsey walks by with his buddies, one hand covering his face, the other pointing a finger in my direction.

I scowl at him, then head to my last class of the day.

With Ashley mad at me and Jodie keeping her distance, I'm officially out of friends. I guess I must be pretty lonely because, at practice, I strike up a conversation with Eve.

"So how was your sister's wedding?" I ask while we stretch, remembering her babbling about it in the past.

She straightens and her mouth opens, ever so slightly. "It was nice."

"When was it again?"

"Three months ago . . ."

"Oh," I say, diving to touch my toes so she can't see how red my face has gotten. "Did you have fun?"

"Yeah. It was really fun. Jerry—that's my sister's husband—is so great. He took her on two honeymoons already. One to Spain and one to Portugal because he said she's so special, she deserves more than one. Isn't that sweet? Two honeymoons in two countries?"

"It is," I say. I don't even bother asking if it was two separate trips because I'm pretty sure I know the answer. Thank God Eve has her athleticism going for her. "What are you doing tonight?" I ask, desperate to move on to a different topic.

"Oh." Eve says, "I'm going to see a movie with Amanda." Hearing her name, Amanda smiles at me from her spot by the wall. I give her a little wave.

"What movie?" I ask.

"*Dance With My Heart.* It's with that blond guy with the big mole? Cute Corey? It's supposed to be really romantic." She stares at me, eyes brimming with unconditional hope. "Do you want to come?"

This isn't going to work. I hate romantic comedies. I hate gushing over guys in public. Unattainable, famous ones even more than the real thing. (Okay, maybe there's one celeb exception: the gorgeous Aidan Duvall from the Leaky Lizards.) Not that there's much of a distinction, anyway. In my case, even before my ID, all guys have been unattainable. I don't need mushy movies to remind me that all the ones I've ever liked have never liked me back.

The point is, Ashley and Jodie know all this stuff about me. They know *me*. As much as I hate to admit it, I can't replace them. And I feel awful for even trying.

"Sorry," I tell her. "I already have plans tonight."

After practice, it dawns on me that I don't have a ride home. Mom dropped me off in the morning and Ashley was supposed to give me a lift home on her way to her shift at the Shack after school. I'm pretty sure that's not going to happen now.

Anna offers to drive me, but I'm extra tired from being extra nice to the girls, and I don't want them to find out I really don't have plans when I told them I did.

So, I decide to walk.

I'm maybe five minutes into my trek when a news van pulls over up ahead on my side of the street. A moment later, it spews out the familiar face of the obnoxious reporter, the same lady who nearly fell out of her car the other day trying to talk to me. Her cameraman is on her high heels within seconds.

I freeze. She looks so hungry to get to me, she might as well be carrying a big black bag to kidnap me with instead of a microphone.

"Ms. Hadi," she says. "We'll blur out your face—how do you feel about your social media campaign?"

I take a step back, managing to choke out a "No comment."

"Why were there Inexplicable Development researchers at your school today? Did you speak with them?"

I inspect the sidewalk beside her. She reads my intentions and spreads her legs wider. From the corner of my eye, I detect a gray car slowing down, almost to a stop. Wonderful. This is officially becoming a spectacle.

"What have they told you?" the reporter woman presses, the tip of her microphone almost smacking me in the face. "What have you learned?"

"Can you please let me pass?"

But she just keeps spewing out questions: "Did you wish for this, and if so, why? Where do you see yourself in ten years? Where do you get the strength to keep on living like nothing happened?"

This last one feels like a slap to my face. I stand there, stiff as a board, my hands making tight fists at my sides. I think I might punch her.

"Camilla," I hear from my right. In the gray car, a grinning Lauren Batko leans over Alan Nguyen seated behind the wheel. She tilts her head toward the back seat.

I'm perfectly capable of handling the reporter on my own; I don't need to be saved like some damsel in distress. Plus, I barely know these two. Yet I find myself trotting over to the back door and gripping the handle. When I slip inside, the stench of weed hits my nostrils. I think I might gag.

The car jerks and we're speeding away. Lauren's arm is stretched out the window, middle finger aimed at the news people growing smaller and smaller behind us.

Drawing her arm back inside, Lauren turns to look at me, a big grin plastered on her face.

"What did those assholes want?" she asks, her bad-girl gaze burning into me. It makes me feel really self-conscious.

I exhale, realizing I've been holding my breath, and drop my gaze to the greasy Burger King wrapper between my feet. "It doesn't matter. Thanks."

"No worries."

"Why were you guys still around school?" I ask.

Lauren glances over at Alan and starts giggling. The expression looks out of place on her usual I-don't-give-a-single-fuck-about-any-of-you face. "We were hanging out," she says, "and then lost track of time, I guess."

"I bet," I say, exaggerating a sniff.

Grinning, Lauren pulls a crisp, white joint out of the front pocket of her flannel. I watch her light it. She takes a hit and offers it to me.

I push myself as far back as my seat allows. "I don't really smoke."

"It'll help."

I'm about to say, "I'm A-okay, I don't need any help," but I pluck the joint from her hand and stare at the smoke snaking away from its tip. Of course by "I don't really smoke," I meant "I've never smoked in my life." The idea of tarnishing my lungs with anything other than air has always bothered me. But then again, don't knock it until you try it, right?

I bring the joint to my lips and suck like my life depends on it. Which, of course, results in a coughing attack. I cough so hard, my throat begins to hurt. But I'm determined not to quit until I get it right. I try again. And again. All while Alan and Lauren snicker from the front seat.

Once I catch my breath, their laughing becomes infectious. I'm giggling along, unable to see anything through my watering eyes.

Lauren was right. It does help.

Apparently, while I was practicing my stoner skills, Alan pulled the car into the old supermarket's parking lot. The abandoned brown building looms on my right. Lauren's talking about this girl she met online who turned out to be a forty-three-year-old army veteran. "She's kind of a MILF, though," she says.

"I think the word you're looking for is *cougar*?" Alan offers.

"No," I say. "The word she's looking for is child molester."

We're laughing. Together. And I realize these two haven't brought up my ID even once yet. They're not judging me. They're not pretending to be nice, like the rest of the world. They're just being themselves. And that makes me feel comfortable.

"How come you guys don't hang out with Konrad Wolnik anymore?" I ask before my brain can properly process whether I should or not.

The car goes silent. Lauren sighs. "Oh, Konrad."

"What?" I ask, a stray cough catching up with me.

"Pretty Boy thinks he's too good for us now."

Alan looks over his shoulder at me and smiles sadly. "His ID gave him more than big muscles. He's got a bigger head now, too."

"Tell me about it," I say.

Alan shrugs and turns back to face the front. "He just needs some time."

"You guys know him pretty well, right?"

"Yup," Lauren says, trying to create circles out of smoke.

"What's he like?"

Alan's eyes meet mine in the rearview. "Why?"

"Oh, come on," Lauren says, poking him with her elbow. "If anyone deserves to know the real Konrad, it's this chick."

"I'm just curious," I say. "He seems so perfect. Especially now."

"He's not," Lauren says.

I'm intrigued. And suddenly, surprisingly lucid. "How so?"

"Well, for example, the boy might act all smooth, but he can be such an emotional mess. Like when he didn't make the soccer team in junior high. Oh God . . . Or when he almost ran over that cat on the way to the city? Remember that, Alan?"

Alan snorts. "Yeah."

"And you should've seen him when Sara broke up with him. *Ugh.*"

My heart beats faster. "What happened?"

"He begged her to keep him," Lauren explains. "Like, crying. *On his knees.* Which was so weird because she treated him like shit from the beginning." Lauren stops and sighs. "She was obviously just using him. We tried warning him, but hey, whatever. I guess you can't control who you love. Even if that person is a total bitch."

Alan nods in agreement. "I think that's why he told us to fuck off after his ID. It's like he developed a phobia of rejection or something. Because of Sara. I was just being real with him and he took it the wrong way. He probably thought I was friend-dumping him, so he panicked and dumped us first." Alan pauses. "At least that's my theory."

My brain gathers this new information. Every last piece. I feel like I'm listening to something forbidden. Something not meant for my ears. I'm not sure what I'll do with this intel just yet, but I'm more than sure that I've stumbled upon a gold mine.

CHAPTER 17

KONRAD

BECCA INTERRUPTS OUR FACE-SUCKING SESSION by cupping my face in one of her hands. Her grip is pretty tight.

At first, I assume this must be some aggressive sex thing—which I wouldn't be surprised Becca was into, and which I'm surprisingly down for. But I'm very wrong because, tilting her head back and staring me in the eyes, she asks, "Are you sexually attracted to Handy Ashley?"

I yank my face away. "What?"

Becca leans back on her bed. She's still in her cheerleading outfit, and the sight of it makes the thought of the oncoming blue balls even more excruciating.

"Carrie saw you talking to her," she says.

I rest my elbows on my knees and sigh. "When?"

"After you beat up that skinny kid."

I narrow my eyes at her. I'm still unhappy about how my encounter with Eric played out, and I don't appreciate Becca bringing it up so casually. "I didn't beat anybody up."

"Whatever," she says bitterly. "Answer the question."

"All right, fine." I take a deep breath. "Ashley Solomon? She's okay, I guess."

This is apparently the wrong answer.

Becca sits up and folds both of her feet under her in a this-is-about-to-get-more serious manner. I catch a glimpse of her underwear and clench my teeth.

"Look," she says, donning the perfect poker face. "I know you're new to this whole popularity thing. You're getting a lot of attention now, and you probably have all these urges to experiment with different girls, especially since they're, like, *drooling* all over you and stuff." She clears her throat. "I get that. It's human nature."

Heat climbs to my cheeks. To cover it, I aim my gaze at her lower half and bite my lower lip suggestively in a last-ditch attempt to both cut this talk short and prevent the blue ball disease. "I'm perfectly happy experimenting with just you."

Becca glares at me and pulls at the hem of her skirt. "I think it's time I gave you a lesson about high school society."

My upper lip stretches back into a grimace. "Are you serious?"

"Yes," she says, sticking her neck out like I'm saying something illogical. "You're new to this. I've been living this life for a long time."

"I'm sorry, I didn't know there was a science behind being popular."

"Of course there is."

I stare at her. Okay. She's serious.

I shift to relieve the strain in my pants. Even though all hope's officially lost, my little big guy is still fighting for it. Maybe he'll get another chance later tonight at Carrie's party? And to think that up until Becca's out-of-left-field question, I was in such a good mood, too. Earlier today, Camilla had sent me a message asking me to hang out tomorrow. *She* invited *me*, not the other way around. It's the best thing I could've asked for on our way to becoming friends, and I was hoping for a little celebration with Becca, not an argument.

"I'm doing just fine," I say, "but thanks."

Becca ignores me. "Social status is as integral to human society as anything else," she says. "Being really good-looking gives you a huge advantage, yeah, but it's not everything. You have to nurture it and you have to respect it."

I just keep staring at her.

"Everyone's eyes are on us," she continues. "Your status affects mine. I can't have you associating with the cheapest whores at school."

My mouth pops open. So much for a lesson. If I've ever seen jealousy, this is it.

I don't want to tell Becca I only talk to Ashley Solomon because of Camilla. She doesn't need to know that. But she does need to know she sounds like a bitch right now. "How can you say awful shit like that about people?"

"What awful shit? She's practically a porn star, Konrad. There are *videos*. *Videos*, okay? And that's fine—I'm all for girls owning their sexuality. But not everyone is as open-minded as I am. That kind of stuff still affects reputations." She crosses her arms and takes a deep breath of disappointment. "All I'm saying is that I'm your girlfriend. You better start appreciating me."

I'm about to say, "I don't remember making any promises," but doing so would definitely annihilate my chances of getting under her skirt later so I keep quiet. Having sex with Becca is by far my favorite thing since my Development. I'm not ready to part with that just yet.

"You're really cute, and we look perfect together, but you need to start putting some effort into this relationship."

"Okay," I mumble.

"Why don't you hang out with Mike and Tom and the guys more?"

I look up at the ceiling. "Um, because I don't like them?"

"Why? They've been nothing but nice to you. Try out for the football team. You'll get to know them better."

"I hate football."

Becca's quiet. When I glance her way, she catches my eye. "Why haven't you asked me to homecoming yet?"

"What? I don't know. That's like a month away, isn't it?"

"See? That's your problem right there. You're holding on to your past when you should only be thinking about the future. You need to get your shit together, Konrad."

The words sink in, hitting a sensitive spot I didn't even know was in me. I start picking at my palm with my fingernails.

Becca sighs. "I don't want to fight. I don't want to be *that* couple. Just promise me you'll actually try to have fun tonight."

I think for a moment. As ridiculous as she can sometimes sound, maybe Becca's right. My past has turned its back on me; why shouldn't I turn my back on it as well? Maybe I just need to worry about what happened and what people think of me a little less, and focus on what *will* happen a little more. Maybe then I'll actually be happy. Things are already looking up, aren't they? Tomorrow I get to hang with Camilla Hadi. If *she's* giving me a chance, I can do the same for others.

And so I do: I promise Becca and I promise myself that tonight, at Carrie's birthday party, I'll give this popularity thing my all.

Carrie's family is loaded. You can tell by the grand living room with the high ceilings and the even grander backyard that's set up like a wedding reception. I'm pretty sure Carrie had it catered because there's not one, but two tables stacked with snacks, and the snacks, in this case, are more platters of sushi and tiramisu than pretzels and chips.

Every member of our school's royalty is here. People I don't recognize, too, so I assume they're queens and kings from neighboring kingdoms. This is the kind of party you hear rumors about, secretly aspire to attend, and never get invited to if you're an average kid with a big nose.

Honestly, though, I can't say I've been missing out. The guys all wear different shades of the same T-shirt and hat. The girls are carbon copies of that ex-Disney chick who screams instead of singing. Everybody's recycling the same exact dance moves.

I think Becca might be right. There is a science to being popular. And this science is just as boring as the one Mr. Sanchez drones about in class.

With Becca's fingers in my left hand and a bottle of beer in my right, I travel from couch to chair to kitchen counter. I let her lead me, even though I kind of feel like a six-foot diamond ring she's showing off. I smile politely at all the people she introduces me to, secretly wishing Alan and Lauren were here so we could smoke weed and talk shit about them.

Carrie shuffles up to us. It's still early, but her gaze is already lagging.

"Hi, Konrad," she says, her words slurring together.

"Hi, Carrie," I say. Becca's elbow jabs me in the side. "Oh! Happy birthday!"

"Thanks. Glad you could make it. All my friends have been asking about you!" She pauses. "Camilla Hadi, too, actually. I'm thinking maybe I should've invited her."

I give her a skeptical glare. "I don't think she would've come, anyway," I mumble. Birthday girl or not, if Carrie's going to start making fun of Camilla, I'm going to call her out.

But then Carrie's face goes serious. "Have I ever told you guys about the ID that happened to my cousin's mother-in-law's boss's son?"

"Um," I say. "I don't believe you have."

"So, her son, right?" She goes on. "He really loved scuba diving. He'd spend all his money on traveling to all these exotic locations and stuff. Anyway, he really wished he could breathe underwater because he really loved being with the fishes and stuff."

"Uh-huh."

"And guess what?"

"He woke up one day and he could breathe underwater," Becca answers, bored.

"Exactly! But there was a catch," Carrie says. My skin crawls and I lean in a little closer so I can hear her over the music. "After his ID, he could *only* breathe underwater."

A chill runs through my bones. "What do you mean?"

"He couldn't breathe regular air anymore. He almost died that morning! So then they had to build him this big aquarium in his yard and he lives inside it now."

"That's . . . insane," I say.

"Right? I mean, he's going to move to the ocean soon, and he's really happy, so it's fine. But, man, some of these wishes come true in unexpected ways."

"Yeah..."

"So yeah," Carrie finishes. "Maybe what happened to Camilla Hadi is a good thing and she doesn't even know it yet. At least I hope so."

"Yeah, maybe," Becca says, yanking at my arm. "We're going to get some drinks, Carrie. See you in a bit, okay? Bye!"

When we get to the huge coolers sitting between the tables in the yard, Becca says, "You're taking Camilla Hadi's ID way too personally. Your body language changes every time somebody brings her up. You need to let it go, Konrad. I told you, it's not your fault."

Am I that obvious? "Yeah, I know. Thanks."

She digs among the bottles, ice crunching, glass clinking. "What do you want?"

At that moment, my phone buzzes in my pocket. "Um..." I say, fishing it out. On my screen there's a notification from a concert app I have installed. The message flashes the words "The Leaky Lizards" so I tap it out of instinct. Tomorrow night, the Leaky Lizards are doing a surprise set at a small venue downtown.

My heart rate accelerates. Before I can think about it, I tap a couple more times and reserve two tickets. When I look up, Becca's holding out a bottle and eyeing me suspiciously. "Who was that?"

"Nobody," I say, returning my phone back to my jeans. I'm not sure why I feel a little guilty, but I'm sure my mood's about a hundred times better than it was a minute ago. I smile at Becca and take the beer. It's a European one I can't even pronounce.

"Carrie is totally wasted already," Becca comments. "I give her twenty more minutes before she passes out."

I'm about to agree when I hear my name shouted from the deck. I look in that direction and my eyes lock onto Mike's.

"YO!" he yells. "Stop drinking those pussy drinks and get over here!"

Shooting me a tight smile, Becca takes back the beer she just handed me. I know what this means, and I'm already regretting it, but I promised both her and myself I'd make an effort tonight, so I grudgingly make my way up the steps.

As soon as I'm within reach, Mike's arm flies around my neck and he pulls me into an uncomfortable bro hug. His breath reeks of alcohol. "This way, playa!" he says.

I shuffle along, having to huddle because Mike's a few inches shorter. While he guides me inside, I rack my brain for potential topics of conversation. Maybe I can ask him about weed? Jocks smoke weed, too, right? And right about now, I could definitely use a hit or two.

In the living room, a bunch of guys stand in a half circle. Sara's off to the side by herself, sipping on something from a red Solo cup. She glowers at me before looking away. Mike's buddies start hooting. He moves me closer so I can see what's happening.

Tom's on his knees in the center. From the fist around his mouth protrudes a long tube that ends in a funnel that sits in Ryan Campbell's hand. In Ryan's other hand, I notice another object: a bottle of whiskey.

"That's pretty dangerous," I say.

"DO IT!" Mike yells. He lets me go and smacks Ryan's back, prompting him to pour a good amount of the honey-colored liquid down the funnel. A couple of seconds later, it explodes out Tom's mouth and he collapses onto his back, howling.

Mike turns to me. "You want to go next?"

"I'll pass."

Mike's fingers snap and this short, freckled dude I've never seen before hands me a full shot glass. I down it. Then I down another one. And another. And with each new one, mingling with these guys becomes easier and easier.

Before I know it, Becca's hand is in mine again and I'm back outside in the yard with Mike and Tom and Carrie and everybody else and we're playing a weird mash-up of "would you rather?" and "truth or dare." I'm so tipsy I don't even mind Sara being there.

This is the new Konrad Wolnik, I think. This Konrad is a handsome devil. This Konrad parties with the cool kids, the hottest girl within a one-hundred-mile radius at his side. This Konrad should be having the time of his life.

But can he really say that he is? Honestly? If he were, would his mind constantly keep wandering to tomorrow? To the Leaky Lizards concert?

To Camilla Hadi?

"Would you rather," Mike asks Becca, "eat a used tampon you found in a trash can"—he waits for the slew of *eww*s and *ahh*s to quiet down—"or turn your mouth into a urinal for three different truck drivers at a highway rest area?"

Becca squints. "That's a good one," she says. She thinks about it for a couple of seconds. "Truck drivers."

"No way!" Carrie yells, her face twisted in disgust. Sara mimics her like the follower that she is.

"Piss is sterile," Becca explains. Both she and Mike take shots. I'm not exactly sure how this game works.

"Oh," Tom interjects. "I've got one!" He glances my way and winks before turning to Ryan Campbell. I already have a bad feeling. "Would you rather," he asks the kid, "blow Konrad and swallow, *or* go down on Camilla the Gorilla for two hours?"

I suck in a breath and hold it. Carrie laughs.

"Come on, man," Mike says. "That's a little harsh, no?"

"Easy," Ryan answers. "Blow Konrad, hands down."

"ME, TOO!" Tom yells.

"Y'all serious?" Becca asks.

"Hell yeah we're serious," Tom says. "Think about it. If Camilla looks like that where we can see, just imagine what's going on down there."

People start howling, but their voices are drowned out, becoming more distant, as if I dipped my head underwater and I'm listening from below.

They're all looking at me. Mike pats my back, says something about how Tom's only joking, but I don't really hear him. I'm still holding my breath. I feel the veins at my temples bulging. Clenching the muscles in my arm, I ball my right hand into a fist.

And I sock Tom right in the gap between his front teeth.

CHAPTER 18

CAMILLA

Since Mom has the day off, I ask to borrow the car.

Seeing me express interest in something other than running in the neighborhood or bumming around my room, she almost explodes from joy. "Where you off to?" she chirps from the sink when I pluck her keys out of the kitchen drawer.

I'm still pissed at her for taking Jodie's side the other day, so I work to keep my voice neutral. "Just going to hang out with Ashley," I tell her, as if that's even possible right now. "I won't be long."

"Okay, honey. Have fun."

My back toward her, I scrunch up my face. Fun? Please. I'm going to see Konrad Wolnik. What she's saying is just not feasible.

Crushing the keys in my palm, I march to the garage. There's a reason I want the car. I want to be the one calling the shots, and being behind the wheel will help me feel like I am. Even if I did only invite him to get Starbucks and talk. About what exactly, I have no idea. But as long as I get my proof that Konrad is an evil human being, it doesn't even matter.

I can't believe I'm going to do this, actually hang out with him. It's even more baffling that I'm the one who suggested it. The news people would have a field day. I can already see the headline: "Freak and Gorgeous Grab Coffee."

But this needs to happen. I need Ashley to forgive me and I need to out Konrad for who he really is. This is the perfect chance to kill two birds with one stone.

And so, with Jodie's sunglasses shielding my face, I drive to the address he sent me. I've been less and less reliant on the giant shades since I went back to school, but today I'll be in public with a hot guy. I refuse to be a part of a walking attractiveness spectrum.

I kill the engine in front of a plain bungalow with a big tree blocking most of its windows. I take out my phone and text: **IN FRONT.**

While I wait, I pull down the sun visor and, in the tiny mirror, check my hair and face for any inconsistencies. Three seconds later, I slap it shut. I'm here to infiltrate enemy lines, not to impress a boy. I cackle out loud at my own stupidity.

A knock on the passenger window makes me jump. Konrad's stooped over, peering inside. I unlock the door, hating him for sneaking up on me.

"Hi, Camilla," he says, swinging it open.

"Hi, *Konrad*," I grunt back.

"Can I get in?"

"No, you can't. I'll drive and you walk."

Konrad forces a laugh and thrusts his left foot inside. While he settles into the seat, I adjust my sunglasses. My heart is racing. This setup, his proximity, everything about this feels so unnatural. It's like two sworn enemies—a rabbit and a fox—forced into a confined space together. It's blasphemy.

He's rubbing his large hands together, as if nervous. Everything about him is large. His arms. His muscular thighs. The way they're spread apart like he's entitled to all the space in the world.

I feel the burn of resentment building. Some of it is toward my own body, for betraying me, for reacting to his physique and his boy smell. But most of it is toward Konrad himself because this only reminds me that he's the reason I'm never going to be intimate with anyone of the opposite sex for as long as I live.

Also, why is he acting like he's nervous, like he's the uncomfortable one? Am I a nuisance? He's the one who wanted to "be friends" in the first place. Turning to the window on my side, I mumble, "I don't want to be here either."

"Sorry, what?"

I take a deep breath. I don't know how long I'm going to last, but I have to at least try to be nice. "I asked if the Starbucks on North Avenue is okay."

"Actually," he says. "do you mind if we go downtown?"

I whirl his way. My sunglasses cast him in shadow, but even through them I notice the bruise under his eye. "Actually, I do mind." An hour at Starbucks I can handle. There'll be other people—plenty of distractions. Going downtown would mean almost an hour alone in the car with him. That's way more weirdness than I signed up for. And why would he want to spend that much time with me on a Saturday night anyway? Something's fishy.

"Trust me," he says, smiling—actually smiling. "You won't regret it."

I stare at him in disbelief. He's out of his damn mind. Does he think I'm going to clap my hands at an opportunity to hang out with him like all the other girls at school?

It's time to get this shit over with. I was going to wait until after I had my coffee, but I don't think I can survive that long anymore. After he hears what he wants to hear—and I know *exactly* what he wants to hear—he'll be out of here in the blink of an eye. I'll record it so I have proof of his selfish assholery, and then I'll have the rest of my Saturday to myself.

As discreetly as I can, I tap the record function on my phone—all set up ahead of time—and place it screen down on my lap.

"Look," I say, turning my whole body to face him. I try to smile so it looks genuine and everything. "I don't blame you anymore, okay?"

The car is quiet. I let the words sink in and wait for him to leave. To disappear and never talk to me again. Because that's the kind of person Konrad Wolnik really is. Because that's all he really wants.

But he stays put.

"Thanks," he says, staring at me with those breathtaking post-Development eyes of his. "That means a lot."

My mouth peels back into a grimace. "Did you hear me? You don't have to feel bad anymore."

"I heard you."

I shrug impatiently and gesture at the passenger side door. "Okay then. You're off the hook. Leave. Go hang out with Becca or something."

"Nah, let's go downtown."

I start the car. "Just go, Konrad!"

"The Leaky Lizards are playing in about an hour."

I tense, letting the car idle. "No, they're not."

"Yeah, they are."

"If they were, I'd know about it."

"It's a surprise performance."

For a couple of seconds, I don't say a word. His voice carries a hint of mischief. I actually think he's telling the truth. "You're serious?"

"Dead serious."

Great. So now privileged little Konrad has access to information about my favorite band that even I don't. "And you want to go now? With me?"

"Yes."

"Why?"

He shrugs. "You like them, too, don't you?"

Understanding falls over me like a warm blanket. Oh, okay. I see what this is. Getting my pardon isn't enough. Konrad needs to come out of this looking like a sexy Samaritan. "Guess what," he's going to say to his crew of popular friends later. "I took Camilla Hadi out to see her favorite band. Thanks to me, she was able to forget her miserable life—if only for a little while. See? I'm not a self-obsessed, life-ruining prick after all!"

But the Leaky Lizards? Dammit. I've been listening to them since they were doing covers on YouTube.

I could say no, but Konrad already gets to say he's doing a good deed just for being here and inviting me. I might as well get something out of it. And I have yet to obtain any concrete evidence proving his evil nature. Besides, Aidan Duvall, the Lizards' lead singer, would never forgive me if he knew I said no to an opportunity like this.

"Fine," I say, pressing myself against the steering wheel to peel out of my spot. "But you're paying for the tickets."

"Already done."

For the next couple of minutes, we drive in silence. Konrad's left knee keeps bobbing up and down. When he looks out the window on his side, I take the moment to stop my phone from recording since it's pointless for now, then turn up the radio.

"So what made you change your mind?" he asks after a while as I'm pulling onto the main street that will take us into the city.

"About what?"

"About talking to me."

This, I expected, so I came prepared with a nice sarcastic answer. "Because you're so good-looking even *I* can't resist you."

He laughs. "Yeah, right."

More minutes pass with neither of us saying a word. The pressure to fill the silence swells within me. "What happened to your face?" I ask.

His hand flies to his bruise. He turns toward his window again. "Nothing. Just had a little too much to drink at Carrie's party last night."

"You were at that party?" I blurt out, but realize it's a stupid question as soon as I say it. Of course he was there.

"Yeah," he says. "It sucked."

Behind my huge sunglasses, I roll my eyes. Please. People had been talking about Carrie's birthday party since school started. It's the stuff of legends. He would've killed to be there before his ID—all of us lesser folk would've, even if we'd never admit it. Now he's pretending to be too good for it? What an ass.

"So," he says after another wordless stretch. "What do you do for fun?"

I know he doesn't care. I know this is all an act. But it'll be another twenty minutes before we get to the club. I have to be civil. "I run."

"Cool. What else?"

I grind my teeth. "I don't know. Hang out with Jodie and Ashley?" I feel a pang as soon as their names leave my lips.

"And do what?" The boy just won't quit.

"A lot of things!"

Konrad falls silent. Just when I think he finally got the hint, he opens his mouth again. "You don't draw anymore, then?"

I grip the steering wheel tighter. "What are you talking about?"

"You used to draw in your notebook. In physics."

"No, I didn't."

"Yeah, you did. You used to draw faces."

My cheeks turn into wildfire. I did. But not faces, plural. Just one—Lance's. Not even Jodie or Ashley know about those drawings. Why does Konrad? "I was just doodling," I say, secretly praying my artistic skills were bad enough to make Lance unrecognizable.

"Alan and I tried to make a comic book once," Konrad says. "Only neither one of us can draw for shit. It was about this dude who could shape-shift, but only into a giraffe."

I snort—because I'm relieved we're moving on from the topic of my unhealthy obsession with Lance, not because what Konrad said is kind of funny. Konrad doesn't get to be both gorgeous and funny.

I can feel his eyes on me. "It's getting dark," he says. "You sure you want to keep driving with those on?"

"Why?" I ask. "Scared I'll crash and ruin your precious face?"

"No," he says flatly. "Never mind." He turns back to the window, and finally shuts up.

As expected, finding parking downtown ends up being hell. We circle by the Well, the club where the Lizards are playing, four times before I spot a car pulling out. I turn my blinker on and stop, suddenly too aware of the city and all of its happenings around me. Parallel parking freaks me out. Especially on big streets and especially at night.

"Want me to do it?" Konrad asks.

"I got it."

But a minute later, when I'm backing into the spot, I'm too slow. My bumper connects with the car behind me. I hit the brake and the car jerks. As my knuckles turn white on the steering wheel, Konrad laughs. "Don't worry," he says. "You barely grazed it."

I whip my head this way and that, looking for accusatory eyes. But I don't see any. People stroll by on the sidewalk, unconcerned. I take a deep breath and straighten the car out. Satisfied, I kill the engine.

Konrad's snickering.

"What?" I demand.

"Nothing."

I yank out the keys and open the door. When I walk around the hood, I see the sidewalk sitting about a mile away from my tires.

Whatever.

A line of mostly college kids snakes away from the club's entrance. Konrad takes a spot at the end and I stand behind him. Every girl who passes us—and every other guy—glances his way. The girls smile, the guys nod. I, on the other hand, draw as much attention as the red bricks that make up the wall we're standing against.

A part of me is grateful. With Konrad around, I'm practically invisible. But every glance he gets also chips away a shard from the statue of hate I'm making for him in my mind. Because somebody enlighten me: How is this fair?

When he cranes his head to see down the line, I yank out my phone and snap a picture of the back of his head.

He turns around. "Did you just take a picture of me?"

"Pff, no," I say, flustered. "I was taking a picture of the line." I want to add that the world doesn't revolve around him, but it clearly does. Finding Ashley in my contacts, I send her the photo without an explanation. She'll know this is my peace offering.

I wait for Konrad to seize the opportunity, to whip out his own phone, start a photo shoot, and immediately post the pictures online for everyone to see. To show the world what a great guy he is for hanging out with Camilla Hadi.

But that doesn't happen. It's bound to, though, and at some point tonight, it will. And then I'll finally have proof of his true intentions.

After a couple of minutes of shuffling forward, the bouncer wiggles his finger at us. He checks our IDs and plants red UNDER 21 stamps on the outside of our left hands. We walk past him. Konrad leads the way and starts descending inside, but I stop at the top of the dark stairs. I think I know why the club's called the Well now.

"What's wrong?" he asks from three steps below me.

I hesitate, pushing my sunglasses farther up my nose. "Nothing."

"Here."

I look up from my feet. Konrad's hand is extended in my direction. If he thinks I'd rather take it than tumble down these stairs to my death, he's insane. "I can see just fine," I lie, dismissing his self-serving excuse at being chivalrous. Clinging to the wall, I slowly make my way down to the entryway at the bottom.

Preshow DJ music blasts through the dingy space. Bodies mill around me. Someone steps on my foot. After a struggle to get as close to the stage as possible—because the Leaky Lizards!—I give in and remove my sunglasses. The venue is dark anyway. I look around, expecting Konrad to be nearby, but he's nowhere in sight.

Standing on my tiptoes, I scan the area. I spot him by the bar, back by the entrance, talking to a pretty girl with a raven-colored bob.

Aha! Finally, Konrad's showing his true colors.

Content, but also irritated for some reason, I face the stage and writhe free of my flannel. If I know anything, it's that it's only going to get hotter in here as the night goes on.

"There you are."

I spin around. Konrad's standing with two plastic cups in his hands. He pushes one toward me. "What is that?" I scream over the music.

Konrad wiggles his eyebrows and leans in a bit. "Beer."

My gaze travels to the stamp on his hand. I can barely see it in this awful light but it's definitely there. "How'd you get beer?"

Shrugging, he looks at the floor. "Some girl bought it for us."

I stare at him, my lips twisted to the side. For us? Yeah, okay. I glance over to the bar. The bob girl sees me and smiles. I don't smile back. I shake my head and give Konrad the cold shoulder. "I'm driving, remember?"

"I thought you might say that," he says, smugly. "That's why yours is a Coke."

I snatch the cup and gulp half of it down, just because I want him to shut up.

"Whoa," he says, laughing. "Easy."

Stop talking to me, I think, just as the music cuts off. The silence is then replaced with shrieks and screams from the crowd. My heart skips a beat. The Leaky Lizards are about to go on.

Konrad squawks a *woo-hoo!* into my ear and stands right beside me. There's so much adrenaline pulsing through me, I don't even mind. As throngs of people move in closer to the stage and the space fills with more bodies, Konrad's elbow presses against my arm. I jerk away, annoyed at the tingle it causes, but forget about it as soon as the opening beat of "Disrupt You!" reverberates in my ears. The Leaky Lizards!

The spotlight hits and the four band members come into full view. "AIDAN!" I yell at the stage. "I LOVE YOU!" I can't help myself.

"Disrupt You!" has a very danceable beat. It's no surprise they chose it as the opening number. Before I know it, I completely lose myself in the music.

For the duration of the song, I forget about everything else. There's just me, the Leaky Lizards, and the fan-wide kinship in the air. My ID slips from my mind. I'm part of one entity, where the way you look doesn't matter. The only thing that does is how you feel.

When the Leaky Lizards transition to "We're Never Gonna Disappear," Konrad prods me with his elbow. I look up at his smiling face. Everything is so surreal and perfect, I smile back.

It's so weird. In the past, I've imagined losing my inhibitions at a Lizards concert, but it was always with a boy I liked. Not someone I despised. But, on a positive note, if I can still feel this good, this free, then maybe my life isn't over after all. Maybe there's still hope. And, heck, maybe even Konrad's not as evil as I thought he was.

Who knows? Right now, I don't even care. Right now, I feel like anything is possible.

By the middle of the fourth song, my bladder reminds me of the Coke I chugged earlier. Using my fingers to point because it's too loud to talk, I let Konrad know I'm going to the ladies' room. He gives me a smile and a thumbs-up and continues dancing.

Since the band is in the middle of a performance, the line isn't too bad. After I force the quickest pee of my life—I want to miss as little of the show as possible—I let the next person in. I hold the door so she can slip inside, but when I turn back, I realize Konrad's girl with the raven bob has taken her place. This time, she's not smiling.

I'd rather just leave without acknowledging her, but one, I'm too nice, and two, she's kind of right there in my face. "Um, hi," I say to her. "Thanks for the drink earlier."

"You're welcome," she replies flatly, giving me the once-over. "So what's a girl like you doing with a guy like that? You can't possibly be related."

My polite smile falls. She may be older, but that doesn't give her the right to talk to me like that. "We're just friends," I say, and add, because I can be spiteful, too, "With benefits."

The bitch guffaws in my face and I immediately realize what a stupid, unrealistic joke I made. "That's funny," she barks. After she calms down, her expression turns to stone. "But, seriously, are you paying him or something? Blackmailing him?"

The temperature in my face skyrockets but, at the same time, something inside me cracks. For the life of me, I can't summon up a good comeback. "No . . ."

Bob Girl crosses her arms. "Huh. I guess he must be a saint then."

I stare at her. She's not even worth it. And it's not like her reaction is totally out of left field, either; I'd be wondering the same thing if I were in her shoes. Probably not out loud, because I have a soul, but I would be, nonetheless.

Konrad, on the other hand, is *why* she's saying it. Why Ashley's mad at me. Why my whole life exists squashed under a giant pile of shit now. I can't believe that, for a moment there, by the stage, I actually thought he might be an okay person.

The sting of tears ambushes me by surprise. I turn away. I don't want this skank to think she's made me upset.

"Anyway," she says. "Can you tell him I'm looking forward to hanging out?"

Her words root me to the floor. I whirl back around. "I'm sure he is, too. And it might happen sooner than you think."

Not even caring if I'm pissing people off, I push my way through the swaying bodies. I get to the dark stairs and race up and up and up until the club spits me out onto the street and into lights of the city. Fumbling with my keys, I march toward the car.

I know I'm crossing a line, going against everything Mom's ever taught me about good manners, but I don't care.

I've reached my limit. I need to get out of here as soon as possible.

"What's going on?"

Spooked, I look up. Konrad's panting a couple of feet away. I stare at him, stunned that he even noticed I left. I stab the key into the door. "I'm going."

His eyes are wide. "Are you . . . crying?"

"NO! GO AWAY!"

"No, seriously, Camilla. Are you okay?"

My face throbs with frustration.

"What happened?" he asks.

You happened, I think and swing open the car door. But before I slip inside, I say, "I'm sure your new friend will give you a ride."

Once I'm in, I start maneuvering the car out of the spot. It takes a while, and I hate him for standing there, watching me do it. Why does he have to ruin my dramatic exit, too?

But it doesn't matter in the end. Because when I finally pull out, I press the gas pedal all the way and speed off in a cloud of fury.

And boy does it feel good.

CHAPTER 19

KONRAD

AFTER CAMILLA LEAVES ME STRANDED, I call Dad. He picks me up in his taxi when the concert is over.

Most of his days are spent behind the wheel, so I should be feeling bad about making him drive back into the city in his off-hours, but I'm not able to because, holy shit, tonight was a hell of a lot of fun and Camilla is awesome.

Yes, she ditched me. Yes, she's as mean to me as hammer is to a nail. And yes, she's not answering my messages. None of that matters. Thinking about her makes me feel like a kid again. Like I'm on an adventure. And every time I do, my heart rate picks up and I get a stupid smirk on my face. I know this because Dad asks why I have a stupid smirk on my face.

"No reason," I tell him. "I just had fun, I guess."

"Hmm. Even though your friend ditched you?"

"Yup."

"Who is this friend anyway?"

"Just a girl," I say.

"Just a girl," he repeats, shaking his head.

But she's more than just a girl, isn't she? If she weren't, I wouldn't already be trying to figure out how to see her again, would I? "What's new with you, Dad?" I ask him, both because I'm in a good mood and because I want to make up for wasting his evening off.

"Oh," he says, his mood instantly improved. "Not much. Had two customers go to the airport this morning. Both generous tippers."

"Nice. So dinner's on you, then?"

He laughs. "I already had Mom's schnitzel, but I can get you something on the way if you want. Hungry?"

"Nah," I say. "I'm kidding. I'll grab something at home."

For a while, we drive engulfed in a comfortable silence. The streetlights outside dance across Dad's face, casting shadows across his proud, hooked nose. I feel a pinch of regret. I look nothing like him, and for the first time since my Development, I'm not happy about that.

"It was Camilla," I say because I feel an urge to share something personal with him. Something that will underscore the fact that he's still my father and I'm still his son.

"What's that?" he asks.

"The girl I was with tonight. It was Camilla Hadi. She's the one who had the other Inexplicable Development."

Dad's quiet for a moment. His expression suggests he's connecting the dots. "Oh," he says. "That's very nice of you to be spending time with her."

"I'm not doing it to be nice. I don't really care what she looks like."

He's quiet again. When I glance his way, I see that he's fighting back a smile.

"What?" I ask. "Funny, right? Especially coming from me?"

He tilts his head. "A little bit." There's a pause before he speaks again. "So why did she leave you stranded tonight?"

I sigh. "Because she hates me."

Dad nods like he expected to hear just that. "She blames you for what happed to her," he says, like it's fact.

"She told me that she doesn't, but she obviously does. And I get it, I'd blame me, too, if I were her." I let out another sigh. "I don't know how to get her to like me."

"Why do you care so much if she likes you?"

My voice shrinks. "I don't know. She's cool, I guess."

The car slows a bit. "What makes her cool?"

"She's just so *real*," I say. "So *passionate* about things. She's confident and determined, even though she had this terrible thing happen to her. She's brave—she's not afraid of anything, it seems. I admire her for that. She always tells it like it is. Doesn't care about what people think, doesn't suck up to people. Doesn't pretend to be something she's not. She's just *interesting*. I'm interested in her." I stop, suddenly embarrassed, not only because I realize I'm rambling, but also because I hear the implication behind my words.

"Well," Dad says, chuckling, "she sure does sound cool."

I'm glad it's dark, because I'm clearly blushing. "I mean, I don't know. I just want to get to know her better."

Dad's nodding. "Sounds like you should." He pauses. "By the way, what happened to that cute cheerleader you're supposedly dating?"

I look at him. "Becca? How do you know about that?"

"Arthur."

"Oh."

"So?"

"Nothing happened," I say, realizing I haven't thought about Becca once today. "We're still together, I guess."

"So what's wrong with her?"

I don't answer right away. "Nothing. She's ambitious. And superintelligent, actually; she wants to be a brain surgeon. And obviously she's beautiful. Everybody wants to date her."

"But you don't?"

I look out the window as Dad stops at a red light. In another car, a middle-aged woman is picking her nose. "I thought I did . . ."

We start moving again. "Well," he says, "if you like this Camilla girl, and I think we already established that you do, then don't give up."

I remember Camilla dancing next to me at the concert. Smiling. Happy. I got a glimpse of a side of her I'd never seen before. I turn to Dad and ask, "Is that how you got Mom to talk to you again after the whole Aunt Elizabeth debacle?"

Dad chuckles. "Mom told you that story?"

"Yup."

"That's funny. But yes. Exactly. I didn't give up." His brow knots. "You have to play it cool, though. Can't be too desperate. Desperation is a turnoff. Women can smell it a mile away."

A pleasant warmth sparks in my chest. This type of bonding is new territory for us. I think I like it. "Noted."

"Oh. And surprise her," he adds. "Women love surprises. The bigger the better."

Smiling, I look out the window on my side. "*Dzięki, tato,*" I say, switching to Polish. I don't use it very often, and I'm not very good at it, but I know that saying "Thanks, Dad" in our native tongue will feel that much more special to both of us.

All throughout Sunday, I heed my dad's advice and give Camilla her space. I have to play it cool and not act desperate, which means no more "Are you okay?" messages and no more checking my phone every five seconds.

This is a lot harder than I thought it would be.

Monday is even worse; I see her between classes, and all I want to do is go up to her and apologize for the mess Saturday night turned out to be. There are other things I want to do as well, but I'll keep that between me and the almost-empty box of tissues in my room for now.

Camilla doesn't even look in my direction once. Clearly, she doesn't seem as interested in me as I am in her (*yet!*), but, judging from the way her face tenses and the slight wrinkle on her forehead when I'm looking at her, she's definitely aware of me and is only pretending I don't exist. I choose to take this as a positive sign.

At lunchtime, I position myself at the edge of the cafeteria table. Becca sits next to me, nibbling on one greasy french fry while she talks to Carrie about Coachella. From here, I have the perfect vantage point of the whole room.

Camilla's sitting with the girls from the track team, no Jodie or Ashley in sight. She seems captivated by her salad. I'm staring at her when Mike and Tom arrive balancing burgers on their trays. If Tom's eyes could murder, I'd be dead by now.

Oh yeah, there was that one other thing that happened over the weekend.

Becca gets up and steps out from behind the table. "Tom," she barks, making him freeze just before he can sit down at the other end. "Come here," she orders, her arms crossing under her breasts. With a flip of her finger, she urges me to stand up as well. I sigh, but oblige. "You were both drunk. Things got out of control. Let's forgive and forget," she says, flawlessly executing her role as mediator.

I glance over at Tom. His lip is still a little swollen, but other than that, he looks fine. I guess I did more damage in my head than in reality. His eyes meet mine and we both look at the floor.

"Let's go," Becca commands. "Shake on it."

My hand is the first to extend. I shouldn't have punched him. Violence is bad. Tom was just being the idiot he usually is. Blah blah blah. I still think he's an asshole for talking about Camilla that way, but I made that more than clear with my fist.

Tom takes my hand, but something in his eyes tells me he's not ready to go skipping around in a meadow with me just yet.

"Great," Becca announces, plopping back into her seat.

As if on cue, Sara shuffles over to our table with her own tray and glues herself to Mike's side. She gives Becca and Carrie a small wave, but they only reply with obligatory nods. I must be in a grudge-dismissing mood because I find myself sending her a smile.

What can I say? I'm starting to feel bad for the girl. When we dated, she took up ninety-nine percent of my brain. Now she's at zero. It's almost sad how someone can cease to exist for you like that. In a sense, I should be grateful to her, too. She did teach me that being in love can be incredible. I still want that from life. Only, in the future, I want the real, two-way deal.

She doesn't smile back, but her face flushes and she drops her gaze to her plate.

I redirect my attention to the track table. The girl next to Camilla, the one who always looks like she's about to throw up—is her name Eve?—catches me gawking and smiles. I look away, embarrassed, and my eyes land on Alan and Lauren. This time, I curb my gaze to my lap. My ears get even warmer. I wish my issues with them were a grudge I could dismiss just as easily.

"All hail the Queen of the Nerds," I hear Tom grumble.

Jackie Baker strides over to his side of the table. I haven't talked to her much since she conducted her interview for the school blog about my ID. For a second, I wonder if we did it again today, if I'd still answer her questions the same way. Taking off her glasses, she stands over us and wipes them down with a handkerchief. "Hello," she says.

"Hi, Jackie," Becca chirps on everyone's behalf. She's being nice, but the air of charitableness she's exuding is not lost on anyone.

"So," Jackie continues, "as you may know, the daily themes for Spirit Week are listed online. Also, congratulations Mike, Konrad, Becca, and Carrie." She makes sure to look at each of us as she says our names. "You're all official nominees for the sophomore homecoming court. The winners will be announced at the dance on Friday."

Carrie and Becca high-five each other. Mike leans toward me, fist first. I bump it half-heartedly. "I'm nominated?" I ask no one in particular.

Becca gives me a look I can't quite decipher, but if I were to guess, I'd say she's thinking about cutting my chest open and making holes in my heart with the fork she's holding. "Why wouldn't you be?" she asks, almost offended.

"When did this happen?"

Jackie shows a little more compassion. "When did what happen?"

"When was I nominated?"

"Last week."

"Oh..."

"Right," Jackie says with a note of finality. "I'll go notify the freshman nominees now."

"Thanks, Jackie!" Carrie yells after her, giggling like we've just had an encounter with a different species. I tune her out, though, because I'm freaking nominated for homecoming king. Or is it prince? Whatever. It doesn't even matter. All that matters is that my heart is pounding super hard because I finally know what I can surprise Camilla with.

"Okay," Carrie says, suddenly captivated by her phone screen. Becca's head is hovering over it, too. "Monday is Pajama Day."

Becca rolls her eyes. "Boring."

Carrie clears her throat and continues. "Tuesday, Drag Day—yass! Wednesday—Looks Don't Matter." She pauses and glances at me. I feel a burn of embarrassment. "Thursday is Sports Day and Friday is School Colors," she finishes with a shrug. "Pretty standard stuff."

"Except for Looks Don't Matter," Sara mumbles.

"What?" Mike complains. "My Lingerie Day didn't make it?"

"And thank God for that," Carrie says. "I do not want to see some people in their underwear." Instinctively, her comment makes me look at Tom. Just as expected, he's glaring at me. I glare right back. Carrie turns to Becca, face lighting up. "Oh! Did you decide if you're going to wear the strapless blue or the silver?"

Becca's reply is much less enthusiastic. "The blue, I think,"

"What's Konrad wearing?" Carrie asks. "Are you guys going to match?"

Becca looks over at me, her glare even more intense than Tom's. It dawns on me that I still haven't asked her to the dance. Dread presses on me like a heavy leather jacket.

I still haven't asked her. And I'm not going to. Not today. Not tomorrow. Not ever. I'm going to ask Camilla Hadi, and if I have any hope of her saying yes, of her taking me even a little bit seriously, I'm going to have to break up with Becca first.

CHAPTER 20

CAMILLA

ASHLEY'S NOT AROUND WHEN I try to find her at lunch, so I decide to wait for her in the parking lot after school.

Leaning against her car, I cross and uncross my arms. I have no idea what to expect. It took her fourteen hours to write me back after I sent her that picture of Konrad before the Lizards concert, and all I got in return was a thumbs-up emoji.

I really hope she'll talk to me. I need her back in my life. I need my rock.

Through Jodie's sunglasses, I watch kids get into their cars and drive off. Two freshmen I don't even know do the hand-on-the-face thing. It pisses me off, so I give them the finger. When will this end? When will I be able to come to school and not be reminded of what I look like?

My stomach grumbles. It's not that I've been starving myself—although Mom would probably disagree. I'm just trying to get my body into the best shape it can be. It might be time for a slipup, though. As soon as I get home, I'm whipping out the Oreos.

After what feels like an eternity, Ashley steps out of the building. My heartbeat shifts into a higher gear. She's not blinking, and her eyes are aimed at the ground, like she's lost deep in thought. She only notices me standing there when I say, "Hey."

Startled, she looks up. Her face relaxes, but she looks almost disappointed to see that it's just me. "Hey," she replies.

"What's wrong?"

She shakes her head but can't hold my gaze. "Nothing."

"You sure?" I catch her eye and feel a chill slither down my spine.

"I'm sure."

I nod, eager to move on, but also hurt. I hate this wall that's sprung between us. "So," I say. "I hung out with Konrad over the weekend."

She sighs, like this conversation—or maybe the person she's having it with—is tiring her out. "And?"

"*And* I still think he's a self-indulgent jerk."

Ashley shrugs. "Maybe he is. Maybe everyone is. Who knows?"

I try to read her expression. This is so unlike her. She's either not telling me something or she's even more pissed at me than I thought.

"Ashley," I say, quietly. "You can talk to me."

She makes her way to the driver's side. "I know," she replies, but it doesn't sound like she believes it. Before I can say anything else, she adds, "Sorry. Can't give you a ride today. I have to go to work early. Bethany begged me to cover for her."

"No problem," I say, like it's no big deal. Even though it is.

"I can give you a ride," chirps a male voice behind me.

My skin tightens. *Jesus Christ. Why him? Why now?*

"No thanks," I say, without even turning. I wonder how much he's heard. Not that it would matter. It's not like it's a secret that I hate his guts.

"See you guys later," Ashley calls as her head disappears under the car roof.

"ASHLEY!" I yell, refusing to believe she's about to strand me here alone with Konrad Wolnik, but she starts the car, an unlit cigarette already in her mouth. I watch her drive off, hoping, praying, that Konrad will be gone when I turn around.

"Congratulations on your homecoming nomination!"

I cringe, recognizing this voice, too. Dammit. That means Konrad's still there. "I'm definitely voting for you," Eve tells him as she heads toward her car followed by Amanda.

"Thanks," he answers.

Eve waves to me with something like awe, or maybe envy, in her eyes. "Bye, Camilla! See you tomorrow!"

I wave back half-heartedly.

Konrad and I are now officially alone. Slowly, I turn to face him. My eyes take in his height, his broad shoulders, the perfectly messy lock of hair decorating his forehead. I stare at him longer than I should, and curse myself for my weakness.

"What else do you want from me?" I ask, a little too loudly. "I don't get it."

He's grinning. Like the concert disaster wasn't such a big deal. Like he has no idea my life would be better if he had never been born. "You missed a great show on Saturday."

"Stop it," I say, boring my eyes into his. "I ditched you, remember?"

He winces, his grin wavering. "Let me give you a ride."

"No."

"All right," he says, shifting his weight from one foot to the other. "How about we make it more than just a ride? There's this little Polish joint I know. Their *naleśniki* are delicious."

I stare at him. Not because I have no idea what the hell *naleśniki* are—although the word delicious did catch my stomach's attention. I'm staring because I'm trying to figure out why he seems to think I'd ever want to spend another second with him.

"They're like Polish crepes," he explains, even though no one asked him. "I think you should try the white cheese ones. With blueberries on top. They're the best."

The invitation seems genuine. His temple is even glistening with sweat, which makes me think he's nervous and might be taking this seriously. But there's no way, absolutely zero possibility, that a guy who looks like Konrad would genuinely want to hang out with a girl who looks like me. Best to remain neutral until further notice.

"I'm walking home," I say. "I need to get back in shape, anyway."

That last part slips out unintentionally. I feel my face flash with heat. I don't want to allude to my ID. Not with him.

Konrad's quiet. His eyes travel down to my toes and back up to my face. His cheeks pink up and he says, "I think you look great."

My blood boils instantly.

Oh. Hell. No. Of all people, how dare *he* say something like *that* to *me*? I curl my fingers into fists to get my body's shaking under control. My chin snaps up. "Well, I think you don't," I spit. "You're too perfect. Perfection is boring. No one's ever told you that?"

Konrad's smile instantly falls. He looks hurt. Like a helpless little boy. Like this is the cruelest thing anyone's ever said to him. This just annoys me even more.

"No," he says.

I blink. "Huh? No, what?"

"No one's ever told me that. But I've been thinking the same thing."

I flash him my teeth, not in a smile. More like a grimace of repulsion. "Good!" I say. "First time for everything." And then I start walking away.

"Camilla! Come on. Just let me give you a ride."

The desperation in his voice makes me stop. It makes me feel powerful.

I could turn around, tell him to fuck off. It would sting, but he'd get over it. *Or*, I could let him take me home. Make him think he's getting his way and *then* tell him to fuck off. He'd still get over it, but it would carry more weight and I'd be getting a ride.

I practice a smile. It takes a few tries to get it to look just right. It needs to be subtle. It needs to say: *Okay, you win.* When I spin around to face him again, Konrad's holding his breath.

"Fine."

He exhales. His features gather into a huge smile that lights up his face from one ear to the other. "Cool. So yay or nay to the *naleśniki* idea?"

I'm about to say no, but my stomach grumbles so loudly Konrad can hear it. My eyes bulge. I'm frozen with humiliation. Konrad's smile only grows bigger.

A minute later, I'm in a car with him. Again. And again with his body so close to mine I can smell his stupid boy deodorant. Ten minutes after that, we're perched atop metal stools at a tiny window counter. I only agreed to make this little detour because he's paying.

The Polish bakery is tiny all over. There's a cake display with a pretty young woman in a white apron behind it; two round tables—both taken up by older men in hats; and our two stools, which couldn't be any closer. Serious design flaw.

If I didn't have my crooked legs turned away from Konrad, I'd practically be sitting on his lap.

The smell in the air, a blend of powdered sugar and blueberry jam, is amazing. I've had three bites of my rolled-up Polish crepe-thing, and I have to admit, it's heavenly.

"You're Middle Eastern, right?" Konrad asks through a full mouth.

I sigh, trying to ignore yet another double take from a passerby outside. This time, it's a college-aged guy with shoulder-length surfer hair. *Yes*, I think, glaring at him through the window. *I'm ugly, Konrad's hot, and we're hanging out together.*

"Yeah," I answer. "Half-Turkish. My dad's side." After a moment, I add, "But I know next to nothing about the culture, unfortunately." As I say the words, I feel a prick in my chest. My dad's never going to have a chance to teach me. And I'll never have another chance to ask. I should've asked. I had so many opportunities to ask.

"I'm sorry about your dad."

I freeze in surprise. My dad's death didn't make waves in school. I made sure it didn't. Konrad must remember me saying it when the ID specialists came to see us. I don't like that he knows some of the most intimate things about me. First my doodles of Lance's face in physics, now my dad. "Yeah," I mumble.

He's quiet for a minute. "When did it happen?"

What is his problem? I don't talk about my dad. Even Jodie and Ashley know better than to bring him up. Why should I share this information with a guy who ruined my life? Especially since I don't plan on ever speaking to him again after today.

"Last year," I say, and before I can catch myself, I blurt, "It was a car accident. Totally his own fault. He drank too much."

Pressure explodes in my ears. What the hell am I doing? Maybe it's *because* I'll never speak to him again that the words are able to flow so easily. But that doesn't mean they should. I bring another forkful of crepe to my mouth and chew vigorously.

Konrad is silent. This is not the way this ride home was supposed to go. I'm about to tell him I'm ready to leave, when he says, "That sucks." He pauses, but something in his expression tells me he has more to say. I don't know why, but I let him. "The only funeral I've ever been to was for Alan's sister. I'm sure you heard about it. She was sick for a while. Alan took it pretty hard. I tried to help make him feel better, but nothing worked."

"Like how?" I ask, but I'm not sure why I'm even bothering. I can tell you from personal experience that nothing works. Nothing makes you feel better except time.

"Mostly, I just tried to distract him, you know? Like, he loves video games. We both do. Especially the old-school stuff. Downtown, there's this bar with old arcade games— *Pac-Man*, *Street Fighter*, all the goodies. Lauren's dad's friend owns it, so he'd let us go there in the afternoons. For a while, after his sister died, we went every single day."

"Huh," I say. Another moment of silence stretches between us. My eyes travel from the stubby fingers around my fork to Konrad's toned forearm. "Sucks that you guys aren't friends anymore. You and Alan, I mean."

Konrad's brow knots and his gaze drops to his plate. Guilty pleasure shoots through my body like a dose of morphine. I watch his Adam's apple rise and fall.

"Anyway," he says. "You should come with me sometime. Play some games. It's fun." He looks me in the eyes. "Are you free this weekend?"

I see the plea for me to say yes etched all over his face. It looks so real it almost gives me shivers. Why is this kid acting so desperate for me to hang out with him?

And that's when it hits me. Finally, I get it. Finally, I understand what's going on inside Konrad Wolnik's head.

He's not acting at all. The desperation is *real*.

I was wrong. Or rather, I wasn't entirely right. Konrad doesn't just want my pardon. He doesn't just want to show everybody what a good Samaritan he is with a one-time good deed. That's not enough for him. No, he wants the world around him to be as perfect as his face. Ladies and gentlemen, Konrad Wolnik needs everyone to like him, and he can't handle the fact that I don't. After all, to this kid, nothing matters more than appearances. How did I not see this before?

But guess what? I can play the appearance game, too.

I can give him that perfect world. A world where he thinks he gets to have it all. And then I can take it away, and

humiliate him in the process. Forget posting yearbook photos online and waiting for the kids at school to turn against
him. I have a better plan.

I'm going to pretend to be Konrad Wolnik's friend. And
just when he thinks everything's going his way—to borrow
Alan's words—I'm going to "friend-dump" him. Only I'm
going to do it with a bang. If what Alan and Lauren say is true
and Konrad hates rejection more than anything, I'll make
sure it's the most public, most splashy rejection ever.

Oh, it's going to be glorious.

I can already hear Ashley's voice, loud and clear in my
head, like there's a tiny version of her sitting on my shoulder,
nagging, scolding. But Ashley doesn't know what I'm going
through. Nobody does. People just assume they know what's
best for me. They think I'm this poor little thing who needs
their help. They think they can speak on my behalf.

Well, guess what. I don't need anyone's help and I don't
need anyone to speak for me. This time, I'll make sure everyone hears what I have to say.

Plus, if Konrad's dumb enough to believe that I'd actually
want to be his friend, he deserves every last thing coming his
way.

Slowly, I turn toward him. And I smile. Because I actually
feel like smiling.

"Sure," I say. "Let's do it."

CHAPTER 21

KONRAD

"WHAT'S YOUR PROBLEM?" BECCA SCREECHES. "You've been avoiding me all week. Now you don't even want to have sex? Are you gay?"

At this point, I'm totally regretting my decision to come up to her room. I figured it'd be easier for everyone involved to break up with her in a safe space. But this is our sex den. We only come up here to have sex. I don't know what I was thinking. I guess I must've felt a little sentimental since—if all goes well—I'll never be coming up here again.

I exhale. "You know I'm not gay."

"Then you have someone on the side," she says. She glares at me, arms crossed over her cheerleading top. She's trying to appear calm, but her nostrils are flaring. "It's the only logical explanation. Guys your age don't turn down sex from girls like me unless they are gay or getting it from someone else. Who is it? It's Handy Ashley, isn't it?"

I rub my face down with my hands. "Stop it with Ashley already."

"Wait," she says. "Carrie? Oh my God, I knew that skank was making eyes at you!"

"It's not Carrie."

Becca jumps from the bed and starts pacing around her room. "You know what, Konrad? If homecoming wasn't around the corner, I would so consider breaking up with you right now."

She stops moving to gauge my reaction. This is good. This is my chance.

I'm about to speak when her stern look morphs into a sad puppy face. She falls to the bed and glues herself to my side, her head tilting onto my shoulder.

I freeze. I did not see this coming. Her breath tickles my ear, and her fingers run up and down my arm. "It's okay if you did it with Ashley," she near-whispers. "Just don't do it again, okay? And don't tell anybody."

I jerk away. "You wouldn't mind if I was sleeping around?"

"I'm not saying I wouldn't mind." She shrugs. "But there are a lot of studies out there that prove humans aren't meant to be monogamous."

"What about your reputation? What you told me? You're kind of contradicting yourself right now, you know."

"You and me going to homecoming is a lot more important to my reputation right now." Sighing, she grabs for her laptop, and flips it open. "This is the jacket I want you to get." She leans in closer, her big eyes rolling over the screen. "We can go downtown tomorrow. I want to see it on you first. Everything has to be perfect."

I shoot up to my feet. When I put enough distance between us, I turn to face her.

"Also," she adds without lifting her gaze from the screen, "we need to talk about what we're wearing for Spirit Week."

"Becca," I start, and then I pause, taking her in. Her long brown hair, which I've thought about putting in my mouth more than once because it smells *that* good. The always too-short cheerleader skirt. Those breasts—God, I'm going to miss those breasts.

But what has to be done has to be done.

Last Saturday, just as she'd promised, Camilla came with me to the barcade. We played *Frogger* for almost two hours and feasted on the best vanilla ice cream floats I have ever had. This morning, I picked her up for school because I knew she didn't have a ride. So far, I have seen her smile a total of twenty-four times. (Yes, I counted.) I don't want to jinx anything, but I think Camilla is starting to like me back. And just thinking about all this has me convinced that I'd rather spend a minute in her presence than a whole hour making out with Becca.

"Becca," I try again, and this time, succeed. "I can't."

She looks up. Her blue eyes darken. "You can't what?" she asks, even though I know she knows exactly what I mean.

"I want to break up."

Becca's hand reaches to shut the laptop, but her eyes never leave mine, not even for a millisecond. Her beautiful chest rises and falls as she takes one deep breath after another. "Can't this wait until after homecoming?"

"No," I say firmly. "I'm sorry."

"You're making a mistake."

I slip my hands into my pockets. "I don't think so."

"You are."

"Okay," I say with a shrug. "I guess I am." I wish I could feel bad, but honestly, I don't, so why force it? Weeks of dating this girl and there's nothing that even remotely resembles a flicker of sadness within me. "Look, you can say you broke up with me if you want to."

Her lips form into a smile so cold, it literally gives me a shudder. "Oh, I plan to."

"Okay."

Becca's hand flies up and does that condescending Muppet wave where your fingers tap the base of your palm. I lift my eyebrows and walk through her door.

Only when I'm striding out of her house do I feel a pinch of doubt. Am I making a mistake? Just because I feel this way about Camilla doesn't mean Camilla feels the same way about me. Or that she ever will. What if I'm wrong? What if she still hates me? What I've just done is irreversible. Becca and me are over, and Becca is so damn hot.

But this doubt is only a pinch. A tiny black splotch on an otherwise colorful canvas of relief and excitement and hope. Becca talks. Camilla listens. And when Camilla talks, I actually care about what's coming out of her mouth. Camilla's the one for me.

I'm going to do it. I'm going to ask Camilla to homecoming.

And I'm going to do it right now.

I reach for my phone and start typing, but immediately delete what I've written and put it away. My dad's words echo in my head: *Surprises. Girls love surprises.*

On the way to her house, I consider buying flowers. Do you buy flowers when you ask someone to homecoming? God, I have no idea. How funny is it that I'm racking my brain over something as stupid as a school dance—an event I couldn't have cared less about a week ago.

No flowers. Too cheesy.

Across the street from Camilla's house, an empty spot calls my name. I fill it with my Toyota and cut the engine. The car goes silent and still. My palms are covered in sweat. Reaching up, I pull down the visor and study my reflection in the little mirror.

When I look at Camilla, I don't see her ID anymore. I see Camilla. But I know it's not the same for her. This, right here in the mirror, the result of my ID, is the very thing Camilla dislikes most about me. The thing that reminds her of her pain.

But, then again, it's also the thing that brought us together.

Tilting my head back, I check for boogers and get out of the car. Downstairs, her house is enveloped in darkness, but there's an orange glow coming from Camilla's window upstairs. I ring the doorbell and wait.

The lock on the other side of the door clicks. She appears in front of me wearing sweatpants and a black T-shirt. The second I see her, my heart flutters.

"Oh, hey," she says, pushing her hair behind her ear. Her forehead wrinkles a bit. "It's you. Again."

I laugh. I love her sense of humor. "What are you up to?" I ask.

She looks over her shoulder and shrugs. "Just hanging out."

"Cool."

Both of us wait for the other to say something. One of her eyebrows lifts. "Do you want to come in or something?"

"Sure."

She backs into her living room, holding the door open for me. I step inside, immediately comforted by the coziness of the place. It's nothing like Becca's huge, piano-decorated living room. Nobody plays piano at the Lipowska house. I asked. I kick off my sneakers and line them up against the wall. "Your mom here?"

Camilla's eyes linger on my shoes. "No," she says and looks up. "But she should be back soon." Her hand gestures to the couch. "Um, sit down? Want some water?"

"That would be great."

But she doesn't get it right away. "Did something happen?"

No, I think, *but it's about to!*

I make a face like *what are you talking about?* She hesitates, as if not entirely convinced, but disappears into the kitchen to fetch my drink.

When she returns to the room with a glass, I'm sitting on the couch, smack in the middle so she'll have no choice but to sit close to me. "I thought you'd be hanging out with Becca tonight," she says, passing me the water.

"I did. For the last time ever."

Her eyes brighten with curiosity. "What do you mean?"

"We broke up."

"Huh," she says. "Sorry to hear that." But Camilla doesn't look sorry. My stomach twists in delight. This is a good sign. She crosses the room to the dining room table and pulls out a chair. *Damn. One step forward, one step back.*

Lowering herself, she adopts a perfect sitting posture. One of her hands squeezes the other. I observe her, entranced.

After having just seen Becca, it's hard not to compare the two. Take their reactions to my gaze for example. When she knows I'm looking, Becca basks in it, lounging around like it's an extension of her natural habitat. Like she's entitled to it as much as she's entitled to air. But when Camilla catches me looking, there's a guaranteed retraction. Whether it's a tiny blush or a shift in her body weight, it's as if my gaze is a luxury she feels unworthy of.

And I can't stop looking at her.

"So something did happen," she says. "You lied." Her lips turn inward and disappear in a brief smile. "Why'd you guys break up? You were, like, the perfect couple." She says the last part like the words have left a bitter taste in her mouth. Another good sign.

"Nah," I answer. "Appearances can be deceiving."

Camilla's cheek twitches under her left eye. She shifts in her chair and clears her throat. "Yeah," she says. "They sure can be." If she wants to hear more about Becca, she doesn't ask. Instead, she sighs. "So, Pajama Day on Monday, eh?"

"Yup."

"You dressing up?"

"I think so."

She nods and looks around the room. This is my chance to dive right in, to ask her before her mom gets home and potentially ruins my game.

I'm about to open my mouth, when I catch Camilla's expression twist as if in irritation. Next, her eyes latch onto mine, piercing and accusatory. "You have to cut that shit out," she says.

Blood drains from my face. "Cut what out?"

"Staring at me like that. I wanted to tell you yesterday. It makes me uncomfortable. I know I look like a freak, but if we're going to be ID buddies, we need to set some boundaries."

I want to scream at her for calling herself a freak. Instead, I gulp down the rest of my water, slam the glass on the coffee table, and say, "Will you go to homecoming with me?"

For a couple of seconds, it's as if all the sound is sucked out of the room. My body temperature rises at least a hundred degrees.

Even though she just told me not to stare, I keep doing it. Her face smooths over, but the neutral expression only lasts a second. The skin around her eyes crinkles, her teeth flash, and she's laughing like I've never heard her laugh before.

I'm too shocked to speak. When her laughter dwindles into sporadic spurts, she looks at me and her eyes widen. "You're serious," she says.

"I am."

She thinks for a moment. "What's the catch?"

"What? There is no catch."

"No."

A knot forms in my chest. "No, what?" I ask. Did she just reject me?

"No, there definitely has to be a catch. Are you trying to make some kind of statement?"

"No."

"You can take any girl you want."

"That's what I'm trying to do."

"It's fine," she says, suddenly very serious. "You can tell me what you're plotting. Does this have anything to do with you breaking up with Becca?"

"Yes. That's *why* I broke up with Becca."

Camilla's upper lip curls back. "I don't get it."

"I broke up with Becca so I could go to the dance with you."

She chuckles again. "Yeah, okay."

"Camilla, I like you."

She laughs again. But not as freely as before. "Come on. I like you, too, but that doesn't mean we should go to homecoming together."

"No," I say. "I *like* you."

She goes quiet for a moment. Then, "Did your mother drop you as a baby or something?"

"I don't know. It's possible."

For a moment, she disappears somewhere else. Not literally, because she's still sitting there across the living room from me, but her eyes glaze over and her line of sight drops to the floor. Heart pounding in my ears, I sit still. I don't say anything. The longer I wait, the longer I can hope she'll still say yes.

When Camilla looks at me again, there's decision in her eyes.

"Okay."

I don't know what to do with myself. I stand up. Sit back down. Then stand up again. Never has a single word affected me this much.

"Thank you," I say.

"Um, you're welcome?"

I'm thinking about walking over to her—maybe giving her a hug, shaking her hand, something—when I hear the clank of keys on the kitchen counter and freeze.

"Camilla?" calls Mrs. Hadi, strutting into the living room. As soon as she sees me, she halts. She looks from me to Camilla and back to me again. "Oh," she says.

Camilla stands up. "Hi, Mom. Maybe I should officially introduce you two?" Her head tilts in her mom's direction. "Konrad, this is my mom"—her head tilts in mine—"Mom, this is Konrad. My homecoming date."

Mrs. Hadi's mouth opens, but nothing comes out. She looks like Camilla just told her she's pregnant and she's keeping the baby. My face is on fire, like I am the father of said metaphorical baby. "Nice to officially meet you, Mrs. Hadi."

Mrs. Hadi doesn't answer. She's trying to smile but can't quite form her lips into the right position.

This is way too intense for me. I turn toward Camilla. "I think I'll head out," I say. "Pick you up again Monday morning?"

"Yeah," she says. "See you then."

Backing out of the house, I nod at her mom. "Have a good night."

Camilla walks over to close the door behind me. When I glance in Mrs. Hadi's direction one final time, her mouth is still open.

CHAPTER 22

CAMILLA

WHOEVER DECIDED PAJAMAS AND SCHOOL are a fun mix is an idiot. It's uninspired, unappealing, and most of all, unhygienic. Also, it's drizzling today, which amplifies all of those things a hundred times over.

Unfortunately, our school is pretty spirited when it comes to Spirit Week. If I didn't dress up in my blue polka-dotted footies, I'd only be asking for more attention. And we all know I get plenty of that as is. Although, now that I'm going to homecoming with Konrad Wolnik, I'm not sure any extra precautions will even matter.

Shoes already on my feet, my backpack and jacket waiting on the couch, I peek between the curtains. Konrad should be here any minute.

After he left on Saturday and Mom got over the whole homecoming thing, she sat me down for a serious conversation.

"Are you sure about this?" she asked.

"Don't worry. I know what I'm doing."

"I think you're mature enough and know enough about the world that I don't have to tell you how unusual this is."

"I know."

She frowned, picking at nonexistent lint from her scrubs. "I just can't help thinking he has some ulterior motive."

He does, I thought to myself. *But then so do I.*

"It's fine," I told her. "None of it will matter after the dance."

"Why?"

"Because. We're just going to the dance. And that's it."

I didn't elaborate in case she thought I was showing symptoms of a disturbed mastermind. And boy do I feel like being a disturbed mastermind. MUAHAHAHAHA!

Oh yes. Everything's falling into place. I couldn't have asked for a better setting to execute my glorious rejection of Konrad Wolnik. I mean, I wanted public and splashy, and what's more public and splashy than homecoming? And as his date? This is just too good.

Konrad's obviously counting on the power of spectacle himself. Think about it: Is there a better way to display his heroism and selflessness than by taking me to homecoming? Absolutely not. It's a smart plan. But, if he thinks I'm going to fall for it, he's not a very smart guy.

Can you believe his audacity, though? Thinking he just gets to say he likes me and I'll do whatever his beautiful highness desires? I cannot wait to humiliate him.

The rumble of an engine out front yanks me out of my thoughts. Slipping into my jacket, I grab my stuff and head out. The misty rain hits my face as I cross the front lawn to his car. I swab a film of water off my forehead.

"Hi," I say, slamming the door behind me.

"Morning," Konrad replies, his gaze burning into me—all of me—making me uncomfortable. As usual. "Nice threads," he says.

"Thanks." My eyes travel to the monkeys, barrels, and bananas on his black pajama pants. I recognize them from one of the arcade games I watched him play the other day.

"*Donkey Kong?*" I ask.

"Yup," he says proudly, swinging his long legs open and closed.

"Cute," I say. I've got to give it to him—he thought his outfit out. The Andy Warhol banana T-shirt peeking out from his open hoodie is a great touch. Cute, hip, and sexy at the same time. Of course, I'm not about to say any of this out loud.

"How was the rest of your weekend?" he asks.

"It was fun," I reply, all friendly and polite. I have to stay on his good side. I can't give him a reason to change his mind about taking me to the dance on Friday night.

We get to school and walk in together, side by side, like there was never a time when we hadn't. People shoot us curious looks. Usually, we go our separate ways as soon as we step in the building. Today, he walks me all the way to my locker. Today, he leaves no doubt that we're more than just polite toward each other.

Adrenaline sneaks into my veins. It has begun.

"Yo," Mike Rogers yells in our direction. At first, I hold my breath, thinking he doesn't have any clothes on below his waist—all I see is his bare thighs. But then I realize he's wearing a thong and exhale in relief.

"Hey," Konrad says.

Mike jogs up to us in his red see-through baby doll, the muscles in his thighs contracting. From this up close, I have the perfect view of the very detailed outline of his you-know-what. Blushing, I yank my eyes away. There's no way he walked into school like that, so my guess is he'd just removed his pants. He's got, like, ten seconds before one of the teachers catches him.

"Very nice," Konrad says, looking him up and down. Tom Dempsey, in more traditionally male nighttime attire, sneaks up behind Mike and crosses his arms. He nods at the pair of us, but the icy look he gives Konrad isn't lost on anybody.

Mike holds the hems of the barely-there dress and does a little Southern belle curtsy. "Thank you," he says. "I'm making the case that lingerie and pajamas are the same thing." He eyes Konrad's T-shirt. "I really like your bananas, Mr. Wolnik."

He straightens and looks at me as if he's only just noticed me. I raise my chin and smile—partly because I'm enjoying the confusion I see etched across his features, and partly so it's harder for my eyes to steal involuntary glances at his crotch.

"Camilla," he says, pressing his palm to his face. He peers through his fingers and points at my chest. "Respect."

"Come on, man," Konrad says. "That's so old."

Just then, Principal Marks turns the corner. Her face twists at the sight of Mike's naked ass. "MR. ROGERS!" she yells. "PANTS! NOW!"

Mike does a little *oops* face and trots back to his locker. Tom lingers, but only for a moment. He turns away without a word. I can't help but wonder what happened between him and Konrad. You could cut the tension between those two with a knife.

Since Ashley's taking her time replying to my texts—like always these days—Konrad and I reunite at lunch. I'm under the impression that we're just walking to the cafeteria together and will sit separately once we get there. And then he says, "Want to eat together today?"

"What about your friends?"

"I'd rather eat with you, trust me." The look in his eyes is convincing, and maybe it's true, but I suspect he just wants to avoid Becca.

When we walk in, at least thirty percent of the kids are looking in our direction. The rest are either stuffing their faces or playing with their phones.

I scan the crowd, but Ashley's not around anywhere. My heart sinks a bit, until I see Jodie.

She's sitting with Joe Park, this geeky-cute Korean kid. I knew they had a class together but I didn't know they talked outside of it. I guess a lot has happened since Jodie and I last spoke.

Jodie's eyes meet mine. At first, there's shock on her face—probably at seeing Konrad stand so close to me—but she gets over it and waves at me.

I drag my eyes away. It took her awhile, but just as I predicted, she's acting like nothing ever happened. Like her words didn't hurt me. Finally, I get my chance to ignore her. Finally, I get to make her reflect on what she did to me.

So why doesn't it feel as good as I want it to?

My chest tightens as I realize how much I miss her. For a moment, I even consider inviting Konrad along and sitting with her. But it's too soon. The part of me she hurt is still too fragile. I scan the cafeteria some more. My eyes land on Alan and Lauren.

Excitement races up and down my body.

This must be fate. I rarely see those two in the cafeteria. Is it because it's raining today? Whatever. Looks like Konrad and I won't be sitting with the track team after all. I just figured out how I'm guaranteed to stay on Konrad's good side until Friday.

After Konrad and I get our food, I balance my chicken rice bowl on my tray with one hand and grab Konrad's elbow with the other. This is the first time I touch him of my own free will, but I ignore the tingle radiating in my fingers and keep pulling. The thirty percent has turned into at least fifty, but I'm too focused on my mission to make a more accurate estimate.

"Follow me," I say to him. I might not be ready to make up with Jodie just yet, but someone is definitely making amends today.

Halfway across the cafeteria, I start feeling the first signs of resistance.

"Where are you going?" he asks. In response, I tighten my grip.

As we near the table, our destination now clear, Alan's mouth stops moving, Lauren's eyebrows hike up, and Konrad's feet stick to the cafeteria floor.

I let him be for a moment and go up to them alone. "Mind if we sit with you?" I ask.

They exchange a glance. Alan looks down at his sandwich. Lauren shrugs and sweeps her hand as if to say, "Do what you like." I look back at Konrad. His face is red and panicked. He might as well be showing symptoms of malaria.

Setting my tray down, I slip my legs under the table, one at a time. Alan's in some game-inspired pajama set, I'm assuming, but Lauren's wearing her usual ensemble: a tight leather jacket over a tight white T-shirt. Apparently, Lauren doesn't do Spirit Week.

"Hey," she calls past my shoulder to Konrad, her gaze unflinching.

Konrad limps over but remains vertical. "Hey," he replies, his eyes catching mine. There's so much pleading in them I almost give in and stand back up so we can go somewhere else. But this is a one-chance type of deal. I shoot him a pleading look of my own.

It seems to work. His face twitches in defeat. He hesitates but presses his lips together and lowers himself to the seat.

Lauren's eyes shift from Konrad to me. "Now I've seen everything," she says.

I laugh. Her no-holds-barred honesty really is refreshing. If the circumstances were different—if I weren't trying to ruin Konrad—I could totally see us becoming friends.

Alan's looking at me, a hint of a smile on his lips. "What game is that?" I ask, pointing to the little pixelated creatures on his shirt.

"*Space Invaders.*"

"Nice," Konrad says to no one in particular, extremely busy as he unwraps his cheeseburger.

"Thanks," Alan mumbles to the table.

I turn to Konrad. "Did we play that one?"

"Nah," Konrad says, his cheeks turning even redder. "They don't have that game."

I face Alan. "Konrad took me to that arcade bar."

"Wait," Lauren says. "You guys, like, *hang out* together?"

"Yeah," I say. "And he talks about you two *all* the time."

Everyone goes silent. The tension around the table thickens. I've gone too far too soon. Just when I start to think my plan's gone to hell, Konrad saves us all. "I, um, didn't know you guys all knew each other."

"We do!" I say. "They gave me a ride home the other day."

"Yeah," Lauren adds. "She got as high as a kite."

Konrad's head snaps my way, his eyes about to pop out of their sockets. "You did?"

"She's being dramatic," I tell him. "I was totally in control."

"That's not what the lawn said when you rolled out of Alan's car."

"I tripped! The marijuana had nothing to do with it."

And then we're laughing. All four of us.

For the next couple of minutes, Konrad, Lauren, and Alan reminisce about their weed escapades of the past. I ask a question here and there, but mostly just listen. More and more of our food disappears from our trays. By the time we're finished eating, nothing but empty plates and wrappers before us, I know my plan is a success.

Konrad, Lauren, and Alan are friends again.

Of all people, Alan's the one to officially confirm it. "We're driving down to Six Flags on Saturday," he says. He looks from me to Konrad. "You guys should come."

Heat travels to my cheeks. I have to cut eye contact with him. Alan is almost making it sound like Konrad and I are a couple.

Lauren stares at Alan's ear for a minute, clearly surprised. But then a smile sneaks onto her lips. She turns to me and Konrad and nods in approval. "Yeah," she says, "come."

"I'm down," I say, feeling a strange tug. I can actually see the four of us hanging out. Maybe even having fun. But, of course, I'm lying. I'm not down. I can't be. The dance is on Friday night. By Saturday, Konrad and I will no longer be speaking.

"Me, too," Konrad says, flashing me a big smile. I doubt he's actually excited about the prospect of having to continue our so-called "friendship" beyond the dance, but the gratitude in his eyes for what I did for him today seems genuine.

All in all, my plan couldn't have gone any smoother, and I would've kept riding the high of my success for the rest of the day, except, after school, Konrad decides to take his gratitude to a whole other level.

We're walking side by side on the way to his car, when his hand reaches for mine.

I'm so flustered, I don't know what to do. My own hand stiffens but doesn't move. His fingers wrap around it. He gives me a little squeeze and then lets go.

My skin is on fire. I'm too stunned to look around, to confirm if anybody saw. And then, his eyes on the pavement, our shadows drifting across it, he says, "Thank you for that. At lunch."

And for a brief moment, as I watch him open the door on the other side of the car, he almost makes me believe that this—our friendship, all of it—is real.

Almost.

CHAPTER 23

KONRAD

"Dude," Mike says. "What did you *do*?"

I look up from my textbook. Framed by his giant blond wig, Mike's eyes are chock-full of mischief. Crumpled tissues peek out from the black bra under his tight tank top. I'm ninety-nine percent sure I had previously removed this very same bra off of Sara.

"What did I do what?" I ask. Ever since Mike and I became friends—if you can even call it that—we've been pairing up in Mr. Connick's class. Working with him feels like having your very own monkey assistant, i.e., he's fun but not very helpful.

He leans in and looks around like everyone might be listening. "Becca, man," he whispers. "It's like she's out to get you."

My gaze drops back to my book. "I didn't do anything. It just didn't work out between us."

"Come on, you can tell me. Did you dip your Polish sausage in someone else's mustard?"

I chuckle. I have to admit, as douchey as Mike can sometimes be, he's growing on me. "No," I say. "But maybe I will."

His fist rises. I bump it as discreetly as I can. "That's what's up!" he says.

"Shhh!" I glance over at Mr. Connick, whose eyes meet mine. I'm pretty sure he knows we're not discussing an influential person from the Depression Era. I send him an apologetic smile and turn back to Mike. "Come on." I slap my pen on my book. "We have to finish this."

Mike leans in even closer. "She's going to homecoming with Tom now."

My head snaps back up, rattling my clip-on earrings. "I thought Tom was taking Gina."

Crossing his arms, Mike leans back. "He was. Until Becca asked him."

"Interesting," I say. I'm surprised Tom would throw Gina to the curb like that. But then again, I guess not a lot of guys can say no to Becca. I would know. I was one of them.

"You're still going though, right?" Mike asks.

"I think so."

"Who you taking?"

"A friend."

"Who? That fiery lesbian chick?"

"No," I say. "Lauren wouldn't go to homecoming if you put a gun to her head."

"Then who?"

I look him in the eyes and grin. "You'll see."

After class, Mike walks with me to my locker where Alan's already waiting. As soon as I see him, I smile. I threw my Drag Day outfit together at the last minute: an old flowing dress my mom dug out from a box in the attic and a pair of clip-on earrings she picked up for me at the mall. Alan, on the other hand, went all out in an anime-inspired blue wig and a matching navy schoolgirl uniform. On his tall, lanky body, it's a priceless look.

Mike gives him a nod of acknowledgment. "Sexy," he says. "Got a drag name, Nguyen?"

Alan flinches in surprise. "Uh, yeah. Sailor Swift-Lee."

"HA! That's good," Mike answers. "Aight, see you ladies later!"

"Uh, bye?" Alan's gaze follows him as he walks off to join Becca and Tom. I glance over, too. Even with painted-on facial hair and baggy basketball shorts, Becca looks stunning.

She looks in my direction. I look away.

"Everyone's talking about her breaking up with you," Alan says, probably detecting the miles of shade Becca just threw me from across the hallway. "Supposedly, she's going to homecoming with Tom now."

"Yeah," I mumble. "I heard."

Alan turns to me, readjusting his backpack. "You're not just trying to be friends with us again because the cool kids are shunning you, are you?"

"What?" I ask, not quite sure if he's joking or not. "Nobody's shunning me. You just saw me with Mike."

Alan's eyes narrow. "What about your yearbook picture?"

I tilt my head just a bit. At first, I'm not sure what he's talking about; it takes me a moment to remember Eric's little prank. Ever since I shoved him down to the floor—*by accident*—he's left me alone. And that's fine by me. No matter what Ashley Solomon might've thought, I still think he did it. "What about it?" I ask.

"Becca shared it last night."

I absorb this information and nod. He doesn't have to explain. The first time, when Becca brought it to my attention, the photo kind of died down, just like she promised it would. Now that she's shared it herself, the whole school must've seen it.

"Tom made some pretty nasty comments on it," Alan adds. "So yeah, I stand by my opinion that you're being shunned."

"Whatever," I say, and mean it. I really don't care about what Becca thinks and what Becca does. Alan's my friend again. Lauren's my friend again. Camilla agreed to go to homecoming with me. What more could I want? A little bit of passive-aggressive bullying is to be expected after you turn down the most influential girl in school.

"Why'd she break up with you, anyway?"

If I can't confide in Alan, I can't confide in anybody. Plus, now I kind of feel like more people should know the truth. I face the lockers and lower my voice. "I'm actually the one who broke up with her."

Alan's eyes grow to twice their size. "For real?"

"For real."

"Why?"

I urge him to walk with me. Once the throng of people around us thins a bit, I tell him. "I like someone else."

Alan stops in his tracks. "Who?"

I stare at him, fighting a smile. With Alan, we've been friends for so long, I'm positive he'll be able to read it right off my face.

"I don't get it."

I lower my chin and raise my eyebrows.

Alan gasps. "No," he says. Then adds in a whisper, "*Camilla Hadi?*"

I exaggerate a blink, our signal for yes since we were seven.

His mouth opens, and his eyes jump all around us. He looks lost and confused. "Nope. Not falling for that. No way."

I give him a little push toward the stairs. "Come on."

"Really?" He's shuffling along like a schoolgirl zombie. "*Camilla?*"

"Really," I say. "By the way, she can't come to the Shack with us today. She said she's got homework to finish. Where's Lauren?"

"Working from home," he mumbles as quickly as possible so he can get back to the topic at hand. "I just don't get it," he says once we get to my car. "You can have anybody."

"I don't want anybody."

"But why? I mean, she's cool and chill. But—"

"She's cool and chill. Period."

That shuts him up.

As usual, the Shack is packed with kids from school, and considering most of them have dressed up for Drag Day, it's quite a scene to behold. Lots of messy makeup and badly placed wigs on the guys. Crooked shoulder pads under jerseys on the girls. It's a teenage invasion of french fry-loving drag kings and queens.

Alan and I order our chili dog combos and find a table. The exact moment I sit down—which is so much harder to do in a dress—someone behind me screams, "UGLY FOREVER!"

I turn around. Familiar faces stare back. Some have stupid grins, but others are straight-out shocked in that I-can't-believe-someone-just-said-that way. Failing to find the culprit, I smile at everyone, shrug, and face Alan again.

He's peering past my shoulder. "I think it was that kid Julian."

I slap my palm on the table to get his attention. Kids without the balls to insult me to my face are going to have to try harder if they want to leave a dent in my good mood today. "SO! How've you been, man?"

He looks at me and grins. "Play, school, play."

I chuckle with nostalgic relief. It's been a while since I heard Alan's life motto: one *play* is a reference to video games, the other to the anatomical joystick guys carry around.

"Oh," he adds, "Mom's in Vietnam to see Grandma. Other than that, same old shit."

"Yeah," I say, nodding. "Me, too."

He laughs, like full-on laughs, all the way from his stomach.

Warmth fills my chest. "Dude, are you ready to do the drop tower again at Six Flags on Saturday?"

Alan's thumb springs up. "I'm definitely going to puke again. Puke or faint, one of the two. You should film it either way this time."

I pretend to be offended. "You think you have to ask?"

A frown replaces his smile.

"What?" I ask.

All of Alan's attention is suddenly taken up by the ketchup he's spraying all over his chili dog. "Sorry I wasn't very supportive when your ID happened."

I shake my head. "Sorry I made such a big deal out of it. It's not."

He looks up and forms his mouth back into a grin. "Says the best-looking guy in school who's hooking up with the best-looking girl."

"*Used to* hook up," I say. "Past tense." I glance past him, toward the entrance to the restaurant. My smile falls. "Speaking of which."

Becca struts through the door. Her eyes fix on me immediately. With a cold smile, she hangs herself on Tom's arm in an obvious attempt to make me jealous. I keep staring at them, but it's not because her plan is working. I'm more concerned with what Tom's wearing.

Over his right hand, he has on a giant glove shaped like an exaggerated fist with a hole in the middle. It looks like a perfect fit for a can of beer, so I assume it's a koozie.

"What's up with the giant fist?" I say to Alan, monitoring Tom the whole time as the douche orders his food. Something about his big Afro wig strikes me as not only racist, but also, combined with the clothes he's wearing, uncomfortably familiar. I just can't quite put my finger on it. "Seems like an odd choice for a Drag Day accessory."

"No idea," Alan says. But I get my answer as soon as Tom sits down. Everyone does. Because Becca jumps onto his lap and he jerks the koozie over her crotch in a way that leaves very little to the imagination.

The restaurant erupts in laughter.

My blood turns to ice. His T-shirt, the black pants, the wig. I know why it all looks familiar now. It's Ashley from the video at Gina's party. He's impersonating Ashley. And now that I think about it, Becca is supposed to be Lance Dietrick.

I shoot up from my seat, my chair scratching the floor.

"What are you doing?" Alan asks.

"I'm going over there."

"Dude," he starts, his voice streaked with worry. But I'm already walking in Tom and Becca's direction.

I know it's just a tasteless prank, I know it's just idiots being idiots, but Ashley is a human being. A human being I happen to like. And, in addition to that, she's a human being the girl I *really* like cares about. Camilla reunited me with my best friends. There's no way I'm letting these assholes disrespect one of hers.

"You think that's funny?" I ask, glaring at Tom.

His eyes run up and down my body, reminding me I'm standing over him in a dress. I puff out my chest to look as threatening as possible.

"I do, yeah," he says, revealing the gap between his teeth.

"So does the whole restaurant," Becca adds.

I don't break eye contact with Tom. "Take that thing off."

"What's it to you?"

Becca speaks again, cheerful, as if this was the cue she's been waiting for. "Konrad's just being chivalrous, protecting his new girlfriend."

I rip my eyes away from Tom and plunge them into Becca's. Now I know whose idea this was. "You're mad at *me*. Why get Ashley involved?"

"So you do admit that you cheated on me with her?"

"If I say I did will you ask him to take that off?"

"I do what I want," Tom says.

I snap at him. "Tom. Dude. Becca doesn't care about you. You're just a last-minute rebound."

Tom shoves Becca off his lap and stands up, eye-to-eye with me. "I might be a rebound," he says, "but at least I'm not an ungrateful fake like you. You might be good-looking, but you'll never be good enough for her. For us. Once a loser, always a loser."

"Okay," I say, nodding. "So what's your point?"

"So fuck off and leave us alone!"

"Not until you get rid of your racist, unimaginative getup."

He laughs, burger breath hitting my face.

My fists clench at my sides. We're not on school grounds. He knows it, and I know it. If we do get into a brawl, neither of us is going to get suspended—I'll still be able to take Camilla to homecoming. I'm about to snatch the koozie away when a hand lands on my shoulder. Surprised, I turn. It's Alan. "Come on," he says in a firm tone.

Tom flashes his tooth gap and raises his hand in a little wave.

I exhale at Tom and turn to Becca, realizing I just gave Becca exactly what she wanted: a reaction. "You know what?" I say to her. "You do what you've got to do. I don't care. At all."

"Great," she says, but she definitely flinches. "Neither do I."

"I don't get it," I say to Alan once we get back in my car. "Becca's so smart. Probably the most logical person I know. She doesn't need me at all. I didn't exist to her before. Why can't I just not exist to her again?"

Alan's shaking his head. "You really *don't* get it."

I tense and stop fiddling with the key. "What do you mean?"

"Dude," he starts. "Looks have power. Even if you say they don't matter, they do. And it's *because* she's a logical person that she's doing this. By rejecting her, you disrupted everything she knows. She's probably just trying to make sense of her place in the world." He shrugs and faces the window. "Like the rest of us."

CHAPTER 24

CAMILLA

I'm with Konrad and Lauren in the hallway when I spot the first mask.

My gaze latches on to the photo on a stick, holes cut out for eyes, as it swings away attached to a freshman's hand. Noticing me staring, the kid's face turns red before he hides the mask from view and runs off. A cold chill strikes my spine. "What the hell is that?" I ask, even though I don't have to. I saw very clearly what it was. *Who* it was.

"Just assholes being assholes," Lauren says, picking at her nails.

I glance up at Konrad. He's looking at me. Like he's not seeing anything but me. "Who cares?" he says, flashing me a smile.

"I'll see you guys later," I say and sprint off, trying to look like I'm in a hurry and not frustrated to the marrow in my bones. *Who cares?* Someone just ran by with Konrad's old yearbook picture. On a stick! Why is he pretending like it's nothing? What's wrong with him?

It took a while, but thanks to Becca Lipowska, Konrad's old photo and the accompanying hashtag finally took off. The photo *I* uploaded and the **#uglyforever** hashtag *I* came up with. On top of that, Becca and Tom have exiled Konrad from their group. Everything's going the way I'd hoped. Even better. Konrad's reputation is going down the drain.

So why am I not enjoying it more? What's wrong with *me*?

I round the corner, breathing hard, when I spot another mask. And then another. I keep walking until I find their source.

Becca and Carrie hold batches of the things to their chests. With their free hands they wave down anyone who passes by, handing them out. And people take them. Like the high school sheep that they are, they all take them. Hungry for even the tiniest link to popularity.

I watch this scene unfold, until Becca sees me and approaches.

"Hi," she says in a fake sweet voice. "How you holding up?"

"Why are you doing this?" I ask, staring at the masks she's cradling like a baby. I genuinely want to know. "Just because he broke up with you?"

For a second, Becca looks flustered. But she recovers quickly. "He broke up with me? Honey, I'm the one who dumped *his* ass." When I don't say anything, her weight shifts from one leg to the other. She blinks, slowly. "It's Looks Don't Matter Day," she says. "What better way to celebrate it than by reminding people of Konrad's transformation?"

I tilt my head. "Why didn't you make masks of the old me, then?"

Fake shock takes over her face. I make my eyes into slits and glare at her.

She rolls hers and exaggerates a sigh. "Okay, fine. You got me. Looks might not matter, but humility does. Konrad thinks he's better than all of us now." She says this like it's the most unthinkable thing in the world. And by *us*, I know she means *me, Becca.* "He should be a little more humble, don't you think? Especially considering he used to look like this." She points to the masks. "Here. Take one."

She shoves one into my hand. I take it absentmindedly.

"You can tell him I'm responsible," she says. "In fact, would you do me a favor and do that? I know you and Ashley Solomon hang out with him now."

"Yeah," I mumble. "I will."

When she dashes off to flag down another person, I raise the photo faceup and stare at it. To make these things, she had to blow them up, print them out, and attach the wooden sticks. That's a lot of work. I should be thanking her. She not only hates Konrad, but she's unwittingly helping me ruin him.

This is good, I tell myself. *This is what I wanted.*

The warning bell rings, and I start walking. But I don't go to class. I don't go to the bathroom to revel in this turn of events and evilly laugh in a private stall. I swerve into the counselor's office and shut the door behind me.

"Camilla," Ms. Hughes says. Surprise makes her big eyes and tiny downcast mouth look more like a rabbit's than usual. I plop into the chair and cross my arms.

"It's today's theme, isn't it?" she says. "'Looks Don't Matter'? Honestly, I have no idea how the school even approved that."

"It's not that," I say. "That's just a bunch of kids with messy hair, stained clothes, and Hunchback of Notre Dame masks. It's all too stupid to even think about. I'm over it."

"Then what is it? Are the media people bothering you again?"

"No." I look at her. "I haven't been harassed in a while. Looks like they moved on to covering that already rich California lady who won that multistate lottery."

"Oh yes. I read about that. And what about the **#IStandWithCamilla** hashtag?"

"That's dying down, too," I say. I don't add that **#uglyforever** is taking its place.

"People's concerns can be so fickle, can't they? It seems like, in this society, as soon as something new comes along, everything that came before it is all but forgotten. Either way, I'm sorry you had to go through those things."

"It's fine."

She observes me. "And what about the government offi-cials? Are they still in touch?"

"Yeah. They reached out to my mom. Doesn't really mat-ter, though. I still don't have anything new to tell them."

"I see." A few beats go by in silence. "What would you like to talk about? We can talk about anything, Camilla. Anything you need to get off your chest."

What *do* I want to talk about? I don't even know why I came in here. I couldn't care less about confiding in this stranger. And yet, words pour out of me. "Everything is going the way I want it to and I'm not enjoying it. Why am I not enjoying it?"

Ms. Hughes crosses her arms and leans back. "What do you mean?"

"I mean the universe is smiling down on me for once. That doesn't happen very often these days. And I can't even enjoy it."

She lowers her chin. "Are you allowing yourself to enjoy it?"

I lower mine. "What do *you* mean?"

"Camilla, sweetheart," she starts. I grind my teeth, but stay quiet. "You've been through a lot. I know it sounds cheesy, but life really is full of mountains and valleys. You were thrown into a valley, a very deep one—I hope you don't think I'm being insulting."

"I don't."

"Maybe now that you're on a mountain, you're afraid of falling back in. Either that or you don't want to believe that you're finally out."

She's right about it sounding cheesy. But she might also be on to something. I nod.

"Don't look back," she goes on. "Only forward. Don't doubt yourself. Good things can and will happen to you." Her rabbit mouth turns into a tiny smile. "Sounds like they already did."

I nod again, even returning a meek smile out of politeness.

"Don't be afraid of good things. You deserve them all. As much as any other student at this school. Don't ever forget that."

I feel my cheeks go red and look down at my lap.

"Do you want to share what these things are? These good things happening to you?"

My head snaps back up. There's no way I can tell her about my plan to publicly humiliate Konrad Wolnik. "Nope."

She winks at me. "I didn't think so."

"Sorry. I *do* feel better, though."

"Great. Do you want to talk about anything else?"

I shake my head. "No. I think I'm good."

"Everything okay at home?"

Mom and I talk. Things have settled down after what Jodie did. We're a functioning two-member family again. As functional as a two-member family who used to be a three-member family can be, anyway. "Yeah, everything's fine. Thank you."

"How's track?"

"Good."

"You look like you're in great shape."

I can't look her in the eye. I am in better shape than immediately after my ID. Much better. I worked hard to get here. But I'm not ready for compliments yet. I don't know if I ever will be. "Thank you," I say anyway.

She gives me a satisfied smile. "I'm happy for you. I really am." Ms. Hughes leans forward. "Now go out there and enjoy yourself."

When I leave her office, I feel a little lighter. She's right. I need to look forward. Focus on the final goal. I shouldn't doubt myself before I get what I'm after. Doubt could lead to quitting and I'm not a quitter. All I have to do is free my mind of distractions.

Distractions like the way Konrad looks at me sometimes and makes my heart jump. Like how I laugh a little too loudly when he calls me—actually calls me on the phone—and tells me about something stupid that happened on some show he saw. Or distractions like Alan and Lauren, who treat me like I'm one of them. Like I'm a friend.

Distractions. Obstacles. Tricks. All of them leading to doubt.

This is all part of Konrad's selfish plan. I can't allow myself to forget that. Questioning if there's a chance his actions are genuine is dangerous and I need to stop.

Because Konrad Wolnik is not kind and thoughtful. He's a slick manipulator, who is only making sure everything goes his way. That everything benefits him and him only.

Two more days.

Two more days and Konrad will feel like I do all the time: *not good enough*.

Before I go back to class, I realize I forgot to get a slip from Ms. Hughes, so I head back to her office. On the way, I check my phone. There are two messages from Jodie.

My heart starts beating faster.

The first: **How are you?**

Twenty minutes later: **I know you're mad, but we should talk about Ashley.**

Ashley's face flashes in my mind. I see her features molded in disappointment, her head shaking in disapproval.

I stick my phone back in my pocket.

After homecoming, after all of this is done and over with, after Konrad Wolnik finally gets what he deserves, I'm going to talk to Ashley and Jodie. I'm going to get my friends back.

Until then, though, no more distractions. And no more doubt.

CHAPTER 25

KONRAD

Sneakers pounding into the track, Camilla runs like an explosion's been set off behind her. She reminds me of those superconfident chicks in the movies: Wonder Woman, Lara Croft, or Ripley from the *Alien* series—only with even more poise and control.

The football team is giving it one final push before the game tomorrow, so the field—and the bleachers, as a result—is seeing a lot more action than usual. You can almost feel the excitement crackling in the air.

I couldn't care less about the game. Even if today is Sports Day and even if I did come to school wearing my dad's old football uniform. Before my ID, it would've been a perfect fit. As is, it's a bit too snug, especially the pants. I pull on the material to give my crotch some breathing room and turn my attention back to the female Flash owning the track.

Now Camilla I do care about. A lot. So much so, in fact, that I'd love to scream her name right now, right from up here where I'm sitting, and ask her to be my girlfriend. Make things official. Let the world hear.

But I'm not ready to do that. Not just yet.

At homecoming, as soon as a slow song comes on, I'll lean in and whisper the question in her ear. She'll sigh and say *Fine, whatever* or some other quintessentially Camilla phrase. We'll kiss the way we have so many times in my head, and the Konrad and Camilla saga will officially begin.

And it will be legendary.

On her final lap, Camilla runs up to the bleachers. "I'm just going to shower real quick," she yells up to me. "Meet you at the car?"

Like the dork that I am, I give her a thumbs-up—feeling stupid even as I do—and push myself past knees and backs so I can get down to the ground.

People go silent when I approach. Apparently, I've been designated the new school asshole. Cocky, ungrateful, disloyal. A cheater. A loser. At least that's what Becca and Tom and their friends—*my* former friends—want everyone to think.

Not that it's working. Sara's probably loving it, I'm sure, and my yearbook picture was a hit, but I can tell the rest of the school is unsure about me. For one, Mike still talks to me. Which, by the way, is beyond weird. The douchebag who used to make me cringe more than anyone—the guy my ex-girlfriend left me for—is the only popular kid who stuck around. Mike Rogers is someone I actually don't mind calling my friend now. Who would've thought?

Then, of course, people see me with Camilla. They love her. More than they ever loved me. And if Camilla herself doesn't mind me, then I can't be that bad, right?

Except for Alan and Lauren, nobody knows I'm taking her to homecoming. And I want to keep things that way. When the time comes, when I'm holding her in an embrace as we dance, let people gasp. Let Becca's jaw drop. I'll enjoy watching her scrape it off the gym floor.

"Thanks for waiting," Camilla says, throwing her backpack and duffel bag in the back seat of the car. Her hair is still damp. What is it about wet hair that makes women look so much sexier? The door *thwacks* as she pulls it shut.

"That was fast," I tell her, genuinely surprised at her speed.

"I don't like keeping people waiting," she says, leaning back into her seat. She turns to me, eyebrows arching. "So the mall, right?"

"Yes, ma'am," I say and turn the key.

Today, I asked her to help me pick out an outfit for homecoming. Dad even let me borrow his debit card for the occasion. Obviously, I couldn't care less about what I end up wearing. It's just an excuse to spend time with her.

Before I back out of my spot, I grab my phone and pick out a song. All Camilla needs is a millisecond to realize it's the Leaky Lizards.

"Nice," she says. I catch a small smile on her face, but it quickly disappears. Too quickly.

"You all right?" I ask.

"Of course. Why wouldn't I be?"

If there's one thing I learned about Camilla Hadi, it's that it's best not to pry. I stay quiet and bob my head to the music as I try to focus on driving the car with my clumsy shoulder pads and the smell of Camilla's shampoo in the air.

"Those pants look really tight," she says.

A grin weaves its way onto my face. Is Camilla paying attention to my lower half? If so, I'm definitely not against it.

At the mall, I suggest we get smoothies. Organic ones because I know she likes to keep healthy. Slurping on them, we walk around, side by side, not unlike a real couple. Even though my legs are much longer than hers, I love how she never falls behind. She saunters with her chin high, ignoring the stares we draw from the people we pass.

We. Us. The confident short girl and the tall, fake football player with a stupid grin that refuses to leave his face. "How about this place?" she says, veering into a store without even waiting for a response. I follow her and we wade through the racks. Or, rather, she does. All I'm really doing is watching her. She turns and says accusingly, "You're not even looking."

"Yes I am!" I shuffle my hand through a nearby display.

"I don't think you need a down jacket for homecoming."

My lips pull back in a guilty, five-year-old grin. "Whatever you pick, I'm going to wear."

Camilla shakes her head in warning. "Not a good idea. I've never shopped for a guy before."

My eyebrows hike up. "Really? What about ex-boyfriends?"

"Nope." Her face hardens and she turns away.

I never heard anything about her dating anyone from school, but I assumed there must've been *someone* in her past at some point. My whole body starts to pulse as a thought enters my mind: Am I going to be Camilla's first boyfriend? What if I'm her first *everything*? That's a lot of pressure. The prospect both scares and thrills me.

"Pants size?" she asks.

"28-30," I blurt, realizing as soon as it's out of my mouth that I'm giving her my pre-Development measurements. "Sorry," I say, quickly. "I mean 32-34." My cheeks sear. Everything's going so well. Why did I have to bring up our IDs?

She nods to herself, clearly understanding the slipup. Because she does. Better than anyone. But if the reminder bothers her, she doesn't show it. She grabs a pair of black dress pants and throws them over her elbow, adding them to the blazer and white button-down already hooked there. "I'm wearing navy," she tells me, passing the bundle of clothes over to me. "Go grab a tie that matches and try 'em on. I'll be by the fitting rooms."

Once I find a classic navy tie—with the help of an unusually touchy-feely female sales assistant who ambushes me out of nowhere—I spot a very shiny, silky-looking yellow dress shirt hanging nearby. Without a second thought, I snatch it, hiding it under the other clothes.

Camilla's in front of the fitting rooms as promised. "She's pretty," she says without looking at me, continuing to pretend-browse through a rack of T-shirts.

"Who?" I ask, catching on about the clerk a beat too late. Is Camilla jealous? To be jealous, you have to care. I feel a happy little tickle inside.

Camilla doesn't answer. She plops onto a nearby bench and pulls out her phone, then shoots me a look like, *What are you waiting for?*

"I think I'm going to try these on," I say.

"Yup," she answers without looking up from the screen.

Inside the fitting room, I pull myself out of my dad's jersey. The T-shirt I have on underneath goes off with it. Next, I squeeze out of the football pants until I'm standing in front of the mirror in my briefs and socks.

My new body's not as toned as it was when I first saw it from the top of my bathtub. Unless you count playing video games and walking up stairs at school, I haven't exactly been taking care of it. The bigger appetite I've had for the past few weeks clearly hasn't helped either. But although it's obvious I've been slacking off, one thing is still certain:

I'm still hot.

And I still don't look like I'm related to anyone in my family.

A sigh sneaks past my lips. When I'm alone, I don't take selfies anymore. I don't check myself out in every reflective surface I come across. I guess you could say becoming superhot is like getting money as a gift. You love it, you're excited—you think you can get anything you want. It's great. For a while. But with time, you forget you ever got it in the first place.

I slip my legs into the pants and push my arms into the sleeves of the shiny yellow shirt I managed to sneak in without Camilla seeing—which, by the way, turns out to have a giant frill on the chest. It's even more flamboyant than I thought.

Unbuttoning the shirt's top three buttons, I step out from my fitting room. "What do you think?" I ask, Don Juan-style, my hands on my hips, my face aimed into the distance.

Camilla rolls her eyes, but she's fighting a smile. "You look like a tacky flamenco dancer," she says.

"That's *exactly* what I was going for."

Her eyes narrow. "I dare you to wear that."

I narrow mine back at her. "To the dance?"

"Yup."

I nod. "We wouldn't really match. As you can see, this isn't exactly navy."

She shrugs, smirking. "As you can see, I don't care."

I don't falter. "Okay then," I say, popping back into the fitting room to change back into my football gear. When I come out, I beeline straight for the register.

"I was kidding!" Camilla says running up behind me. But there's a snicker in her voice.

The girl who helped me with the tie rings me up. She looks at the yellow shirt, at me, at Camilla, then at me again. "I was kidding," Camilla repeats from beside me, officially chuckling now. "We're going to look like the Chiquita banana lady split in half."

With a lift of my chin, I urge the clerk to continue. Her face twists in confusion, but she completes the transaction anyway. The yellow shirt must really be silk, because it's a lot more expensive than I anticipated. Dad will definitely regret lending me his card when he sees the bill.

"You're an idiot," Camilla says as we walk out of the store, a big paper bag swinging from my arm. But she's *still* laughing.

I'm in such a good mood, I want to commemorate the moment. I *need* to commemorate the moment. So I put down the shopping bag, take out my phone, sweep her in closer, and snap a photo. When I let her go, I'm disappointed to find that Camilla's no longer smiling.

We walk back the rest of the way to the car in silence. Shopping bag in the back seat, I turn to her and announce my secret surprise plan for the evening. It'll definitely improve her mood. "There's this great Turkish restaurant downtown. Five stars on Yelp! It's actually not far from the place where we saw the Leaky Lizards. You hungry?"

Camilla doesn't say anything. She's looking straight ahead, but I know she heard me. She's breathing heavily.

"What is it?" I ask.

Still, she says nothing.

"You don't want to go? We don't have to. I just . . . I don't know. I love Turkish food and thought we could try a bunch of different things together." I pause. Panic zaps through me. "Oh God, do you hate it? We can totally go somewhere else if you hate it."

More silence. She turns away.

"Camilla?" I try to take her hand, but she snatches it away. She slips both of her hands between her thighs, where they're clearly off limits.

I slump in my seat, ashamed. "Did I do something? Was I being racist? I'm sorry, I shouldn't have assumed . . . It's just . . . you mentioned that—"

"No," she finally says. "I don't think you were being racist. It's actually very sweet. It's just that . . . I can't. I have to study tonight."

"Oh, okay. No problem. You want me to take you home?"

She's still looking out the window. "Yeah, thanks."

Five minutes later, I tighten my grip on the steering wheel. "It's because I made you think of your dad, right? I'm sorry. It was a stupid idea."

"It's fine," she says. "Really. Don't worry about it."

"I don't know what I was thinking."

"You didn't do anything wrong, okay?" she says, shaking her head. But there's anger in her voice now. Despite the big knot in my chest, I don't say anything else because I know she doesn't want me to, until I pull up in front of her house.

"See you in school tomorrow?" I ask.

"Um," she says. "I don't think I'll go tomorrow. My mom's got a day off and we're supposed to see my aunt."

The knot tightens. I'm finding it hard to breathe.

"What about the game?" I ask. "And the dance?"

Hand on the door handle, ready to pull, she turns to look me in the eyes. "I'll be back in the afternoon. But I don't think I'll make it to the game." She forces a smile. It's utterly unconvincing. "I'll meet you at school for the dance? Say, eight o'clock?"

I nod. "I'm really sorry," I manage to spit out, my voice catching in my throat. But the words are too weak, and the slam of the car door mutes them anyway.

My heart pounding in my ears, I watch her scurry away, willing her to look back at me before she disappears behind her front door. She doesn't. And I know—as painful as it is, as much as I wish it weren't true—that tomorrow, at eight o'clock, she won't be showing up.

CHAPTER 26

CAMILLA

LET ME TELL YOU A sweet little story.

Once upon a time, a boy—the most beautiful boy in the world—talked to a girl. A girl so ugly that, when she looked in the mirror, her own eyes glazed over and she didn't see a girl at all, but only parts. Flat, unremarkable hair that always needed brushing. A unibrow lurking under the surface. Crooked teeth only braces could save. Un-kissable, thin lips.

But the beautiful boy talked to this ugly girl anyway. And he kept talking to her, day in and day out. He took her to see her favorite band, told her she looked great—even though she obviously didn't. He made her laugh, held her hand, made her feel special. He was thoughtful, attentive. Against all odds, the beautiful boy and the ugly girl were happy together.

The end.

This is not a realistic story. This is a fairy tale.

But I'd be lying if I didn't admit that, for a moment there yesterday, at the mall with Konrad Wolnik, I almost believed it to be true myself.

Thank God he took that photo of us. Thank God he reminded me of his true character. I mean, a Turkish restaurant? What fucking high school guy is that thoughtful? Even the boyfriend of my fantasies—and I'm an expert at fully realized, imaginary boyfriends—isn't that sweet. I can't believe I almost fell for it, almost believed he *actually* likes me.

This morning, I ran in the park until I could no longer bear the excruciating stitches in my side. At lunch, I blasted the Leaky Lizards while I made chicken salad. When five o'clock came along, I whipped out the makeup kit Jodie had left me soon after my ID, and at six thirty, I slipped into my navy dress. When Mom got home at seven, I lied about my day, failing to mention the little tidbit about ditching.

And now it's five to eight, and I'm here, behind the school I didn't go to today, hanging from the steering wheel of Mom's car.

I really do hope that photo Konrad took of us has over a thousand likes by now. I really do hope he thinks his plan is working. It'll only make his humiliation burn that much hotter.

This is it. Tonight's the night. Tonight, things don't go Konrad Wolnik's way. Tonight, Konrad Wolnik's life stops being perfect. Tonight, Konrad Wolnik has to face the fact that his despicable selfishness ruined someone's life.

And it's all going to happen in front of the entire school.

The parking lot is crowded with other cars. Couples mill around the back entrance, colorful ties and dresses galore. Lights flicker out through the gymnasium windows. It's strange seeing the building so alive this long after last period.

I don't see anybody I know—anybody I'd have to stop and talk to, anyway—so I seize the moment and get out of the car. Heels clicking on the pavement, heart thudding, I make my way toward the commotion. My arms, I realize almost too late, are covered in a layer of perspiration. I wipe one against the other.

Mom bought me this little navy evening purse to match my dress. I feel stupid carrying it, but at least it gives me something to do with my hands. Besides, there are plenty of other reasons to feel stupid. Every girl I see has exposed shoulders. Every dress ends above the knees. Mine not only has elbow-length sleeves, it flares out to mid-calf. It's an outcast. Just like its owner.

"Camilla!" I hear halfway up the stairs. I turn to see Eve's hand hooked into Scott Jenkins's arm. "You came!" she says. But I bet that's not what she's really thinking. Really, she means *You came?* Very emphatic question mark.

"Of course," I say, a little too defensively. But that's not a good way to start the evening, so I make up for it with a smile.

"You look great," she tells me, her eyes gleaming in the stream of light from inside. The V-neck black dress she has on complements her runner's body perfectly, displaying her collarbone in the most elegant way. I'm ambushed by a pang of envy and my smile falls.

I don't look great. She does. I might look better than usual, but looking great and Camilla Hadi are opposing forces now. Unfortunately, if I'm going into this building tonight, I have to forget about semantics. "Thanks," I say. "I love your dress."

"Aww!" Eve says. "Thank you! Did you come by yourself? Why didn't you call me? We totally would've picked you up." She looks up at Scott, who is standing there awkwardly like humans with penises tend to when I'm around. He fires off a few nods for my benefit.

Maybe I'm combative, maybe I'm desperate, or maybe tonight I just want to be on a mountain and not in a valley, but their forced kindness triggers something inside me. "I'm here with somebody." I say. "Konrad Wolnik? You know him?"

Eve and Scott are staring at me like I just spat out a chunk of gibberish. Eve's about to open her mouth, but before she can, I quickly add, "Yup. Konrad Wolnik is my date tonight." I turn my back to them and walk through the door.

"Good evening, Ms. Hadi," says Mr. Connick, clearly on chaperone duty. I flash him a brief smile and hurry on. I'm too busy trying to control my pounding heart and dodging all the stares. They're almost tangible, like I'm walking against a heavy wind. Still, I show Mr. Connick my ticket, hold my head up high, and strut through the gym doors.

Inside, it's darker than I expected. Above me, strings of white light bulbs hang from the middle of the ceiling in two symmetrical arches. The lights reflect off the shiny floor like it's a giant wooden mirror. White balloons are scattered everywhere you look.

People line the walls, especially near the drink area. A group of brave seniors has ventured into the middle of the floor, the guys waving their arms to the hip-hop music, but it's clear the party's still far from full swing.

I'm looking around, searching for Konrad, when I spot Alan Nguyen. Solo cup in hand, he's heading straight for me, with—and this is pretty random—Jackie Baker, our school journalist, on his tail. He has a huge smile on his face. "Camilla!"

"Hey, Alan," I say as Jackie catches up. "Hi, Jackie." I eye them both with curiosity. "Let me guess, Lauren's not coming tonight."

Alan laughs. "Good guess."

"Did you guys come together?"

Even though it's dark, I can see Alan's face flush. "As friends."

Jackie nods emphatically. "As friends."

I don't want to make them any more uncomfortable, so I decide to change the subject. "Did we win the game?" Looking relieved, Jackie quickly shakes her head. "Well, darn," I say.

Alan grabs my elbow. "Come on." He weaves us between dresses and neat, buttoned-up shirts, all the way past the drink tables. There, against the wall, my eyes lock on to a frilly yellow shirt. For a couple of seconds, I feel like my heart stops.

Head down, elbows on his knees, Konrad sits in one of the chairs, holding his phone with both hands. The light from the screen illuminates the concentrated frown on his perfect face.

My throat goes dry. I stop, willing him not to look at me, but it's like he can feel my presence. His eyes jerk up and crash into mine. Instantly, he stands, the biggest smile I've ever seen stretching across his face.

"Hi," he calls over the music.

"Hi," I say back.

His hands slip into his pockets. "I was sure you wouldn't come."

"Why wouldn't I? I told you I would."

He smiles, another huge grin. Then his eyes start shifting, running up and down my body. He's looking at me, taking me in. All of me. My ugly calves. My small breasts. My thick layer of makeup. It's torture.

"You look beautiful," he says.

"Thanks," I mumble, my insides twisting with humiliation. I motion to his shiny yellow shirt. "You actually wore it."

He glances down. "Why wouldn't I? I told you I would." He shoots me a smirk.

I feel a warm tingle in my chest. It rises up into a smile. I quickly suppress it.

"You look absolutely ridiculous," Alan says with a snort. But if Konrad hears him, I can't tell. Instead, Konrad moves closer, stopping right in front of me.

"Want to dance?"

Shaking my head, I say, "I just got here." I glance over my shoulder at the near-empty space in the middle. "No one's dancing, anyway."

"Good," he says, "more room for us." He extends his hand.

I take a deep breath. Do I have to roll out my plan already? If we go out on that dance floor, we'll have everyone's attention. It's the perfect opportunity to humiliate him.

But I hesitate. It's not the idea of all those eyes being on us that bothers me. It's the thought that, deep down, a part of me—a part that dreams of beautiful boyfriends and true romance—actually *wants* to take his hand, follow him out on that dance floor, and just *dance*.

I suck in a breath and place my hand in his. As he pulls me to the center of the room, the stares pile on us. It doesn't help that the music transitions into a cheesy eighties pop song.

Smiling, Konrad turns to face me. His neck starts twitching from side to side, his mood immediately contagious. Unable to look away, I start copying his moves, making my own shoulders shimmy back and forth.

And for a moment—our hands interlocked, swinging to the beat, both of us owning our dorky moves, not a care in the world—I allow myself to pretend. I let myself believe that the fairy tale where I'm here, all dolled up, dancing with the hottest guy at school is real. That this stunning guy—for inexplicable reasons—actually likes me.

Me.

"What's wrong?" Konrad yells, still swaying. "Why'd you stop?"

"Um," I mumble, realizing I've completely frozen. "Let's get something to drink."

He leans in. "What?"

"LET'S GET DRINKS!"

Slowly, he reins in his dance moves, reminding me of those battery-powered toys that take a few seconds to go still after you turn them off. He looks disappointed but nods.

Back on planet Earth, I remember where I am. The music gets louder in my ears and I'm again aware of my surroundings.

"BEAUTIFUL FOREVER!" one of the seniors yells in our direction, hands cupped around his mouth. "I STAND WITH CAMILLA AND KONRAD!" screams the girl next to him.

Someone whistles. I scan the crowd and see Becca and Tom. Becca's arms are crossed under her cleavage. Tom is whispering something into her ear, scowling.

Eyes. Eyes as far as I can see. All filled with glee and support and optimism. All looking at Konrad and me.

This is the perfect moment to make a scene. To do what I came to do tonight. And yet, a lump forms in my throat. I can't bring myself to take the next step. I need more time.

"Damn," Alan says when Konrad and I rejoin Jackie and him. "You guys got this party started." I follow his gaze to the crowd on the floor, which is growing bigger by the second.

"That's how we roll," Konrad replies.

The two of them start chatting about a video game that's coming out soon, and Jackie asks me something about PSATs, but I'm not really listening. I'm busy watching the other side of the gym, where Jodie and Ashley are hugging. Ashley must have just arrived.

My heart contracts. They both look so beautiful. Ashley's got on a white chiffon cocktail dress, the hem flowing above her knees. Jodie's enveloped in a short black sheath, Audrey Hepburn-style. Next to her, Joe Park hovers protectively in his black blazer.

I wonder if Jodie's officially dating him now. I wonder why Ashley isn't smiling. I wonder why I don't know these things and why I'm over here and not there with them.

Jodie looks at me and my breath catches. Even though I promised myself to wait until the night is over, I smile at her.

She looks away first. Cold. Indifferent. Ashley doesn't even glance my way.

"You okay?"

I blink and look up into Konrad's eyes.

No, I'm not okay, I want to say. *I'm not okay with you sabotaging my friendships. With you making me feel like you can have everything this world has to offer, while I get nothing. I'm not okay with you making me feel like you care when I know you don't.*

I yank my eyes away from him. I need a distraction, so I search for Jackie, but she's not around. Before I can ask Alan where she went, I get my answer.

The music cuts off. A spotlight illuminates the back of the gym. Everybody stops what they're doing and crowds toward the makeshift stage that's set up there.

"You guys having fun?" Kendra McKenzie, the senior class version of Jackie, asks into a microphone. The floor erupts with hoots of confirmation. "Great!" she says. The microphone—too close to her mouth—hisses and crackles. "Oops!" The microphone lowers. "So," she says. "Who wants to know this year's homecoming court?"

More squeals and cheers. Beside me, Konrad reaches for my hand. I bring my hands up to clap, as if I didn't notice, and pretend to crane my neck to get a better view.

First, a freshman announces his grade's prince and princess to wide applause. Once the two are crowned, he passes the microphone to Jackie. Jackie clears her throat. "And now for the sophomores." She pulls out a white card from an envelope, makes a show of reading it, and looks out at the floor. "Please give a warm round of congratulations to our sophomore prince, Konrad Wolnik, and our sophomore princess, Becca Lipowska."

I hold my breath. There are no hoots this time. The only people clapping—besides me and Alan—are the ones who didn't get the memo that Konrad and Becca broke up.

"I'm not going up there," Konrad mumbles.

"Dude!" Alan says, clearly enjoying this. "Don't be a dick."

Gently, I place one of my hands on Konrad's back. "Come on." I force out a chuckle. "Go get 'em, Prince Konrad."

The muscles under my palm stir as he takes a breath. "Fine." He snakes his way past the mob, taking his spot next to Becca onstage before accepting his little white sash.

More people clap and cheer now, likely in response to Konrad's ridiculous shirt as much as anything else. Alan puts his fingers in his mouth and whistles and a sense of pride warms my chest. I can't help it. My date is homecoming prince.

After the juniors are crowned, the senior emcee makes an extra-dramatic spectacle of announcing the king and queen. Konrad doesn't even glance at the other winners. He's politely clapping along, but they don't seem to exist to him. No one does. Not even Becca, making a sour face beside him. There're hundreds of kids here in the gym, but he keeps looking only at me.

His gaze is so intense, I take a step to the side so I can hide behind the girls in front of me. But every time I peek out from behind them, his eyes lock on to mine immediately.

Why is he doing this?

The applause dies down as Kendra McKenzie raises the microphone to her lips. "Okay!" she says, ready to wrap things up, when Konrad dashes forward from the line of royalty.

"Sorry!" he says, getting all up in Kendra's personal space. "Can I? Just for a second?" Without waiting for her answer, he confiscates the microphone. All Kendra can do is watch in shock along with the rest of us.

My heart is thumping. *Don't do it*, I think. *Whatever it is, just don't do it.*

He clears his throat. "I just need a minute."

Silence falls over the entire room. Konrad's eyes are on me again. I really, really don't like what I see in them.

"Camilla," he starts and I hold my breath. Curious heads turn toward me. Konrad clears his throat, and says, "I don't want to be your homecoming date."

The gym erupts in a giant, simultaneous gasp.

I exhale.

Konrad sputters into the mic. "I mean—I DO! SORRY! Thank you for coming with me tonight. What I mean to say is, I want to be *more* than just your homecoming date. I want to be your date every day after tonight, too."

More gasps. Panicked, I look around. Becca's mouth is gaping open. Alan is speechless. The entire school is staring at me.

Even though he's far away, Konrad must see my expression, because after a crackle of the microphone, he adds, "Sorry to embarrass you like this. I just really wanted you to know—everyone to know—that I'd be honored if I could be your boyfriend."

It's as if my mind completely resets.

My feet are moving, marching, straight ahead. I'm running on auto. Bodies shift to open up a path before me. I push the ones that don't out of the way. With each step, Konrad's smile grows bigger. Still holding the mic, he waits for me.

Only when I enter the light does his smile falter. My eyes burning into his, I climb onto the stage and I get up in his face until it disappears completely.

"You think I'm that stupid, *asshole*?" I say, with as much conviction as I can muster.

Konrad's eyelids flutter as his lips form into a sheepish smile. Shame stabs my heart—he looks so taken aback. But I can't allow myself to think right now. I can't back out of this. So I just raise my voice to quiet all the conflicting ones within me. The microphone amplifies it.

"You're the most *selfish* human being on this planet. All you care about is *yourself*. You pretend to be a good person, but YOU'RE NOT! You manipulate people, use them, just like you're using me right now. Just to make yourself look better."

The gym goes completely silent. Someone coughs.

I turn toward the faces in the crowd. "Actually, that goes for a lot of you. So many of you made my ID about yourselves. About how it made *you* feel. You didn't even bother to ask *me* about it. Hashtag #IStandWithCamilla? You're SO FULL OF SHIT!"

My face snaps back to Konrad. "But none of these people are as bad as you. Because you're using me for your own benefit after you did this to me." I spread out my arms. "YOU DID THIS TO ME!" I stop and shake my head in disgust. "You want me to be your girlfriend? I don't even LIKE you! Never did, and I never will."

Pain creeps into Konrad's eyes. I can't bear to look at him. So I don't. Instead, I focus on the silly frill of his shirt. I cup my hand over the microphone and lean in. "Also," I whisper. "I'm the one who posted your yearbook picture with that **#uglyforever** hashtag."

And then I turn my back to him.

My whole body shaking, I walk back the way I came. This time, everybody moves aside to create a path. When I reach where Alan's standing, I walk right past him.

Out in the hallway, a whimper escapes my lips. Then another. I feel dizzy. The next thing I know, my hands are on my knees. I'm gulping for air, my insides in total chaos.

Konrad *couldn't* have been telling the truth. Konrad *couldn't* have meant it.

But, deep down inside, in a place where there's no room for doubt, I know he did.

I think I'm going to be sick.

No, I'm definitely going to be sick.

"Come on," I hear from around the corner where the bathrooms are. "Just a little. I know you want to."

My turmoil goes on mute.

"Stop," another voice—a female one—answers. I'd recognize that voice anywhere. "Don't!" Then, "FUCK OFF, will you?"

Again, my mind is a blank.

Again, I'm moving. Only faster, this time. Faster than I ever have before.

I round the corner.

A guy stands there, his back to me, his shirt half untucked. Facing this guy—and facing me—is Ashley. My Ashley. But she doesn't see me. Not at first. She's too busy fighting off the guy's invasive hands. Poking, prodding, trying to find their way under her pretty white dress.

Ashley's palm arches through the air, connecting to his cheek with a loud *smack*. Then she thrusts both of her hands into his chest, making him stumble backward.

The guy's head tilts. I catch a glimpse of his profile.

Tom Dempsey.

I take my rage, fuse it with the self-disgust I'm feeling, and jolt forward, pouncing onto his back. And then, with my legs wrapped around him, my elbow under his neck, I'm scratching, pounding, kicking with every last drop of energy I have.

CHAPTER 27

KONRAD

ON THE OTHER SIDE OF my wall, swords clash and voices scream in a foreign language.

Arthur's watching one of his anime shows.

I roll over in bed and grope around the floor for my phone. There are zero new texts from Camilla. My heart clenches, but I'm immediately angry at myself. Because there are zero reasons why there'd be any. More importantly, there are zero reasons I should want to see them. Camilla played me. She made me look like a fool. So why do I still want to hear from her?

I do, however, see four texts from Alan, two from Lauren, and even one from Mike. I don't read any of them. Instead, I scroll, looking for Eric Stewart's name, only to remember I'd blocked him. I guess I'll have to apologize to him in person for wrongly accusing him of posting my yearbook photo.

It's 12:24 P.M. My stomach rumbles. I drop the phone back to the floor and turn over on my side. Five or so minutes into yet another replay of last night's events, I hear two new voices join my mom's in the kitchen.

Snagging my pillow, I press it over my face and hold still. A couple of seconds later, it skyrockets off me. Lauren leans over me, nose wrinkling. "I'm opening the window," she says. "It smells funky in here."

I don't even have the energy to respond.

She disappears from view. The moment she does, my bed sinks behind me and an arm drapes around my shoulder. "Hey, gorgeous," Alan whispers into my ear. When I don't react, he sits up. The room explodes with brightness and a breeze hits my face. Lauren's butt parks on the sheets, inches away from my face.

I feel a poke in my side. "Come on," she says, prodding me some more. This is the most physical affection Lauren has ever shown me. "There's a nice Polish breakfast on the kitchen table with your name on it. Let's eat it and then go smoke a joint."

I don't reply. I keep staring at the back pocket of her jeans.

"Ham and sausage," she adds in a singsong voice. "And pickles!"

Behind me, Alan sighs. His words fly over my limp body to Lauren. "At least after Sara, he could still talk."

Lauren doesn't reply. Instead, she jumps off the bed and clutches my arm, yanking it toward her. "You're being rude, Mr. Wolnik," she says. "You have guests! Stop being a little baby. Shit happens. Life goes on. Let's go." And then I'm pitching upward, my view changing from Lauren's crotch to the open curtains.

My shoulders hunch. Lauren tugs at my arm again, harder. Next thing I know, there's a thump, a sting of pain, and my face is kissing the floor.

"What the fuck?" I mumble, resting for a minute before hauling myself up.

She's smirking. "You asked for it."

I try to sit back on the bed, but before I can, Lauren grabs hold of me again and propels me through my door into the living room.

In the kitchen, Mom's worried eyes await my appearance. Crossing her arms, she leans against the counter, the frown of the century on her face. "How you feeling, honey?"

I wonder how she knows, but get an idea who she heard about my plight from as soon as Arthur joins us. "Bro," he says, "you're breaking the internet."

Lauren turns to him. "Shut up, you little shit."

"Lauren," Mom warns, fatigue in her voice.

"Sorry, Mrs. Wolnik." She thrusts me the rest of the way to the kitchen table, where my breakfast, currently covered in Saran Wrap, is laid out.

Arthur rushes to sit across from me. "How does it feel to be turned down by the ugliest girl in the northern hemisphere?"

"Arthur!" Mom snaps. "Go to your room!"

We all wait for him to shuffle away. Then Mom comes up behind me, gives my shoulder a little squeeze, nods at my friends, and heads upstairs. Lauren takes Arthur's place on the other side of the table. Alan grabs a chair and they both watch me eat, stealing a slice of ham here, taking a bite out of my mayo-covered boiled egg there.

"You guys can have the rest," I say, pushing the plate toward Lauren. "I'm not hungry."

They both stare at me.

"Let's go for a ride," Alan finally says.

I slouch even lower in my seat. Lauren stands up and pretend-reaches for my arm. I tip away from it and glare at her. "*Stop!* Not in the mood . . ."

She smacks both her palms on the table and adopts an army sergeant tone: "YOU'RE COMING WITH US!"

Alan nods. "You need some medication, and we've got just the thing."

"I still have some of that tequila left," Lauren says, eyebrows jumping.

I think about it. The last time I tried Lauren's tequila I went to sleep and woke up to a whole different life. How awesome would it be if that happened again? What if I chugged the disgusting thing today and woke up my old self tomorrow? Even better, what if the past few weeks got wiped out from my memory?

"Come on," Lauren says, grinning. "Give in to the peer pressure."

I sigh. Alan takes this as encouragement and rubs his hand all over my bed head hair. I slap him away. "Fine," I grunt. I intend to pass on the tequila, but at this point, I'm willing to try *something* to take my mind off what happened. Even if only temporarily. The sun is out. My friends can distract me. "I have to shower first, though."

"You have ten minutes," Alan says.

Lauren narrows her eyes. "Five."

The shower takes eight. And ten minutes after that, my hair still damp, we're parked in an alley a couple of blocks away from my house. Between my fingers rests a nice, fat joint. I suck on it until I can suck no more and a cough attack rattles my entire body.

"That's my boy," Lauren says, lounging in the back seat. She only lets me ride shotgun when I'm down.

The sun ends up being more of a nuisance than anything else. It might be a breezy fall day outside, but the sun decided it's not done with the summer just yet. Even with all four windows open, the glare is cooking us alive.

When my coughing subsides, Alan's hand reaches over and I pass him the joint. Before he brings it to his lips, he smiles and says, "Let's go to Six Flags tomorrow."

It's like he flips a switch.

All of the floodgates keeping my sadness at bay are suddenly wide open. Tears rush up my throat and explode out of my sockets.

If yesterday hadn't happen the way it did—if I hadn't been epically rejected by a girl I liked more than I've ever liked anyone, I'd be at Six Flags with her at this very moment.

"No, no, no," Alan mutters to himself, rubbing my back and dropping ashes all over my shirt in the process.

"Nice going, *ass*," Lauren says as she slaps the back of Alan's head. She shuffles around and hangs herself between the front seats. Stealing the joint from Alan, she puffs and talks at the same time. "Since we're on the subject, though, there's no way Camilla meant what she said."

I hold my breath. Through the blur of my tears, I see Alan tense and give Lauren the eye. "Stop giving him false hope," he growls.

Another wave barrages my insides and I'm bawling. Alan sighs. His hand is again doing therapy work on my back. "Come on, man. If you could get over Sara, you can get over Camilla." He pauses and adds in a quiet voice, "You guys weren't even an official couple."

I slouch into my seat and curl up into a ball, my arms hugging my knees.

"Alan, just stop talking," Lauren says. "Sara's a bitch. He obviously liked Camilla a lot more." Her finger pokes into my back. "Anyway, all I'm saying is, I think there's more to this story than meets the eye."

I sit up. Why can't Lauren just shut up? At least Alan's being honest. Brutally honest, yeah, but it's better than this devil's advocate crap.

"She was pretty clear about how she feels about me," I hiss at Lauren. "She said she never even liked me and never would. Plus, she's the one who started the whole **#uglyforever** thing. She was playing me. This whole time."

Lauren flicks the joint out the window. "Because she thought *you* were playing *her!*" she says, as serious as I've ever seen her. "I don't know what's going on in her head, Konrad, but she had an awful ID experience. If I were her, I'm pretty sure I'd be suspicious of everyone, too. I'd probably assume the worst and hate everything around me."

"Yeah," I scoff. "I'm pretty sure Camilla hates *me* more than anything else."

Lauren sighs. "Maybe she hated the *idea* of you. But I'm one hundred percent sure that she doesn't hate *you*. Not after seeing the way she looked at you."

"Okay, whatever."

A moment passes. Alan's looking at his lap, playing with his fingers. To my surprise, Lauren's hand lands on my shoulder and stays there. "I know you weren't trying to use Camilla," she says. "I know you really liked her and meant everything you said. You're a good guy, Konrad. You're pretty hard to hate."

I feel like crying. "Yeah, well, someone should have told Camilla that."

"True." Lauren gives my shoulder a squeeze. "Someone should have."

CHAPTER 28

CAMILLA

Ashley's fine. At least she says she is. I asked her so many times over the past two days, I don't really have a choice but to take her word for it.

Tom Dempsey is fine. His face is probably scratched up, and he might have a sore rib from when Ashley slammed her fist into it, but after Mr. Connick ripped me off him, and after I spat death threats into his face, Tom ran off like a little lamb being chased by a wolf.

So he's fine. For now. But he won't be. I'll make sure of that.

Jodie found Ashley and me a minute after Tom took off. The three of us gathered into one big hug, pressed our foreheads together, and just stood there. None of us said anything. We didn't need to.

Me? I am not fine. Last summer, I shared a video of my best friend and the guy I had a crush on making out at a party. By doing so, I didn't just put a stain on her reputation. I set off a chain reaction that made that stain grow larger and more vicious with each passing day.

And I didn't even see it. How could I not see it?

Instead of being there for her— of thanking God for having such amazing friends, focusing on the good things in my life—I let my ID consume me.

And then, as if that wasn't enough, I decided to play God by blaming and punishing a boy I had no place blaming and punishing in the first place.

I thought humiliating Konrad, belittling him while the whole school watched, would give me satisfaction and peace. Once it happened, I didn't feel any justice. If anything, it left me with a knot inside so tight, I don't think it can ever be undone.

According to the text Lauren sent me yesterday, Konrad Wolnik isn't fine either.

I didn't need Lauren to tell me that. I knew Konrad wouldn't be okay and that the state of his reputation would have nothing to do with it the moment I looked into his eyes when I confronted him at the dance. No, that's not right. I knew even before that.

I just refused to believe it.

"Why did you do it?" Jodie asked me that night as she, Ashley, and I sat at a booth at the Shack piled on top of each other like puppies, our dresses creasing.

"I thought he was using me." My voice cracked. "I thought I was being duped by a selfish asshole, so I wanted to dupe him first."

"But he sounded so sweet, so sincere up there."

A huge lump filled my throat. "I know . . ."

"So why didn't you believe him?"

I shifted away. "How could I, Jodie? Look at me and then look at him. How could I even *think* that was possible?"

"Camilla," Ashley said then. "Do you really believe that? Look at all the shit happening in the world all the time. At all the things you'd never expect to happen, not in a million years, but that do anyway. I'm not even talking about Inexplicable Developments. A lot of other things are fucking inexplicable. And what? You're telling me you couldn't believe that a good-looking guy could possibly like you? That's bullshit and you know it."

"It's not just that," I explained. "I was convinced that he was responsible for what happened to me. I mean, how can I know that he's not?"

"But he told you he wasn't. And he apologized anyway."

A tear slid down my cheek. "It wasn't fair."

Ashley scoffed. "Oh, *boo-hoo.* Newsflash, Camilla: life isn't fair to *anyone.* Everybody's got problems. You're not special."

"Maybe you can still work things out," Jodie suggested, her mascara in smudges. "Maybe if you apologize, tell him the truth, he'll forgive you."

I closed my eyes and sucked in a shaky breath. "Even if for some reason he magically did forgive me, it still wouldn't work."

"What wouldn't?"

"Me and Konrad."

"Why?"

"Because. He's gorgeous. He'd dump me the first chance he got."

"Maybe he would," Ashley said with a *tsk*. "So what? You don't know that for sure. You don't know anything for sure. Nobody does. You can't assume things before they happen."

No one said anything for a few beats.

"Anyway," Jodie said, cutting the silence, "regardless of how you treated Konrad, the way you called out the whole school up there? On that stage? That was badass."

"Agreed," Ashley added. "That was cool as hell."

Wiping at tears with my fingers, I managed a tiny smile. "Thanks, guys."

After another moment, Jodie asked, "Do you really like him?"

My smile vanished. "It doesn't matter. He'll never talk to me again."

Ashley crossed her arms. "No excuses. You don't get a special pass for what you did to him, you know. You need to make things right."

I didn't say anything after that. Because there is no making things right. I burned everything to the ground and there's nothing left to rebuild with. I don't deserve Konrad. I don't even deserve his forgiveness. I was a terrible friend, a terrible person.

I'm pretty sure I know why my ID happened now.

The outside just needed to match the inside.

It's four o'clock on Sunday when I get home from my run. Mom's in front of the TV watching a rerun of a nineties high school series. As she takes in my sweat-soaked T-shirt, a crease of worry forms on her forehead. "It's too cold to be running in short sleeves," she tells me.

Without a word, I fall into a chair.

She's watching me. "What is it, honey?" she asks. When I don't reply, she points the remote at the TV to lower the volume, then sets it down on the coffee table and waits.

"Mom," I say, looking at her. I've made a decision and I need her to know there's no room for negotiation. "You know that crowdfunding page that Jodie set up?"

Her eyes grow bigger and her jaw tightens. "It's up to thirty-two thousand dollars now."

"I know," I say. "I just looked."

We stare at each other for a moment.

"I want to donate it to charity."

Her eyebrows jump along with her voice. "All of it?"

My gaze doesn't waver. "All of it."

"But—"

"I know which charity, too," I cut her off. "I want it to be Direct Relief. I did my research and I think they do amazing things for the world. They provide medical aid to people who can't afford it and they help out when disasters strike. I want them to have it."

The hushed voices of the TV characters are the only sound in the room. Finally, Mom's shoulders go slack and she leans back on the couch. "Are you sure?"

"Yes. Other people need that money more than I do."

Slowly, she nods. "Looks like there's no changing your mind."

I shake my head. "No."

Mom sighs. "It's your money, so it's your decision."

"And," I add, "I want to transfer to a different school."

Her frown returns. "A different school? *Why?*"

How can I tell her the truth? How can I tell her I can't bear to see Konrad in the hallways? That if I do, the shame of what I've done to him will only eat me up? "I'll wake up earlier," I say. "Take the bus. It's not going to cause you any extra trouble, I promise."

"But why now?"

"Now's the time."

Her face goes stern. It's the same expression she puts on when she's dealing with stubborn patients. "Tell me what happened at the dance."

"I told you already," I say. "I met up with Konrad, we danced, and then there was that awful thing with Ashley and Tom."

"You know that's not what I mean. What did Konrad *do*?"

A lump forms in my throat and I start breathing faster. I have to stop pretending. If I want things to change, I'm going to have to be honest with everyone. Including myself.

"Nothing," I say, my voice cracking. "He was perfect."

Mom shakes her head. She has no idea why I'm acting like this. Or maybe she knows exactly why. Either way, she doesn't say anything. She just stretches out her arm. "Come here."

"It's fine," I say. "I'm fine."

"Come here," she orders again.

The affection in her voice makes me stand up. I shuffle over and fall onto the couch beside her. Her arm wraps around me. She pulls me in, tucking me against her shoulder. The moment she rests her chin on the top of my head, I break down.

I let out a tiny sob. It leads to another, slightly bigger, one. And another. Like a trapdoor opening up within me, the sobs keep coming and coming until I'm crying. Really, truly crying.

As my mom holds me, I don't push the tears back in like I always do. I let them pour out and out and out. They feel like sickness leaving my body.

"Let it out," Mom says into my hair as her hand slides up and down my back. Her shaky voice tells me she's crying, too. "Let it all out."

And so I do.

Minutes later, or maybe even hours, after I'm drained, Mom releases me and holds my face in her hands. "What you went through—what you're going through—it's not fair. I hate myself for not being able to do anything about it."

"It's not your fault," I whisper.

She stares me in the eyes. "Looks aren't everything."

"I know," I say. "They're not even close to being everything. There are so many other, bigger problems to worry about."

Mom's lips lift at the edges. "You've grown into such a smart young woman, Camilla. I'm so, so proud of you," she says. "And I know your dad would be proud of you, too." I try to blink away the blur, but the tears keep coming again. "I want you to be happy," she goes on, "and if you think changing schools will do that, then I'm on board."

I think about Konrad. I may not be able to fix what I did, but I do want to turn things around. I do want to become a better person. And I do want to give myself another chance to love, and, maybe even someday, be loved by someone again.

What better way to do that than by giving myself a clean slate?

CHAPTER 29

KONRAD

HALLOWEEN FALLS ON A WEDNESDAY.

Usually, I'm a fan of the holiday—jack-o'-lanterns and horror flicks, climbing over cemetery fences on midnight dares from Lauren, the general silliness in the air. Usually, it's great.

But this year, I barely register the witch hats and cat ears parading the hallways at school. The whole vibe is lost on me, like I'm on one wavelength and all the Halloween stuff is happening on another.

I didn't even bother dressing up. I've done enough of that for Spirit Week. Besides, you might say I've been wearing a costume for over a month now, and I'll have to keep wearing the same one for the rest of my life.

What I do register, though—what's been dominating my thoughts—is the fact that Camilla hasn't shown up to school since the dance.

I know. She hurt me. Embarrassed me. Used me. I get it. But I can't help flicking my eyes around the halls searching for her anyway, my chest prickling with anticipation of the moment when I see her and she sees me. What will her eyes convey? What will mine?

But as hard as I search, I don't see her anywhere.

Eventually, though, before lunch, I do spot something that makes my stomach lurch.

Jodie Mathews and Ashley Solomon. Talking to Lauren.

"What?" Alan says, stopping a second after I do.

Jodie's the only one of the three in costume. She's wearing high heels, leggings, and a leather jacket—all in black. Her hair is hidden from view under a purple headscarf that drapes down her chest, and her lips are smeared in deep-red lipstick. I have no idea who she's supposed to be, but I have more pressing questions I need answers to.

"What is Lauren saying to them?" I ask.

"I'm going to the library," Jackie Baker says. She gives Alan a shy peck on the cheek.

"Bye, Jackie," I mumble, my eyes attached to the trio up ahead. Jodie looks my way and gives me a weak smile. My heart starts pounding.

"You're being weird and creepy," Alan whispers, but he drags me to the side, out of the way of hallway traffic, and waits with me. After what feels like hours, Lauren finally raises a hand at Camilla's friends and shuffles over to Alan and me.

"What's up, geeks?" she says nonchalantly, her hands tucked in the back pockets of her holed-up jeans, as if having little chats with Ashley and Jodie is totally normal for her.

"What were you guys talking about?" I demand.

"Who?" Lauren asks. I glare at her. She purses her lips into a sad smile and sighs. "Camilla's transferring."

My chest compresses so suddenly it hurts.

Lauren's hands leave her pockets. She performs a dramatic display of cracking her knuckles. "I kind of feel like quinoa salad today. Let's drive up to that spot near the mall."

"Which school?" I ask, annoyed.

She watches me for a moment, lips twisting from one side to the other. "Roosevelt."

"Oh," Alan blurts. "That's not too bad! That's only like fifteen minutes away."

It is, but it might as well be a different continent.

I keep staring at Lauren. "Is she all right?"

Lauren shrugs. "Yeah, I guess." She bares her teeth. "Who's with me? Yes or no to the quinoa salad?"

"What else did they say?"

"Well, Jodie's supposed to be Grace Jones. You know, the legendary singer and supermodel? Studio 54? Pretty cool, eh?"

Shaking my head in disappointment, I turn away.

"Quinoa salad?"

"You guys go ahead," I say. "I brought my lunch today, anyway."

Lauren snaps her fingers. "Dang. Okay, let's just eat in the cafeteria then."

"Nah, you guys go. I'm going to eat in the library."

A scowl forms on Lauren's face. "Depressing much?"

"It's . . . fine."

"You sure?" Alan asks.

But I'm already walking away. "See you guys later."

In the library, I zigzag through the aisles, so I can avoid Jackie or anybody else I may know. I want to be alone, so I'm happy to spot an isolated table all the way in the back. Flopping in the chair, I unwrap my sandwich and stare at the giant pork cutlet jammed between two sourdough slices. After a minute, I wrap it back up.

My face falls into the nook of my elbow. I keep it there until the chair across from mine scratches the carpet and the table wobbles.

When I lift my head, I'm sitting face-to-face with a doctor. No, not just any doctor, I realize. A brain surgeon.

"Hey," Becca says, pulling down her surgical mask with a gloved hand.

I take in her hospital cap and the boxy green scrubs. This is the last person I expected to see right now. And in the library? At lunch? Isn't this the time when Becca Lipowska usually reigns over her minions? I have to give it to her, though. This is the least revealing thing I've ever seen her wear, and yet I've never been more fascinated.

"I like your costume," I say, because holding grudges, I've learned, is a pointless waste of time.

"Thanks." Her cheeks redden just a bit.

I lift my brows. "So . . . what's up?"

She takes a deep breath. "I'm *sorry*, okay?"

The words take me by surprise, but I nod and drop my gaze to the table. "Me, too."

She chuckles, and I look back up at her. Becca's eyes are aimed down at her hands. Her head is shaking. "I'm shallow as fuck," she says.

I shift in my seat. She has a valid point, but it doesn't feel right to agree with her at the moment. "You're not."

"No, it's true. I basically used you."

I take a deep breath of my own. "I used you, too, Becca."

She nods, but doesn't seem concerned by my admission. "You're the only guy who's ever rejected me."

I snort. "Well, you don't always get what you want, I guess."

"What happened, it didn't make any logical sense to me."

I look her in the eyes. "You can't apply logic to everything."

"I know."

For a minute, we sit in silence.

"Funny thing," she says. "After I got to spend more time with you, I actually started to like you. And then you broke up with me, and right before homecoming, too. That's why I acted like a bitch. I think that's my natural defense mechanism."

I chuckle, uncomfortably. "Yeah . . ."

"Anyway," she says, "I hope we can still be friends."

I don't think I've ever liked Becca as much as I do right now. "I don't see why not."

She nods and looks down at her hands again, but her shoulders relax a little.

"How's Tom?" I ask.

"I broke up with him. I don't like him that way. I've decided to try a different approach to relationships. Like a guy first before trying to date him."

I chuckle again. "Sounds like a plan."

"Plus," she says, "Tom's an asshole. I'm sure you heard about what he tried to do to Ashley Solomon at the dance." I nod. "I'm going to apologize to her, too."

"Hmm, yeah. I think that's a good idea."

Becca's eyeing my sandwich. "Can I have some of that?"

I slide it toward her. She takes a tiny bite. I watch her chew.

Through the bread in her mouth, she asks, "So you really liked Camilla Hadi, huh?"

My chest tightens. I focus on a nearby bookshelf. "Yeah."

"Well," Becca mumbles, "I think she's an idiot for turning you down like that, then."

I cringe. "Thanks."

"And I don't just mean because you're the hottest guy at school."

I try to catch her gaze, but she's too busy pretending Mom's sandwich is the most delicious thing she's ever tasted. I smile anyway. "Can I have my lunch back now?"

Becca sighs dramatically before handing the sandwich back to me. She stands up, giving me a better view of her well-pressed green scrubs. "Happy Halloween, Konrad."

"Happy Halloween, Becca."

CHAPTER 30

CAMILLA

The crowdfunding money is officially in the hands of the charity.

I wrote a message and posted it on the site. This is what it said:

> To everyone who contributed to this campaign, thank you. Your act of kindness means a lot. I'm writing this to let you know that I have donated the entire amount to Direct Relief, a nonprofit organization that provides medical aid to those who need it.
>
> Yes, my Inexplicable Development had an unwanted effect on my physical appearance. But

I'm also still healthy, still surrounded by people who love me, and still able to do all the things I was able to do before. There are so many people out there who are much less fortunate.

I'm not saying looks are not important or that they don't affect lives because that would be a lie. But I am saying that if you pay too much attention to them—to this one small part among so many others (SO MANY!) that make you who you are—you might become blind to other things that matter much, much more. And you might not even realize it until it's too late. At least that's what happened to me. I hope you don't make the same mistake.

Yours Truly,
Camilla Z. Hadi
P.S. Jodie, I love you. XOXO.

Reading all the (mostly positive) comments people have left since the message went up has served as a welcome distraction from thinking about Konrad. I try not to, but I keep replaying every interaction I've ever had with him and stalking him on social media—which is totally pointless anyway because he hasn't posted anything in a long while.

I guess this is another thing that only time will help me with. It's only been about two weeks after all.

Today, it's Saturday, and Ashley, Jodie, and I are going to Six Flags to celebrate. Yes, *celebrate*. We haven't exactly defined what it is we're celebrating, but we don't have to. It's a combination of things: our friendship, my philanthropic moment, new beginnings.

As expected, Ashley is right on time. Her incessant honking tells me she's in a good mood. I lock the front door behind me, yank at the doorknob three times to make sure it's really locked, and then glide down the front steps.

The weather could definitely be better, but that hasn't stopped Ashley and Jodie from wearing giant pairs of sunglasses, too. I point to mine (well, Jodie's, technically), they point to theirs, and by the time I slam the car door, we're laughing our asses off.

"Road trip!" Jodie yells. I voice my approval with a loud, "Yay!"

It rains for the first twenty minutes of the ride, but eventually the sun peeks out from behind the clouds. The three of us sing along with the radio. We interrogate Jodie about her bowling date with Joe Park. ("Bowling, Jodie? What are you, five?") I make sure no one's been talking shit to Ashley, and I restate my promise to help her kick anyone's ass again if there's a need. We laugh and laugh and laugh. I haven't felt this at ease in a long time.

But there's one thing we don't do, even though the urge sits on my chest the entire time, like a trapped bunny ready to leap out.

We don't talk about Konrad.

"You're so getting on the drop tower with us, Jodie," I say.

Jodie purses her red lips and shakes her head. "Absolutely not."

Hanging on the back of her seat, I poke my finger into her armpit to tickle her. "You owe me, remember? For saying that I need plastic surgery?"

She recoils, then turns to face the back seat. "Uh, no. You owe *me*, sweetheart. Where do you think you got the money to turn into Mother Teresa? And I never said you *need* plastic surgery. I'm not apologizing for bringing it up. It's a totally viable option. As long as a person is doing it for themselves, if it boosts their self-esteem, then nip and tuck away, baby."

"Touché," Ashley says from behind the wheel. She gives Jodie a high five.

"Stop calling me *sweetheart*," I mumble, but I smile anyway. "And I know that plastic surgery is okay. I might even consider it down the line. But I don't think now is the right time. Besides, you need a parent's permission and all that if you're a minor."

"Oh!" Jodie exclaims, accusingly. "So you *did* look into it."

I wink at her. "Maybe just a little."

Six Flags is full of loud children and even louder roller coasters. The lines are long but the rides are totally worth it. Not to mention the lines are prime locations for people watching.

Through our sunglasses, we check out all the guys, claiming the cuties and making fun of the douchebags. On the way to the third ride—the one where your legs hang loose in the air, which took some convincing to get Jodie to go on— Ashley grabs me by one elbow, Jodie by the other, and they pull me into a little courtyard.

"Pretzels!" Ashley announces.

"You get pretzels and I'll do smoothies," Jodie orders, unusually enthusiastic about carbs. "Camilla, you go find a good spot to sit."

"Got it," I say, slightly bewildered by the random turn of events. I shuffle over to a stone ledge enclosing a little batch of dirt where flowers grow during warmer times and sit down.

The girls return a few minutes later. I attack my pretzel, eager for the next ride's promise of thrills and flushed cheeks. Unfortunately, neither Ashley nor Jodie seem to share my enthusiasm. Jodie's on her phone and Ashley's nibbling on her pretzel, scanning the crowd.

"Hurry up," I tell them. "Jodie, stop texting Joe Park!"

Jodie looks up from her screen and exchanges a look with Ashley. She gives her a weird nod and turns to me. "Oh my God," she says. "You won't believe what he just sent me."

"Who?" I ask, blushing. "Joe?" I never thought about Joe Park that way, but now that she says it like that, I'm kind of curious.

"It's pretty graphic," Jodie warns. "Are you sure you want to see it?"

I shrug and glance at Ashley, but Ashley appears totally uninterested. Her eyes are still checking out the crowd like she's desperate to find a cute boy of her own. Jodie scoots closer, cradling her phone like it contains a CIA secret.

"So?" Jodie asks, pinning me down with her gaze. "Do you want to see?"

"Not really," I lie, but aim my eyes on her phone and wait.

"Come closer and hide the screen," she says. I huddle in, even though nobody's close enough to see it, anyway.

"Okay, you ready?"

I roll my eyes. "Jodie, I've seen a dick before."

Jodie's mouth pops open. She leans away from me. "Really? Whose?"

I glare at her. "Whatever," I say, wiggling my butt away on the stone.

And right then, across the courtyard, standing with a churro frozen on the way to his mouth, I see him.

Heat explodes in my face. The world around me goes silent.

At first, I'm overwhelmed with relief. I resigned myself to never seeing him again. Not in person, at least. And here he is.

Konrad Wolnik.

His gaze is locked onto mine, his expression a reflection of my own: parted lips, burning cheeks, and eyes so round they might pop out of his face.

"OVER HERE!" Ashley yells, her hand flapping through the air.

The silence around me shatters. My heart starts pumping in overdrive. And I realize: there is no dick pic. Jodie hasn't been talking to Joe Park. She was texting Lauren Batko, because just then I see Lauren's red mane right there next to Konrad. Or maybe she was texting Alan Nguyen, who's a step behind them, peeking over Konrad's shoulder.

I'm the victim of a setup. And judging from Konrad's expression, so is he.

Konrad's churro sinks to his side. His lips close. Jodie and Ashley stand up. I can feel their eyes on me, urging me to do the same. Theme park-goers pass through my field of vision like ghosts. Alan leans in and whispers something in Konrad's ear. With her fist, Lauren gives him a little shove. Konrad takes a small step forward.

He stops.

I stand.

Jodie and Ashley are speaking now, but I don't hear what they're saying because my entire world is only Konrad and my thumping heartbeat.

I should run. I want to. That's what the shame I'm feeling is telling me to do. But the desire to be near him overpowers it, so I stay where I am. I want to hear his voice—see his smile—one more time. But why would he even talk to me? And why would he smile?

No. Running is out of the question. At the very least, I need to apologize. A rush of determination makes one of my feet step in front of the other.

Seeing me move, Konrad's eyes widen. Even from here, I can see his Adam's apple rise and fall. He mirrors my action and starts shuffling over.

Little by little, we close the distance between us. When we're only a couple of feet from each other, we stop, face to face. Trembling, I take him in. He's cautious. On full alert.

"Hey," I say.

His reply comes in the form of a polite chin lift. Like I'm a bro of a bro he's not very good friends with. My insides explode with so much guilt and shame my knees buckle. But that's not what makes me want to cry. It's the fact that he acknowledges me at all.

People slow as they walk by, staring at the ugly girl getting all teary-eyed in front of the beautiful boy, wondering what's going on.

I blink away the tears, take a deep breath, and look Konrad straight in the eyes. "I wish there was a word stronger than *sorry*. But there isn't. I'm sorry, Konrad." My voice gets smaller. "I'm really, really sorry."

It feels like I've dropped two heavy dumbbells I didn't even know I was carrying. I wipe my eyes with the back of my hand and take another deep breath.

Konrad still hasn't said anything. *Okay, now what?* I think. But before I can properly read his reaction and decide what to do, I see his foot dash forward. Next thing I know, my face is pressed up against his broad chest, his boy scent all around me.

I'm only stiff for a second, before I melt into him. And it feels so good, I'm crying for real now, my whole body shivering.

"Tell her to stay at our school!" Jodie yells from behind us.

Konrad's embrace loosens. He sets his hands on top of my shoulders and looks me in the eyes. "Stay at our school," he says. "Please."

"What?" I manage a smile. "All the paperwork is done already. I start Monday."

His grip around my shoulders tightens. "If you're transferring to Roosevelt then I'm transferring to Roosevelt, too."

I sniff. "But how can you still like me?"

He cracks a crooked grin. "I wish there was a word stronger than *like*."

"But *why*?"

"Why do you ask so many questions?"

"But I'm evil. I'm an asshole. You *shouldn't* like me. Not after what I did."

His grin stretches wider. "I guess I like evil assholes, then."

My face is burning hot. I see the sincerity in his eyes, the same sincerity they've shown me all along. Only, this time, I let myself believe it.

"Okay," I say. "I'll think about it."

Konrad's grin starts moving toward me. Before I can process what's happening, his lips are pressing into mine, bringing with them the taste of cinnamon churro.

A euphoric tickle scuttles down to my toes.

Forget roller coasters. Forget running. I've found the best thrill yet.

"TOO MUCH TONGUE!" a voice yells. "There are little children around!" It takes me a moment to realize it's Lauren.

Konrad and I untangle from each other. Slowly, the world comes back into focus. Our friends are watching us, giant smiles plastered on their faces. Who would've thought Jodie and Ashley would be there to witness my first kiss?

A lady with an impatient kid hanging off her arm shoots me a wink. I'm too embarrassed to maintain eye contact with anyone for longer than a second, so I snuggle up against Konrad instead. His arms falls around me.

"You guys are so stupid."

I peek out at Alan. His lanky arms are crossed, and he's shaking his head at Konrad and me. If he didn't have a smile on his face, I might've been offended. "Why?" I ask.

"The main Inexplicable Development theory," he says. "It's obviously true."

"What do you mean?" I say, tensing up.

Alan sweeps his arm at Ashley, Jodie, and Lauren, and says, "We've known for days what you guys wished for."

The three all nod in unison.

Goose bumps spring up all over my body. The Inexplicable Development Theory: the theory that says all IDs stem from a trigger originating in the person to whom the ID happens—that IDs are a reaction to a powerful desire. A wish coming true.

In Konrad's case, it always made sense. But I never wished to be ugly. So what powerful desire could possibly explain why this happened to me?

Confused, I tilt my head at Konrad. And in his expression, in his swelling eyes and parting lips, I see it dawn on him at the same time it dawns on me.

I'm suddenly so hot, I duck under Konrad's arm and step away so I can breathe properly.

"You're saying that I wished for . . ." I look at Konrad, the skin on my entire body—especially on my face—on the verge of burning off. ". . . for . . . *Konrad?*"

"Well," Ashley says. "Sure. That's one way of putting it." She looks at Alan and smiles. "We thought of it more like you guys each wishing for, you know, *love.*"

Lauren winks at me. "Cheesiest shit I've ever seen."

Eyes shining, Jodie says, "Most romantic shit ever is more like it."

Alan's singing now: "Konrad and Camilla, sitting in a tree . . ." Jodie and Lauren and Ashley join in. Everyone's laughing and going *aww*. But I'm speechless.

Did I really wish for love *that* much without even being fully aware of it?

Could be . . .

But if that's the case, and my own wish was the reason for my Development, then the universe chose one twisted way to grant it.

It's happened before. With IDs, there are no set rules on how people get what they want. Sometimes, happiness takes a roundabout path.

It would mean that I was partly right from the beginning. Konrad might not have been directly responsible, but he did have something to do with my ID. He was involved, only in a way I could never have imagined.

It would also mean I did this to myself.

I look at Konrad.

Was it worth it?

He's looking at me. His face is redder than ever. I melt under his shy smile.

Fuck. I think it was.

"So we good?" Ashley asks, basking in my state of shock.

"Yeah," Lauren says. "Can we do the drop tower now?"

"YES!" I announce.

"You guys go," Jodie says, tossing her pretzel wrapper into a nearby trash can.

"Jodie," I say, lowering my chin and making my eyes into slits.

Jodie purses her lips and crosses her arms. She makes a show of glaring at me for a moment and then rolls her eyes. "Fine," she says and starts leading the way.

Alan steps in after her with Ashley by his side. With a tilt of her head, Lauren invites me and Konrad to follow.

Konrad takes my hand and he doesn't let it go. Not even when we're free-falling on the drop tower, our stomachs flying up to our throats, air pummeling our faces.

He only holds it tighter.

ACKNOWLEDGMENTS

Melissa Edwards and Alison Weiss. You made this book not only possible but also infinitely better. Thank you for making my freakin' dream come true.

Konrad and Kamila. I like your names. ;) Love you, guys.

Wojtek, Madoka, Alan, Ayumi, Yusuke, Jango, Piotr, Amina, Fleur. Your cheers and support mean the world to me. I'm beyond lucky to have friends like you.

Mamo i Tato. Dziękuję za Wasze wsparcie, wiarę we mnie i zrozumienie. Kocham Was.

Babciu, Dziadziu. Opowiadaliście mi o nocnych tęczach i ufoludkach, które lubią kapustę. Rozbudziliście moją wyobraźnię, za co będę Wam na zawsze wdzięczny.

みちゃん。本気を出して書き始めたのは、お前のおかげだよ。ありがとう。